THE PYRAMIDS
An Enigma Solved

THE PYRAMIDS

An Enigma Solved

Joseph Davidovits and Margie Morris

HIPPOCRENE BOOKS
New York

For information, address:
Hippocrene Books, Inc.
171 Madison Ave.
New York, NY 10016

Library of Congress Cataloging-in-Publication Data

Davidovits, Joseph.
  The pyramids.

  Bibliography: p. 255
  Includes index.
  1. Pyramids—Egypt—Design and construction.
2. Stone, Cast.   3. Masonry—Egypt—History.   I. Morris,
Margie.   II. Title.
DT63.D37   1988   690'.68'0932   88-16568
ISBN 0-87052-559-X

Printed in the United States of America.
Third printing, 1989.

Contents

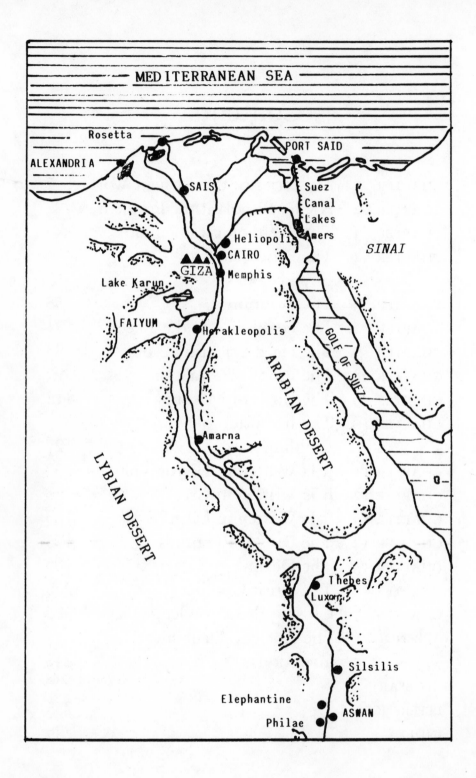

CHAPTER 1

Mysteries of the Ancient World

EGYPT'S LEGENDARY REPUTATION AS MASTER OF THE MA-sonry arts spans almost the entire history of civilization. At a time before hieroglyphs or numbers were written or copper was smelted, prehistoric settlers in the Nile valley either inherited or began a remarkable legacy that has survived for at least 6,000 years. During this era, hard stone vessels made of slate, meta-morphic schist, diorite, and basalt first appeared. All but inde-structible, these items are among the most unusual and enig-matic of the ancient world. In a later era, 30,000 such vessels were placed in an underground chamber of the first pyramid, the Third Dynasty Step Pyramid at Saqqara.

"On examining them attentively, I only became more per-plexed," wrote the renowned German scholar, Kurt Lange, after encountering these stone vessels. "How were they made, the dishes, plates, bowls, and other objects in diorite, which are among the most beautiful of all the fine stone objects? I have no idea. . . . But how could such a hard stone be worked? The

Egyptian of that time had at his disposal only stone, copper, and abrasive sand. . . . It is more difficult to imagine the fabrication of hard stone vases with long narrow necks and rounded bellies." Admittedly, the vessels present a problem that Lange's "imagination could not handle."

Metamorphic schist is harder than iron. The diorite used, a granitic rock, is among the hardest known. Modern sculptors do not attempt to carve these varieties of stone. Yet, these vessels were made before the introduction into Egypt of metals strong enough to cut hard stone. Numerous vessels have long, narrow necks and wide, rounded bellies. Their interiors and exteriors correspond perfectly. The tool has not been imagined that could have been inserted into their long necks to shape the perfect, rounded bellies. Smooth and glossy, these vessels bear no trace of tool marks. How were they made?

An extraordinarily hard diorite statue of Pharaoh Khafra (Chephren in Greek), builder of the Second Pyramid at Giza, was created during the Fourth Dynasty. Acknowledged to be one of the greatest masterpieces of sculpture ever produced, it was found upside down in a pit in the Valley temple south of the Sphinx, which is associated with Khafra's pyramid at Giza. Archaeologists confirm that during the Fourth Dynasty, the Egyptians did not possess metals hard enough to sculpt this diorite statue, and the Great Pyramids of Giza were also constructed during the Fourth Dynasty.

Similarly, small scarab amulets made of diorite date from early times and bear no tool marks. In other parts of the ancient world, tiny stone beads with ultrafine holes for threading defy explanation. Only the most current technology is capable of piercing holes of a comparable minute size in stone.

Mysterious ancient works in stone, ranging from the minute to the gigantic, are a testimony to ancient wisdom. The most enormous stone blocks found in temple construction are in Baalbek, Lebanon, a remarkable ancient center of Sun worship. The magnificent temples of Baalbek, with their vast courts and impressive pillars, are, for the most part, more recent structures than the feature for which the site is famous. In an outer wall of

FIGURE 1. *Diorite statue of Khafra
dates from about 2600* B.C.

the acropolis at Baalbek, three blocks are so large that they have
acquired their own name, "the trilithon." Each of these blocks
measures sixty-four feet long and thirteen feet wide. Estimated
to weigh 1,200 tons apiece, they are situated in the wall at a
height of twenty feet above the ground. It is estimated that it
would require the force of 25,000 men to raise these stones. The
placement of the trilithon has puzzled the most expert engineers.

The older portions of the acropolis wall containing these
huge blocks date to Phoenician or Canaanite times. In the
Roman temple of Jupiter at the site, one of the foundation
stones dating to more ancient times weighs 2,000 tons. The
foundation stones and the trilithon have a common bond with
the millions of enigmatic stones in the Egyptian pyramids.
They have a stellar connection—they were built under the direc-

tion of priests of solar cults during the long era when the Sun was worshipped as the supreme God. Did all the ancient builders use the same construction method as they raised the earth's mightiest monuments for the Sun? There is no doubt that there was cultural and technological exchange between Egypt and other lands.

In Khafra's Valley temple at Giza, blocks weigh up to 500 tons apiece. As will be explained, these blocks were not carved *in situ* from the bedrock as is generally assumed. Who were the men of Egypt who, without powerful machinery, placed 500 hundred-ton blocks in temples? How did they manage to place hundreds of fifteen- and twenty-ton blocks in tiers thirty stories above the ground in pyramids? Before pondering the technology of these ancient master builders, briefly consider some facts about the pyramids for which Egyptologists have no adequate explanation.

The Great Pyramid was built for a pharaoh named Khnumu-Khufu (Cheops in Greek) during his twenty-year reign. During those twenty years approximately 2.5 million limestone blocks, weighing from two to seventy tons apiece, were incorporated into his sacred monument. Large fossil shells make this stone material difficult to cut precisely. Enormous plugs of granite harder than limestone once blocked the ascending passageway. The walls of the so-called King's Chamber are granite, and the latter room contains a granite sarcophagus, which is curious in that it is too large to fit through the adjoining door and hallway.

Egyptologists claim that this unparalleled structure was built using primitive stone and copper tools. Flint tools, though they can be made with sharp cutting edges, are unsuitable for perfectly shaping millions of large blocks. Copper, which the Egyptians smelted and also mined in native form, is a soft metal. Copper saws are suitable for cutting wood, but not the type of hard granite found in the Great Pyramid, and copper implements are not applicable for cutting 2.5 million nummulitic limestone blocks in twenty years. Bronzeworking was not introduced in Egypt until about 800 years after the Great Pyramid was built, during or slightly before the Egyptian period known as the Middle Kingdom. Iron came later to Egypt and was rare even during the New Kingdom.

If the blocks of the Great Pyramid, material of medium hardness, had been shaped using bronze tools, the labor involved would equal that required for shaping all the stone monuments built during the New Kingdom, Late period, and Ptolemaic era, periods which together span 1,500 years. How did Old Kingdom pyramid builders accomplish in twenty years what required successors 1,500 years of labor?

The Great Pyramid is not an aberration. Khnumu-Khufu's (Khufu) son, Pharaoh Khafra, built the Second Pyramid at Giza, which is almost as large as that of his father, during a twenty-six year reign. Khnumu-Khufu's father, Pharaoh Sneferu, was the most prolific builder in Egypt's long history. He built two colossal pyramids, applied casing stone to another, and erected stone monuments throughout Egypt. It is estimated that Sneferu's workmen used 9 million tons of stone during the pharaoh's twenty-four year reign. All of this was expertly accomplished before the invention of the wheel as a means of transportation.

To raise a two-ton portcullis positioned in a narrow passageway in Khafra's pyramid requires the force of at least forty men. The fact that the passageway allows room for no more than eight men to work at once has caused some archaeologists to admit that extraordinary means, about which they have no information, were employed for pyramid construction.

The casing blocks of the pyramids are made of fine-grained limestone that appears to be polished. The Great Pyramid originally possessed about 115,000 casing blocks, some weighing about ten tons apiece, and covering twenty-two acres of surface area. A razor blade cannot be inserted between any two remaining casing blocks. The noted Egyptologist, Sir Flinders Petrie, determined that some casing blocks in the Great Pyramid fit as closely as 0.002 inch. Those covering the pyramid of Khafra also fit perfectly with an additional touch of expertise—they fit together with tongue-and-groove joints. How were these blocks prepared so perfectly? How did workers install them without chipping the corners even slightly?

Twenty-two steps near the top of Khafra's pyramid are un-weathered and in good condition, since the casing blocks which covered them were removed as recently as 150 years ago. In a preliminary study in 1984, I (Joseph Davidovits) measured the lengths of the thousands of blocks in these steps, which make up about ten percent of the area of the pyramid. The blocks all conform to ten uniform lengths. How could a civilization with-out the benefit of hard metals prepare many thousands of blocks with such precision?

Limestone frequently splits during cutting, even with the most efficient modern tools. Faults and strata in bedrock assure that for every block cut to standard, at least one will crack or be improperly sized during quarrying, and this rate of breakage is far more optimistic than realistic. Given the many millions of blocks in the numerous pyramids, there should be millions of cracked blocks lying nearby or somewhere in Egypt, but they are nowhere to be found.

We know that millions of broken limestone blocks were not cut down and used for building monuments when bronze and iron were introduced. By that time only soft varieties of sand-stone and granites were being used in monuments. Ancient historians who documented their visits to Giza have not men-tioned heaps of broken blocks. So this is the technological paradox of Egypt: before Egypt possessed strong metals for stone cutting, hard varieties of stone were employed in monu-ments. As bronze and iron came into use, only the softest varieties of stone were used, with very few exceptions.

Rather than providing a logical solution to the riddle of pyramid construction, investigators so far have succeeded only in challenging the flaws in numerous proposed theories. There are far more complex and perplexing aspects of the pyramid puzzle. Before describing them, let us consider the knowledge of the solar priests responsible for pyramid construction.

The ancient Egyptian town of Anu, called On by the Hebrews and Heliopolis by the Greeks, was a great religious center for thousands of years. The city, located about twenty-five miles from Giza, was erected on holy ground, symbolizing rebirth and creation. Starting at the time of the great Imhotep, the Heliopolitan priest credited with inspiring and engineering the first pyramid, the priests of Heliopolis engaged in raising spectacular pyramids and temples for the Sun. These priests excelled in arts and sciences. They were considered to be the traditional wise men of Egypt throughout that nation's extremely long history. Religious philosophy, mysticism, mathematics, geometry, horology, and astronomy were among the sciences piously fostered by the priests.

Their preoccupation with the heavens is reflected in the orientation of pyramids and temples and stemmed from great reverence for the Sun and other stars. The priests descended from an extremely long and learned line. During prehistoric times, their ancestors invented the first 365-day calendar.

Archaeologists assume that modern science is in every way superior to the science of antiquity. However, with technological and scientific possibilities being as limitless as the human imagination, it is unsubstantial bias to suppose that modern technology is all-encompassing and always superior. The pyramids and other monuments provide a glimpse into a tremendous knowledge gap between ancient and modern science. A vast body of methods and knowledge very different from our own awaits rediscovery. Several thought-provoking examples of ancient technology have been found in many regions.

One striking example of superior ancient technology is the long-term preservation of food and other organic materials. One remarkable example is the tomb of a woman, the Lady of Tai, found by archaeologists in Honan, China. The wife of a nobleman, she died more than 2,000 years ago in about 186 B.C. When discovered, her body was in the condition of someone who had been dead no longer than a week. Most remarkably, her flesh was still elastic enough to return to its proper shape after pressure was applied. Her body was not mummified, embalmed, tanned, or frozen. Preservation occurred with the body immersed in a mysterious brownish liquid containing mercuric sulfide. The coffin was set into other protective coffins sealed with pasty white clay and layers of charcoal. The water- and air-tight chamber kept its contents at a constant tem- perature of 55° F (13° C).

There are also astounding examples of long-term food pre- servation. Until recent years, few archaeologists acknowledged that ancient people successfully stored grain for long periods. In the 1800s European travelers discovered ancient grain silos in Spain. It has since been learned that grain was once stored in sealed subterranean silos universally. Ancient silos have been found in Hungary, Ukrania, Turkestan, India, and several re- gions of Africa. In Central and North America subterranean silos were built by numerous Indian tribes. In France and in England, subterranean silos were found in abundance. Agron- omists were initially surprised to find that sealed silos can successfully store grain.

In the Nile valley, the inundating river made subterranean silos impractical and above-ground silos were constructed. They have been depicted in bas-reliefs and look like upside- down earthenware jars. In the pyramids, too, grain has been found free of mold and in good condition after thousands of years. Though germination was unsuccessful, the condition of the grain was so good that researchers attempted germination.

In contrast, using state-of-the-art technology, the U.S. De- partment of Agriculture can store grain for no more than four years before insect infestation and mold render it unfit for human consumption. Modern storage methods, based on ven- tilation, sharply contrast with the sealed systems used in antiq- uity, demonstrating the vast difference between ancient and modern technology.

The Great Pyramid has a legitimate reputation for its ability to preserve organic matter. Historically, the pyramids were called the storehouses of the Hebrew patriarch Joseph, son of Jacob. The biblical book of Genesis recounts that grain was stored in Egypt by Joseph from seven to perhaps as much as twenty years. The Genesis story has been discounted in modern times because historians are generally unaware that ancient peoples were capable of such technology. The account cannot be doubted in light of the information already presented.

In the 1930s, Antoine Bovis, a Frenchman, observed that animals that wandered into the Great Pyramid and perished before finding their way out did not decompose. He began to investigate, and thus was born the theory of pyramid power. Its advocates attribute the Great Pyramid's ability to preserve organic matter to the alignment and shape of the pyramid itself. However, this theory does not explain why preservation can also occur in other tombs. Some theorists suggest that the pyramids and their surroundings are protected by a mysterious force, but no such force has prevented the pyramids from being raided during antiquity or excavated in modern times.

When tourists enter the Grand Gallery and the so-called King's Chamber of the Great Pyramid for the first time, most are surprised to encounter high humidity. In 1974, a joint research project carried out by Stanford Research Institute (SRI International), of Stanford (California) University, and Ain Shams University, in Cairo, indicated that whereas the bedrock of Giza is dry, the pyramid blocks are full of moisture. The scientists attempted to locate hidden chambers in the Great Pyramids of Giza with electromagnetic sounding equipment but were prevented by the high moisture content of the blocks. The waves emitted by the equipment would not transmit through the pyramid stone. The waves were instead absorbed, ending any chance of a successful mission. The Great Pyramids attract moisture in the midst of an arid desert necropolis. Why? How can the atmosphere in their chambers be conducive to preserving organic matter?

In an attempt to discover ancient secrets of preservation, the Egyptian Antiquities Organization (AEO), in Cairo, assembled an impressive team of scientists from the National Geographic Society and the National Oceanic and Atmospheric Administration. The scientists are studying the air sealed inside the rectangular pit in front of the Great Pyramid—air which is 4,500 years old. Samples of air are being encapsulated using space technology developed by NASA for testing the atmosphere of other planets. Scientists hope to learn from ambient temperatures, pressure, and the air itself, how preservation was accomplished.

Because artifacts begin to deteriorate once they are excavated and exposed to the air, one of the most treasured items of antiquity was placed in jeopardy. In the 1950s, an excavation of one of the pits near the Great Pyramid yielded a sacred funerary boat of Khnumu-Khufu. To the delight of archaeologists, the acclaimed artifact was preserved in perfect condition. The boat, measuring more than 120 feet, had a displacement capacity of over forty tons.

The hull, composed of hundreds of pieces of wood shaped to fit together like a jigsaw puzzle, is cleverly sewn together with a single piece of rope. The boat does not require caulking or tar to be completely water-tight. The design principle is that when wet, wood swells whereas rope shrinks, producing an automatic seal impervious to water.

A specially designed museum was erected under the auspices of the Egyptian Antiquities Organization to house and display Khufu's boat. After the museum opened, serious problems were encountered. The atmospheric control system could not accommodate the vast number of tourists passing in and out of the building. The boat, which the ancient Egyptians had confidently called "Boat of Millions of Years," rapidly began to disintegrate. The museum closed its doors to the public for some time. Subsequently, costly, energy-consuming devices were successfully substituted for the original cost-free, self-powered means that had so subtly and perfectly preserved the entombed boat for 4,500 years.

Khufu's boat is far more seaworthy than any craft of Christopher Columbus's day. The famous mission of Thor Heyerdahl in 1970, from Morocco to Barbados in a papyrus reed boat, makes it clear that ancient Egyptian ships were capable of intercontinental travel. Their seaworthy craft is impressive, but crossing an ocean is a demanding venture. With their knowledge of the stars, it is likely that the Egyptians were excellent navigators, but how would they obtain fresh water at sea? In modern times desalination is achieved through several methods, including distillation, electrodialysis, freezing, ion exchange, and reverse osmosis, all requiring either high-energy input or advanced apparatus or materials. There is evidence that the Egyptians not only possessed technology for perpetually obtaining moisture in the desert, but were able also to extract fresh water from the ocean.

The ancient method was described by the Roman naturalist, Pliny (AD 23–79). In his Latin work *Natural History,* Pliny described curious ceramic vessels, which, during voyages, were tightly corked and immersed into the sea in nets—where they automatically filled with pure, fresh water. When Pliny's text was translated from Latin to French in 1833 by the French Academy of Sciences (to compare ancient science with science of their day), the scholars could not believe the account. During their era, distillation was the only way of obtaining fresh water from salt water.

The Romans occupied Egypt from 30 BC to AD 395 and absorbed some of the technology developed in the country during more ancient times. It seems unlikely that the Egyptians would have built ships capable of crossing an ocean unless they also possessed technology that assured their survival.

Whether ancient Egyptian travelers, or those who may have inherited their technology, influenced other megalithic-building civilizations around the globe is a matter of debate. Enigmatic stone edifices, most often difficult to transport and place and bearing no tool marks, are found in numerous regions. Foundation blocks at Tiahuanaco, Bolivia, weigh 100 tons apiece. The Cuzco walls in Peru are made of enormous stones—spectacular because of their unusual jigsaw joints. The Easter Island statues were studied by a UNESCO-sponsored team, which reported that the oldest statues do not match mineralogically stone of the quarries. Standing stones of prehistoric Brittany tower over sixty-five feet high and one weighs more than 340 tons. Also curious are the Pyramids of the Sun in Mexico, numerous stone sundials in North America, and the stone calendar or observatory of Stonehenge, England.

Of all the mysteries of the ancient world, the Great Pyramids with their adjoining complexes provide the most obvious evidence of sophisticated technology very different from our own. Although the other megalith-building civilizations left no written history holding relevant clues about the technology used, the ancient Egyptians left a wealth of information. Egyptian written history spans a 3,000-year period, and though much has been destroyed, surviving records are a treasure of information on surgery, medicine, mathematics, the arts, topography, religion, and much more. Egyptologists have long claimed that no surviving records describe how the pyramids were built. They are incorrect in this assumption, as will be shown in a later chapter.

Considering the number of workers necessarily involved in pyramid design and construction, the actual building method employed was known or witnessed by enormous numbers of people. Their methods, therefore, could not have been secret and must have been documented. Most hieroglyphic and cuneiform texts were deciphered in the 1800s and have not been updated to reflect current archaeological finds or scientific developments. They cannot, therefore, be completely accurate; so accurate conclusions about ancient technology cannot necessarily be drawn from them.

To discover more about the level of ancient technology, pyramidologists focus their attention on the dimensions, design, orientation, and mathematical aspects of the Great Pyramid. These mirror the level of some of the science of the Pyramid Age, but pyramidologists have overlooked the most enigmatic aspect of the pyramids, the blocks themselves.

Much of the scientific research on the stone of the Great Pyramid raises more questions than it answers. For instance, in 1974, geologists at Stanford University analyzed casing-block samples from the Great Pyramid. They were unable to classify paleontologically the samples containing no shells. This raises the question: Where does the pyramid stone come from? A team of geochemists from the University of Munich, Germany, sampled quarries along the Nile and removed specimens from twenty different blocks of the main body of the Great Pyramid.

To determine the origin of the pyramid blocks, they compared trace elements of the pyramid samples with those of the quarry samples. Their interpretation of the test results is startling. The scientists concluded that the pyramid blocks came from all of the twenty quarries sampled. In other words, to build the Great Pyramid, these geochemists say that the Egyptians hauled stone for hundreds of miles, from all over Egypt—an amazing feat for which archaeologists have no logical explanation.

Geologists do not concur with their findings. They can demonstrate that the source of stone is near the pyramid itself. Yet, they are unable to explain the fact that while the bedrock of the Giza plateau is made up of strata, the pyramid blocks contain no strata.

Although geologists and geochemists cannot agree on the origin of the pyramid blocks, geologists cannot agree among themselves on the source of stone used for the wondrous statues built for the Eighteenth Dynasty pharaoh, Amenhotep III, in the Valley of the Kings. The awe-inspiring statues, the Colossi of Memnon, were originally monolithic and weigh 750 tons apiece. They rest on monolithic 550-ton pedestals. The structures are each seven stories high. They are made of hard, dense quartzite, which is almost impossible to carve. At the beginning of the nineteenth century, members of the Napoleonic Egyptian expedition remarked about these statues and Egypt's quartzite quarries in *Description de l'Egypte:*

> None of the quartzite hills or quarries show tool marks, as are so common in the sandstone and granite quarries. We have to conclude that a material so hard and unworkable by sharp tools must have been exploited by a process other than that generally used for sandstone, or even granite. . . . We do not know anything about the process used by the Egyptians to square this stone, to trim the surfaces, or to impart the beautiful polish that we see today on some parts of the statues. Even if we have not determined the means used, we are forced to admire the results. . . . When the tool of the engraver in the middle of a hieroglyphic character hit a flint or agate in the stone, the sketch was never hindered, but instead it continued in all its purity. Neither the agate fragment nor the stone itself was even slightly broken by engraving.

19

This last observation has profound implications. What masonry process could possibly allow hieroglyphs to be inscribed in this manner? The beloved king Amenhotep III called the production of his statues "a miracle." Hieroglyphic documents written after his time refer to this type of stone as *biat inr,* meaning "stone resulting from a wonder." What technological wonder did Amenhotep behold?

French and German scholars, who will be discussed later, claim that the Colossi of Memnon were carved from a quarry fifty miles away and hauled along the Nile by boat. English and American geologists advocate a feat bordering on the unbelievable. They claim that the statues were quarried and hauled 440 miles down river—against the flow of the Nile. As more sophisticated methods, such as atomic absorption, X-ray fluorescence and neutronic activation are used to study Egypt's most enigmatic monuments, more confusion arises.

The Great Sphinx in front of Khafra's pyramid has become more controversial than ever in light of recent geological studies. Based on the severe manner in which blocks covering the lower layers of the body and paws are eroded, the age of the Sphinx has, once again, come into serious question.

Today, the Sphinx is attributed to Khafra. Earlier Egyptologists believed it was erected a great deal earlier than his reign, perhaps at the end of the Archaic period. The Sphinx looks much older than the pyramids.

No inscriptions connect the sacred monument to Khafra, but in the Valley Temple, a dozen statues of Khafra, one in the form of a Sphinx, were uncovered in the 1950s. Some Egyptologists claim a resemblance between these statues and the face of the Sphinx.

A document which indicates greater antiquity, however, was found on the Giza plateau by French Egyptologists during the nineteenth century. The text, called the "Inventory Stele," bears inscriptions relating events occurring during the reign of Khafra's father, Khufu. The text says that Khufu instructed that a temple be erected alongside the Sphinx, meaning that the Sphinx already existed before Khafra's time. The accuracy of the stele has been questioned because it dates from the Twenty-first Dynasty (1070–945 BC), long after the Pyramid Age, but because the Egyptians took great pride in precise record keeping and the careful copying of documents, no authoritative reason exists to discount the text as inaccurate.

Fragments of early papyruses and tablets, as well as the later writings of the third century BC Greco-Egyptian historian Manetho, claim that Egypt was ruled for thousands of years before the First Dynasty—some texts claim as much as 36,000 years earlier. This chronology is dismissed by Egyptologists as legend. However, ancient Egyptian history is viewed by scholars mostly from a New Kingdom perspective because numerous documents have survived from Thebes. The capital of Memphis, founded during prehistoric times, was a vitally important religious, commercial, cultural, and administrative center with a life span of thousands of years, but unfortunately, it has not been effectively excavated.

The recent geological studies of the Sphinx have kindled more than debate over the attribution and age. The established history of the evolution of civilization is being challenged.

A study of the severe body erosion of the sphinx and the hollow in which it is situated indicates that the damaging agent was water. A slow erosion occurs in limestone when water is absorbed and reacts with salts in the stone. The controversy arises over the source of the vast amount of water responsible.

Two theories are popular. One is that groundwater slowly rose into the body of the Sphinx. This theory produces irreconcilable problems: A recent survey carried out by the American Research Center in Egypt (ARCE) determined that three distinctly separate repair operations were completed on the Sphinx between the New Kingdom and Ptolemaic rule, that is, during a period of roughly 700 to 1,000 years. The study also indicates that the Sphinx was already in its current state of erosion when these early repairs were made. No appreciable erosion has occurred since the original damage, nor is there further damage on the bedrock of the surrounding hollow, an area that never underwent repair.

Knowing this, one must consider that the inundating Nile slowly built up levels of silt over the millennia, and this was accompanied by a gradual rise in the water table. During Khafra's time the water table was about thirty feet lower than it is today. For the rising groundwater theory to hold, an unbelievable geological scenario would have to have taken place. It would mean that from thirty feet lower than today's water table, water rose to about two feet into the body of the Sphinx and the surrounding hollow, where it caused erosion for roughly 600 years, and then stopped its damaging effects.

Historians find the second theory that is offered more unthinkable. It suggests that the source of water stemmed from the wet phases of the last ice age—c. 15,000 to 10,000 BC—when Egypt underwent periods of severe flooding. This hypothesis advocates that the Sphinx necessarily existed before the floods. If it could be proven, well-established theories about prehistory would be radically shaken. The world's most mysterious sculpture would date to a time when historians place humanity in a neolithic setting, living in open camps and depending largely on hunting and foraging.

The age of the pyramids themselves has been challenged by a recent project carried out, in cooperation with the American Research Center in Egypt (ARCE), with radiocarbon (carbon-14) dating. Although limestone contains no carbon for dating purposes, mortar found in various parts of the pyramids' core masonry contains minute fragments of organic material, usually calcined charcoal or reeds. Some fragments are too minute to be dated by standard methods, and therefore, carbon-14 dating was also carried out with the aid of an atomic accelerator in Zurich, Switzerland.

Seventy-one samples were collected from thirteen pyramids or their surrounding funerary monuments. From the core masonry of the Great Pyramid itself, fifteen samples were taken at various levels from bottom to top.

The test results announced by the research team are startling. The team claimed that their tests indicate that the Great Pyramid is up to 450 years older than Egyptology had established from the archaeological record. Most remarkably, the team also reported that the mortar at the top of the Great Pyramid was older than that on the bottom and that the Great Pyramid dated older than the Step Pyramid of Zoser, which Egyptologists have established as the first ever built.

All Egyptologists are in firm agreement that the Great Pyramid was built about 100 years after Zoser's pyramid. Those questioned about the recent carbon-dating project deny the possibility of the accuracy of the tests. The researchers, however, are confident that their sampling was careful and their methods effective. A German laboratory previously sampled tombs at Saqqara and their tests also provided dates of about 400 to 450 years earlier than established dates.

The baffling features of the Valley Temple near the Sphinx deeply impressed members of the Napoleonic expedition at the beginning of the nineteenth century. Francois Jomard, a member of the expedition, at first thought that the enormous temple blocks were protrusions of bedrock that had been rough cut and squared. As mentioned, the blocks are assumed today to have been carved *in situ*. But Jomard noticed cement between the blocks of the temple and realized he was observing deliberately placed blocks weighing as much as 500 tons. Reflecting amazement and admiration, he remarked in *Description de l'Egypt,* "I wonder who these Egyptian men that playfully moved colossal masses around were, for each stone is itself a monolith in the sense that each is enormous."

Engineers have not reconciled the logistical problems that would be encountered by raising stones of this magnitude. To shift them about manually and set them so perfectly in place with cement in their joints in the small work area would have been impossible. A remark that Petrie made when describing stones in the inner gallery of Khufu's pyramid makes this point clear: "To place such stones in exact contact required careful work, but to do so with cement in the joints seems almost impossible." Petrie was referring to stones that weighed sixteen tons—a mere fraction of the weight of these temple blocks.

The floor of the Valley Temple is made of white alabaster

slabs. Interior walls are lined with precisely joined granite facing blocks. The curious tailoring of the corners in the interior is unlike anything found in modern architecture. Blocks curve around the walls and join in a diverse interlocking jigsaw pattern. These hard and beautifully crafted stones exemplify an extraordinary masonry method.

Petrie introduced the puzzles of pyramid construction with the publication of *Pyramids and Temples of Giza* in 1883. The topic simmered in the public mind until the writings of amateur archaeologist Erich von Daniken caused the controversy to explode in the 1970s. In his book *Chariots of the Gods?* von Daniken sought the solution to the numerous engineering enigmas of the past. He wrote, "The Great Pyramid is (and remains?) visible testimony of a technique that has never been understood. Today, in the twentieth century, no architect could build a copy of the Pyramid of Cheops even if the technical resources were at his disposal. How is anyone going to explain these and other puzzles to us?"

Our book reveals the true method of pyramid construction, and, as I will explain, most of the mysteries of the ancient world are finally solved by one major scientific breakthrough. The discovery is so dramatic and far reaching that many important aspects of ancient history will be rewritten in their entirety. First, a deeper look at the unresolved problems of pyramid construction is required.

CHAPTER 2

A Close Look at the Problem

GENERALLY, PEOPLE BELIEVE THAT THE PYRAMIDS WERE built by primitive methods of quarrying, carving, and hoisting huge limestone blocks because they have been conditioned thusly. They have accepted their conditioning because it is handed down through the authority of scholarship. What they generally are not taught is that the evidence for the accepted theory is flagrant.

About thirty theories attempt to explain how the Great Pyramid may have been constructed by carving and hoisting stone, all proposed by intelligent people with academic backgrounds. Yet something is wrong with reasoning that spawns such technological profusion. Nothing is wrong with the logic itself; it is the premise of the logic that is erroneous. Simply, traditional theory has not resolved the problems of pyramid construction.

Common sense rejects as illogical any conclusion accompanied by blatant flaws. And the more closely we examine the issue, the more blatant those flaws become. In my own process

25

of discovering the true method of pyramid construction, my first step was to examine closely the accepted theory. I found myself embarked on a fascinating analytical journey, one that began with a close look at the unresolved problems of pyramid construction.

As mentioned previously, the labor involved in cutting the amount of stone in the Great Pyramid equals that required to cut all of the stone used in the monuments produced during the New Kingdom, Late period, and Ptolemaic period combined, a span of about 1,500 years (1550–30 BC). A calculation of the amount of stone used during this 1,500-year period was made by de Roziere, a geologist with the Napoleonic expedition.

Napoleon's army was stranded in Egypt for fourteen months during the French Revolution. An army of 50,000 men was accompanied by 150 scholars, among them Geoffroy Saint-Hilaire, a naturalist; de Dolomien, the minerologist who lent his name to dolomite; Dominique Vivant Denon, an artist and engraver; Claude Bertholet, a chemist; Dominique Larrey, a surgeon; Guillaume Villoteau, a musician; Marie Jules de Savigny, a botanist; Nicholas Conte, the inventor of the lead pencil; Colonel Coutelle, a geometrician; and de Roziere, a geologist. The academics among the group produced the most impressive study ever of Egyptian monuments.

Between 1809 and 1813, Francois Jomard, general commissioner for the scientific expedition, produced his great work, *Description de l'Egypte,* based on the research of the Cairo Institute, which was founded by Napoleon. In this work de Roziere reported his volumetric approximations of stone used in Egyptian edifices.

Using approximations, I have estimated that the surviving sandstone edifices might represent a total surface area of about one and a half million square meters [125.5 acres], which are covered with bas-reliefs, including columns, pylons, and enclosure walls. This does not include the monuments which were demolished, of which vestiges can still be seen, and those which must have been destroyed completely, which would perhaps form a very considerable amount. And this estimate does not include Nubia, where the sandstone monuments are hardly less numerous and widespread than those of the Thebaid. By similar means, I have estimated the total volume of surviving sandstone monuments to be more than one million cubic meters [35,314,475 cubic feet]. The total would not be doubled by adding those which have disappeared because part of this material was used in succeeding edifices. If we take into account the material used in foundations, floors, roads, quays, and hydraulic constructions, we can estimate at a glance that there must have been at least three or four million cubic meters [141,257,950 cubic feet] of carved sandstone from quarries simply for those constructions in the Thebaid that can be estimated. However large this quantity, it still does not equal half of the material that exists merely in the pyramids of Giza or those at Saqqara.

My following calculation demonstrates the inefficiency of the accepted method of pyramid construction. The calculation is based on the amount and hardness of the stone used and the time required for construction. To balance the equation we will assume that bronze tools were used to prepare the blocks for the Great Pyramid even though they were unavailable. For a given amount of labor, using the same bronze tools as were used to build and decorate the sandstone edifices of the New Kingdom and later periods mentioned, all that could be carved would be half of this amount of a medium-hard limestone, such as that used in the Great Pyramid. Only a quarter of this amount could have been carved of Carrara marble, and scarcely a sixteenth of this amount of basalt. In other words, the labor required to cut, haul, and hoist the 2 million cubic meters (70 million cubic feet) of limestone for the Great Pyramid alone, during twenty years of work, equals the labor used to carve and erect the 4 million cubic meters (141,257,950 cubic feet) of sandstone used for all the monuments built during the 1,500 years of the New Kingdom, Late period, and Ptolemaic period combined **(Figure 2)**.

I use a twenty-year construction period for the Great Pyramid in this calculation for two reasons. First, each pyramid was built during the reign of the pharaoh for whom it was constructed. The reign of Pharaoh Khufu was from 2704 to 2683 BC, or twenty-one years. Second, when the Greek historian

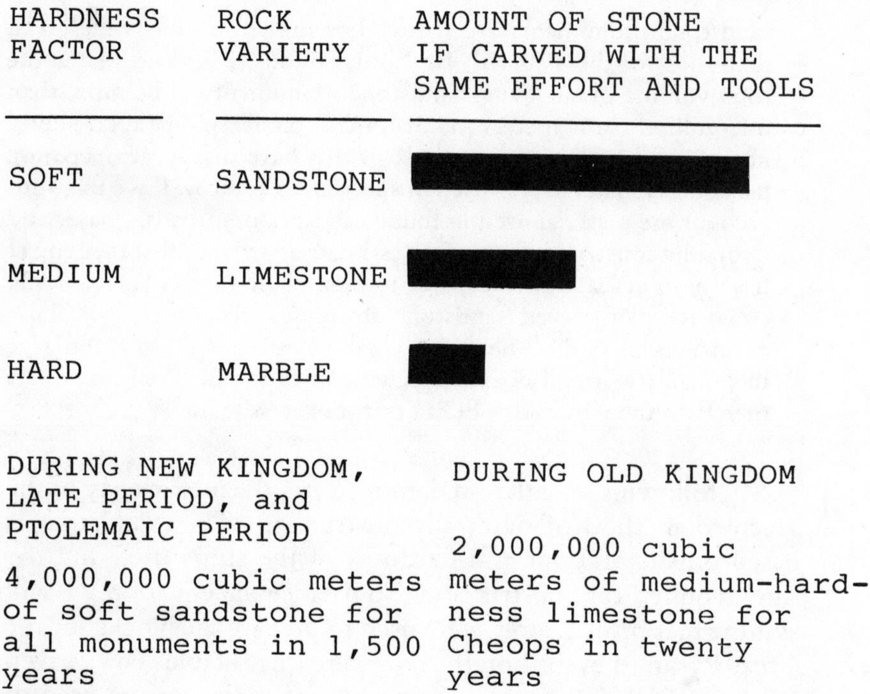

HARDNESS FACTOR	ROCK VARIETY	AMOUNT OF STONE IF CARVED WITH THE SAME EFFORT AND TOOLS
SOFT	SANDSTONE	████████████████
MEDIUM	LIMESTONE	████████
HARD	MARBLE	████

DURING NEW KINGDOM, LATE PERIOD, and PTOLEMAIC PERIOD	DURING OLD KINGDOM
4,000,000 cubic meters of soft sandstone for all monuments in 1,500 years	2,000,000 cubic meters of medium-hardness limestone for Cheops in twenty years

FIGURE 2. *Construction of the Great Pyramid required the same effort as the construction of all monuments in the 1,500 previous years.*

Herodotus (c. 485–425 BC) visited Egypt, he was told that the Great Pyramid was constructed in twenty years.

During the combined New Kingdom, Late period, and Ptolemaic period 4 million cubic yards of sandstone monuments were prepared in 1,500 years. During the Old Kingdom, about 2 million cubic yards of stone for the Great Pyramid were prepared in twenty years. As mentioned, this production period is no aberration because the two pyramids of Sneferu (2575–2551 BC), which have a total volume of 4 million cubic yards, were produced during this king's reign of twenty-four years. And the Second Pyramid at Giza has a volume of 2 million cubic yards and was built during the twenty-six year reign of Pharaoh Khafra (2520–2429 BC).

Because the Old Kingdom limestone is twice as hard as the sandstone used during the New Kingdom and later periods mentioned, the Old Kingdom could have produced 4 million cubic meters of sandstone in twenty years. Therefore, to show how much more productive the Old Kingdom was compared with the New Kingdom and later times, we divide 1,500 years by 20 years, yielding 75 years. Assuming that during the New Kingdom and later as few as 10,000 workers were continuously involved in such labor, then 750,000 workers (75 × 10,000) would have been required to work on the Great Pyramid to achieve the same productivity.

It is ridiculous to suppose that the 750,000 men required could effectively labor together in the work area at Giza; and Egyptians of the Old Kingdom, without bronze tools, accomplished in twenty years what took Egyptians of the New Kingdom, Late, and Ptolemaic periods together 1,500 years. This calculation makes it obvious that the standard construction theory is unacceptable.

Egyptologists are able to make only a poor attempt to settle this issue. Egyptologist Dieter Arnold, in an attempt to reconcile the vast number of blocks that would have to have been set per day, proposed to expand the life span of the pharaohs far beyond that provided for by Egyptology. In *Ueberlegungen zum Problem des Pyramidenbaus,* Arnold calculated that from Sneferu to Khafra, a period he calculated to be eighty years, 12 million blocks were used in pyramids, yielding a minimum of 413 blocks set per day. He recognized that the number of blocks would not begin on the first day of the pharaoh's reign. A site had to be chosen, plans drawn, and the leveling work completed. Depending on when work began on the pyramid itself, the number of blocks would exceed 413 and possibly become two to three times as high, leading to, as Arnold said, "astronomical numbers." Arnold therefore proposed, "There can only be one solution . . . namely to increase the lifetime of the pharaoh. . . ." He proposed life spans which are two or three times as long as those established by Egyptologists from existing records.

It is abundantly clear, however, that even by going against the grain of established Egyptology by vastly lengthening life spans, no appreciable dent is made in the enormous problem. Arnold admitted, "But we cannot deduce from the records how the Egyptian workers managed to accomplish this task. But the fact that they were able to solve the hard problems they were facing is beautifully exemplified by the pyramids of Khufu and Khafra." In this last statement, one begins to see the futility of the typical response to this puzzle. Instead of considering that a different method must have been used, experts throw up their hands and admire the monument in question.

The same type of response has been provided for the problems of quarrying hard varieties of granite and other hard rocks with primitive methods. We have already seen a passage from *Description de l'Egypte* mentioning that the means for quarrying the hard quartzite used for the Memnon Colossi had not been determined. A substantial number of finely jointed blocks of hard granite appear in the Egyptian pyramids. In *The Pyramids of Egypt,* I. E. S. Edwards, retired Keeper of Egyptian Antiquities for the British Museum, writes:

> The methods employed in the Pyramid Age for quarrying granite and other hard stones are still a subject of controversy. One authority even expressed the opinion that hard-stone quarrying was not attempted until the Middle Kingdom; before that time, the amount needed could have been obtained from large boulders lying loose on the surface of the ground. It seems difficult, however, to believe that a people who possessed the degree of skill necessary for shaping the colossal monoliths built into the granite valley building of Chephren were not also able to hew blocks of this stone out of the quarry.

In other words, because beautifully formed granite blocks appear in the pyramid complexes, the Egyptians must have quarried such stone even though expert opinion denies the possibility. Here, results are used as proof of method. This is a useless process when it ignores well-founded arguments to the contrary. Worse, the it-must-have-been-so approach does not settle the issue because the method by which hard granite blocks were shaped for construction remains unsettled.

Although it is taken for granted that the pyramids were erected by workers using simple stone or copper hand tools and primitive quarrying techniques, an examination of these methods will help to show how really limited they are. French archaeologist and architect Jean Paul Adams remarked on the amount of surface area of stone that would have to have been cut for pyramid construction in *Archaeology Face-to-Face with Imposture*.

> It is easily imagined from this, that to obtain one cubic meter [35 cubic feet] of building stone it was easier to make it in one single piece than from a number of smaller blocks which would considerably multiply the number and extent of surfaces to be worked. But before the carving, there was the extraction. Nowadays, it is difficult to imagine workers attacking a rocky cliff with stone axes. It is, however, in this way that numerous megaliths were detached and squared. *

Assuming that the builders aimed for maximum efficiency when carving stone, the first pyramids should have been made of enormous blocks with a relatively low surface-to-volume ratio. As tools improved, the dimensions of the blocks forming the monuments should have diminished, yielding a higher surface-to-volume ratio. The opposite happened. The pyramid of Zoser (c. 2670 BC), the first ever erected, was made entirely of small stones, 25 centimeters (9.8 inches) high, weighing only several dozens of kilograms (50–100 pounds) apiece. Blocks in the Great Pyramid, the seventh or eighth in chronology, are larger, weighing at least two tons apiece. Beams forming the vaults of the inner chambers of the last pyramids of the Fifth and Sixth Dynasties weigh from thirty to forty tons apiece. Monolithic burial chambers produced during the Twelfth Dynasty weigh seventy-two metric tonnes and more. We see that the size of stones gradually increased. Accordingly, the conventional theory does not accommodate the evolution of pyramid construction.

*Translation from the French from *L'Archeologie devant l'imposture*.

Dressing or knapping blocks with stone or copper tools would pose serious problems, and more acute problems would be encountered if another, still cruder, method advocated by Egyptologists was used to produce pyramid blocks. Adams remarked:

> When dressing the surfaces was necessary, two techniques could have been used. The first, already described, consisted of dressing with the aid of hard stones or metal tools, the art of knapping being quite well known at the time. The second method described in Egyptian documents, among other sources, consisted of heating the surface of the stone very strongly with fire, then spraying on water to make it split.

Heating stone and applying water is applicable for reducing large pieces of sandstone, granite, or basalt into small aggregates. But granite blocks, for instance, in the base of Khafra's pyramid have only one flat side, perhaps the result of splitting by the water and heat method. The other surfaces of the stone are irregular, demonstrating that this technique is not applicable for making perfect blocks.

FIGURE 3. *Irregular granite blocks on the west side of the Second Pyramid suggest builders of the Fourth Dynasty were unable to quarry regular granite blocks, if these were part of the original masonry.*

In addition, blocks of the dimensions used for the pyramid of Zoser ($25 \times 15 \times 10$ centimeters, or $9.8 \times 5.9 \times 3.39$ inches) cannot be dressed by heating and applying water without reducing them to debris. Moreover, heating with fire transforms limestone into lime, because the transformation to lime occurs at $704°$ C ($1,300°$ F). This completely disqualifies the use of the heating operation for producing pyramid blocks.

How efficient are flint and copper tools for shaping pyramid blocks? Tools made of hard stone are useful for working softer varieties of stone but are not applicable for producing 2.5 million blocks for the Great Pyramid in twenty years. Copper is a soft metal. Because it is unsuitable for cutting hard stone, a popular theory proposes that the ancient Egyptians mastered a process for giving copper a high temper. This surmise has never been proved, and there is no evidence to support it. No such highly tempered copper has ever been found. It is difficult to believe, when considering the billions of dollars of research money spent on metallurgy in modern times, that the technique would not have been rediscovered.

Although the Great Pyramids were erected during historic times, technically they belong to the Chalcolithic (copper-producing) period, which marked the end of the Neolithic Age. The only metals known in Egypt were gold, copper, silver, and lead, which are all quite malleable. Native copper was available in the eastern desert, and copper was smelted from ores since prehistoric times. A copper arsenate alloy, considered as bronze, was used in Egypt during early times. This, however, was not a hard product.

The type of bronze required for cutting rock of medium hardness is an alloy of copper and tin, such as that introduced at either the end of the Middle Kingdom or in the early New Kingdom, about 1900 BC. In other words, hard bronze was introduced 800 years after the Great Pyramid was built. Some scholars estimate the appearance of iron at about 1400 BC, and others place it as late as 850 BC.

I am not suggesting that stone and copper tools were not used in pyramid construction where applicable. These primitive tools were used for leveling and tunneling work and for sculpting the *in situ* body of the Great Sphinx. Whereas fossil shells in the Giza bedrock make it difficult to cut into blocks, the bedrock itself is loosely bound and easily disaggregated.

However, shaping the Sphinx cannot be compared with building the Great Pyramid. We must appreciate the vast difference between using stone and copper implements for hollowing out tunnels and sculpting *in situ* monuments and for using these same tools to produce 2.5 million blocks for the Great Pyramid in twenty years. Stone and copper tools are not applicable for producing the approximately 115,000 casing blocks that were fit together with tolerances averaging 0.02 inch and as small as 0.002 inch in the Great Pyramid. The scale and precision of the Great Pyramid is simply too grand for primitive tools to have been applicable.

The problems of logistics are far more mysterious and complex than has been realized. The logistical studies established so far have never even considered certain germane issues. The geochemical study mentioned earlier, for instance, by D. D. Klemm, a German geochemist from the University of Munich, presents an unusual new dimension to the puzzle.

Klemm presented data at the Second International Congress of Egyptologists, held in Grenoble, France, in 1979. As mentioned, he attempted to determine which quarries provided blocks for the Great Pyramid. His team sampled twenty different building blocks from the Great Pyramid. The team also sampled twenty geological sites along the Nile, excluding those of Tura and Mokhatam on the east bank, which are in a restricted area. The team then compared trace elements in the pyramid samples with those of the quarry samples.

Based on his analyses, Klemm reported that the twenty pyramid blocks he sampled came from the different geological sites he sampled. In other words, he concluded that blocks for the Great Pyramid were hauled from sites hundreds of miles away from the pyramid itself. This presents a dramatic conflict. Legend has it that the blocks came from Tura and Mokhatam (not tested by Klemm). Geologists who have performed petrographic analyses affirm that the blocks for the Great Pyramid were quarried at Giza. Now a geochemist has determined that the blocks came from sites hundreds of miles away. The paramount problems Klemm's study poses threaten all logistical studies made so far on the Great Pyramid.

As mentioned, the same sort of scientific dilemma is associated with the Memnon Colossi in the Theban necropolis. These remarkable monuments were built during the New Kingdom, a period during which the quality of architecture declined in comparison with that of the Old Kingdom. The colossi are two gigantic seated statues of the great Eighteenth Dynasty Pharaoh Amenhotep III. They adorned the entrance of his funerary temple, which is now demolished but which also must have been spectacular.

The colossi were originally monolithic and are made of exceptionally hard quartzite, a type of stone that is almost impossible to carve. The statues weigh 750 tons apiece and rest on 556-ton pedestals. Including their pedestals, they each originally stood sixty-three feet high or the height of a seven-story building. The width at the shoulders is twenty feet. The length of the middle finger of the hand is 1.35 meters (4.5 feet).

A legend is associated with the statues. The northernmost of the colossi was damaged during an earthquake around 27 BC. After the earthquake, reports say that every morning when sunlight struck the statue, musical tones, like those of a harp, were emitted. The statue was repaired about 250 years after the earthquake by a Roman emperor, Septimus Severus, during the Roman occupation of Egypt. His men repaired the statue by adding blocks, so it is no longer made of a solid piece of stone. From the day of the repair forward, the statue remained silent.

Even more interesting are the features that have mystified those who discovered the colossi and modern scientists alike. The passage from *Description de l'Egypte* describes the fact that none of the quartzite deposits, where the stone had to have originated, exhibit tool marks, and that it was the opinion of members of the Napoleonic expedition, that because the quartzite is so hard, an unknown process must have been used on this unworkable type of stone. Members of the expedition were amazed by the fact that the flint and agate aggregates constituting the stone were never disturbed by the engraving process.

In 1913, French scholar M. G. Doressy and German scholar G. Steindorff proposed that the 750-ton statues were transported along the flow of the Nile from around Edfu or Aswan to Thebes. In 1965, L. Habachi, a German archaeologist at the Cairo Institute, concurred. In 1973, a team from the University of California, Berkeley, proposed a more incredible feat. Based on the team's studies, it was proposed that the statues were quarried at Gebel el-Ahmar, not far from Cairo. In other words, they say that the 750-ton colossi were floated 440 miles along the Nile against its flow!

To determine the source of the quartzite, the French and German teams made petrographic analyses. They analyzed flint, agate, and the other components of the stone. The Berkeley team studied the geochemical aspects of the quartzite, performing analyses on infinitesimal quantities of trace elements with neutronic activation, a method allowing the quantity and type of minerals occurring to be measured. After comparing the quarry samples with samples of the colossi, the team concluded that indeed the stone originates from Gebel el-Ahmar. However, the French and German scientists interpreting these scientists' data arrived at their original conclusion, that the stone came from Syena (Aswan). Even expert scientists with the most sophisticated modern equipment and methods cannot agree on the origin of the stone for the Colossi of Memnon.

The list of anomalies about the Great Pyramid lengthens when we consider the dimensions of the blocks. There is a misconception about the blocks of the Great Pyramid which archaeologists perpetuate. They advocate that the heights of the blocks at the base are always greater than those near the summit. If accurate, this would make logistical problems far less complex.

It is true that the height of the blocks at the base is 1.41 meters (1.54 yards) and that the heights of blocks progressively diminish to 0.59 meter (1.93 feet) in the first seventeen steps. With the exception of the huge cornerstones, the weight of blocks in the first seventeen steps diminishes from approximately six to two tons. Beyond the seventeenth step, however, blocks weigh from fifteen to thirty tons apiece, showing that block size does not consistently diminish as the pyramid ascends.

What most people fail to recognize is that at the nineteenth step the height of the blocks increases suddenly to 0.90 meter (2.95 feet). This is not obvious when you are standing at the bottom of the pyramid looking up because the heights of blocks forming the tiers appear to diminish. From a distance it is difficult to make an accurate assessment. The only way to determine the exact heights of the steps is by measuring them. Because it is difficult and potentially dangerous to climb to the top of the pyramid, it is likely that most specialists have mounted only the first few steps.

M. M. le Pere and Colonel Coutelle of the Napoleonic expedition very carefully measured the heights of the steps of the Great Pyramid one at a time and recorded the exact measurements in feet and inches in *Description de l'Egypte.* I transposed their measurements onto **Graph I** and have made the following observations:

1. Stones more than 1 meter (1.09 yards) high are equally distributed throughout the pyramid.

2. Except for the cornerstones, the largest stones of all are located about thirty stories high in the pyramid, at about the level of the King's Chamber.

3. Small stones are distributed between several successive series of larger stones throughout the pyramid, with many situated near the base.

Why is the misconception perpetuated? Egyptologists rely on the following general remarks by Jomard from *Description de l'Egypte,* which they consider, without further verification, to be precise:

> Finally, in 1801 M. M. le Pere and Coutelle measured all of the steps of the pyramid with the utmost care, using a specially designed instrument. The number of steps counted was 203 and the height of the pyramid itself was 139.117 meters [152.14 yards]. . . .
> It is perhaps worth taking note of the agreement which exists between our measurements and those of le Pere and Coutelle, not only regarding the height, but for the number of steps. Among the various travelers, some have counted 208, others 220, etc. . . . The perfect agreement on this point, together with that of our measurements of the base and height, is important proof (if proof were

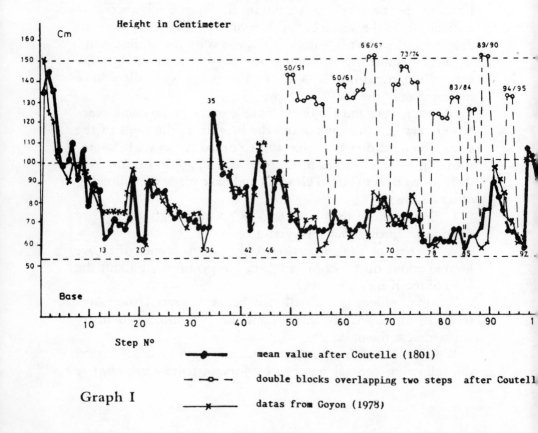

Graph I

mean value after Coutelle (1801)

double blocks overlapping two steps after Coutell

datas from Goyon (1978)

38

necessary) of the scrupulous care with which the engineers and artists of the expedition made their observations. Before deducing measurements other than the base and height, I should point out the differences in the heights of the steps from bottom to top. As is natural, the heights continuously decrease from 1.411 meters [1.54 yards] down to 0.559 meter [1.83 feet], with the smallest stones of all 0.514 meter [1.68 feet] high. The average height is 0.685 meter [2.24 feet].

Jomard's remark that, "As is natural, the heights continuously decrease" was meant as a general statement which was not intended to account for all blocks in the pyramid. It certainly does not apply to hundreds of blocks weighing from fifteen to

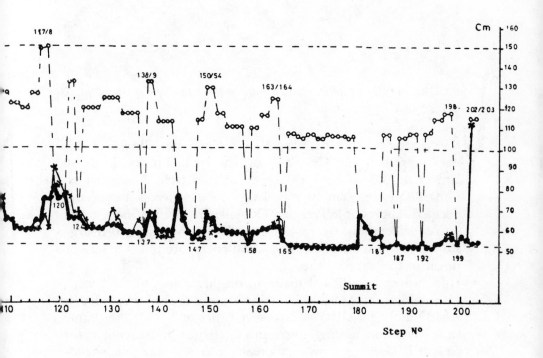

FIGURE 4. *Blocks at Step 35 (A) are so large that one spans Steps 20 and 21 (B).*

thirty tons situated near the King's Chamber. Blocks of this size, represented in **Graph I** and shown in **Figure 4,** are so large that they occupy the space of two tiers. Nevertheless, Jomard's general statement is always cited, whereas the precise, detailed reports of le Pere and Coutelle are rarely, if ever, taken into consideration. Because of the difficulty of raising such large stones to great heights, their detailed report poses a serious threat to the accepted theory.

In November 1984, I made an on-line search in the French archaeological data bank, Francis-H, using the key words PYR-AMID and QUARRY. I discovered that in 1978, at the same time I was transposing le Pere and Coutelle's measurements for **Graph I,** Georges Goyon, a French Egyptologist published a report after climbing the northeast corner of the Great Pyramid and carefully measuring the steps. Comparing his results with the measurements of 1801 reveals that the Great Pyramid has lost steps 202 and 203. The peaks and plateaus charted by Goyon compare exactly with all other data established in 1801. Step heights suddenly increase and diminish in nineteen sharp fluctuations. Goyon could not account for the dramatic fluctuations except to propose that they must conform to the heights of the geological strata of the Giza plateau. His assumption is incorrect. The blocks of both the Great Pyramid and the Second Pyramid of Giza are smaller than the heights of the strata at Giza.

Almost none of the pyramid blocks matches the Giza bedrock. The strata appearing in the body of the Great Sphinx are 1 meter (1.09 yards) high. Those in the quarry near Khafra's pyramid are more than 4.5 meters (4.90 yards) high. Realizing this, we might begin to feel sympathetic toward some of the wildly conjectural pyramid construction theories presented in recent years.

Having been impressed by the high degree of uniformity in the heights of blocks, as can be deduced from **Graph I,** I decided to make a preliminary study of the lengths (or widths). The lengths have never been measured, and I, therefore, photographed the area below the top thirty levels of the south and west faces of the Second Pyramid of Giza. The blocks in the Great Pyramid itself are too eroded to afford accurate overall measurements. The area I photographed is unweathered and in very good condition because the casing blocks previously covering it were removed only within the last 150 years. The area encompasses twenty-two steps, or 1,000 surface blocks per face. The steps photographed represent about ten percent of the area of the pyramid.

I had slides produced and projected them onto a screen, and then I measured the length of each of the 2,000 blocks. I transposed the measurements onto graphs to analyze structural features of the pyramid. Slides made with conventional photographic equipment do not allow the actual dimensions of blocks to be measured in feet and inches. Having used standard equipment, I made relative measurements. I considered that strata and defects make it impossible to cut stone to perfectly uniform dimensions with primitive tools. Therefore, if a low occurrence of uniform block lengths appeared, it would support the traditional carving hypothesis. A high occurrence of uniform lengths corroborate a method affording more precision.

I found that blocks do conform to the same lengths, and not to a moderate degree. As surprising as it may seem, almost all 2,000 blocks conform to ten perfectly uniform lengths. These lengths are distributed in diverse patterns throughout the twenty-two steps. Any possibility that the blocks were cut to the random sizes that would be dictated by cracks and other features of bedrock is eliminated. Anyone attempting to explain the preparation and use of blocks of such highly uniform dimensions based on the carving hypothesis would encounter serious difficulty. This degree of uniformity makes the possibility of carving with primitive tools out of the question.

It might appear that the Egyptians had a taste for performing bizarre and impossible tasks. Another example is the placement of monolithic sarcophagi in confined or otherwise difficult spaces. We can, for instance, appreciate the emotion of Cotaz, a member of the Napoleonic expedition, as he discovered the numerous tombs in the Valley of the Kings.

Cotaz entered the valley on the one road that passed through a narrow access gorge situated between two steep mountains. Cotaz reached the area consecrated to the Ramses pharaohs. He reported:

> The gate through which one enters the valley is the only opening in its entire contour. As this opening is man-made, the valley must previously have been shaped in the form of an isolated basin which could only be reached by climbing the steep mountains. It was perhaps this remoteness which gave them the idea of placing the royal sepulchers there to make them safe from robbery, which the ancient Egyptians so much feared. . . . High mountains crowned with rock are hemmed in on all sides from the horizon, allowing only part of the sky to be seen. Towards midday, when the bottom of the valley has been in the sun for a few hours, the heat becomes concentrated and excessive. Any tempering wind can find abso-

lutely no way into this enclosure. It is like an oven. Two men from the escort of General Desaix died from suffocation. I do not think that it would be possible to remain there for twenty-four hours without the shade provided by the catacombs which offer protection from this overwhelming heat.

Most of the sarcophagi Cotaz discovered in the various tombs had already been destroyed. He described one, belonging to Ramses III, which was still intact and is now in the Louvre:

Imagine a large oblong chamber made of pink syenite granite, ornamented inside and out with hieroglyphs and paintings. Its dimensions are such that a man standing inside can hardly be seen by everyone outside. A blow with a hammer makes it ring like a bell. . . . The sarcophagus must previously have been closed by a cover which has since disappeared. . . . The cover would have formed a considerable mass which was very difficult to move. . . . A comparison between the dimensions of the sarcophagus to those of the entrance to the valley yields a big surprise and a new example of the Egyptian's taste for difficult tasks. The entrance of the Valley of the Kings is not wide enough to allow the sarcophagus through, so that the huge mass must have been hoisted with a crane or pulley up the hills which surround the valley and then brought down along their sides.

The sarcophagus in the King's Chamber of the Great Pyramid is another example of unusual placement. It does not fit through the doorway or adjoining hallway. Egyptologists surmise that it must have been placed before the pyramid was completed. Although this goes against what is known about Egyptian funerary customs, the carving and hoisting theory offers no other alternative. Cotaz suggested the use of pulleys for raising sarcophagi, although Egyptologists have discovered since that pulleys were not known to the Egyptians until the Roman occupation. The matter in which sarcophagi were placed will become clear as we progress.

CHAPTER 3

The Technological Paradox

WHEN CONSIDERING THE HISTORICAL OVERVIEW OF EGYP-
tian art and architecture, one can clearly distinguish the existence of two distinctly different masonry methods. One was
used primarily during the Old Kingdom, and the other, carving
with hard bronze tools, was introduced during the late Middle
Kingdom or perhaps a little later, about 800 years after the Great
Pyramid was built. The distinction between the two methods
can be made based on quality of workmanship, the hardness of
the stone materials worked, and the design and structural features of buildings.

The contrast between the two methods is apparent in large
monuments and small works of art. The quality of sculpture
declined dramatically in the later periods. Nestor l'Hote (c.
1780–1842), an artist who worked with the founder of Egyptology, Jean Francois Champollion (1790–1832), was ecstatic
about the artwork found by Karl Lepsius (1810–1884) and Au-
guste Mariette (1821–1881) in three particular mastabas of the

Old Kingdom. Describing the sculptures in one of the most ancient, that of the vizier Menefra of Memphis, l'Hote remarked:

> The sculptures in this tomb are remarkable for their elegance and finesse. The relief is so light that it can be compared with one of our five franc coins. Such perfection in something so ancient confirms the observation that the further one goes back in antiquity towards the origin of Egyptian art, the more perfect are the results of this art, as if the genius of these people, unlike others, was formed in one single stroke. Of Egyptian art we only know of its decadence.

Egyptian sculpture was so degenerated by the New Kingdom that it fell into irredeemable decadence. Neither artists of Saite nor Thebes produced such masterpieces as the more ancient diorite statue of Khafra or the Kneeling Scribe now exhibited in the Louvre. Remarks by archaeologists and architects Georges Perrot (1832–1914) and Charles Chipiez express awe of the Old Kingdom sculptors:

> How did the sculptors manage to carve into these rocks which are so hard? . . . Even today it is very difficult when using the best tempered steel chisels. The work is very slow and difficult and one must stop frequently to sharpen the edge of the chisel, which becomes dull on the rock, and then retemper the chisel. But the contemporaries of Khafra, and everyone agrees on this, had no steel chisels.

On a grand scale we observe the same scenario. The blocks of the Old Kingdom pyramids exemplify a peerless fit, and Old Kingdom monuments exhibit hard stone materials prepared with ultimate care and perfection. Egyptians of the New Kingdom and later times were incapable of comparable workmanship when using bronze tools. In New Kingdom and later monuments, precision joints and the regular dimensions of blocks disappears. The degradation that occurred after the introduction of bronze tools astonishes architects and archaeologists who have studied Egyptian architecture over the last two centuries. Champollion, for instance, was astonished by the poor quality of the New Kingdom structures erected for Theban kings at Wadi Esseboua. He commented:

> This is the worst piece of work from the epoch of Ramses the Great. The stones were poorly masoned, gaps are hidden by cement upon which decorative sculpting continued, and this was bad workmanship. . . . Most of these scenes are unrecognizable because the cement onto which large parts were carved has fallen and left numerous gaps in the inscriptions.

The Theban kings of the New Kingdom built a prodigious number of edifices from Nubia to the Mediterranean beaches. Surfaces of the walls were nearly always covered with richly colored polychrome decorations that masked imperfections. Perrot and Chipiez commented about this technique:

> But why would they have prolonged their work by patching up, with infinite patience, joints that had to be hidden? Was the purpose of the stucco and paint to hide imperfections? In these edifices we do not see certain combinations of stones which the elegant building civilizations who left the stone undecorated were happy to use. . . . You will search in vain for regularity of construction, perfection in joints, and the perfection of carving and fitting which gives the face of a wall in the fortification of Mycena, even when separated from all to which it belongs, its own nobility and beauty. At Thebes the worker relied on fillers and was content to say, "That should do the trick."

It is assumed that the use of stucco and paint made it unnecessary for joints to be perfect. In my opinion, it was because the carving method was used, and I think that it was to mask imperfections that the polychrome coating on a stucco base was developed. There was no matter of laziness. Ramses II drafted masses of Asian and African slaves in order to dot the land with temples, palaces, and cities bearing his name. As frantically as he built, he simply could not compete with his illustrious ancestors.

47

Egyptologists usually explain the difference between the workmanship of the New Kingdom compared with that of the Old Kingdom by saying that Theban kings built more edifices than did their ancestors. I have already shown that by de Roziere's estimates there is far more stone in the Giza pyramids alone than in all the construction built during the New Kingdom, Late period, and Ptolemaic period combined, that is, in 1,500 years.

Furthermore, New Kingdom and later monuments were made, with few exceptions, of very soft varieties of stone, but since the inception of Egyptology, a common misconception has been widely perpetuated in literature, which is that monuments built during the New Kingdom and later are made of hard stone materials. De Roziere commented:

> It would be hard to believe that such famous monuments, famous for their age, richness, and the multiplicity of their ornamentation were built with rough, common materials. Most travellers, using their imaginations more than their eyes, believe that they have seen in the layers of the land, and in the monuments themselves, hard, precious granites from the Syene environment, the porphyries and variegated rocks of Arabia, and sometimes even basalt. Others are content with the use of marble, inspired by what they have seen in the ancient monuments of Greece and Italy. The truth is that there exists in these quarries, and in the edifices of the upper Thebaid, neither porphyry, nor basalt, nor marble, nor any kind of limestone. All that can be found in this entire area, on both banks of the Nile, are layers of sandstone . . . and it is with this stone that, almost without exception, all of the still surviving monuments from Syene to Dendera were built.

When making the latter remark, de Roziere was not referring to hard sandstone such as that in the pavement of Fontainebleau, near Paris, withstanding generations of wear. He was talking instead about a particular soft variety called monumental sandstone. To avoid confusion, he distinguished it as psammite, since, having been a Parisian, the word sandstone suggested to him a dense material consisting of grains of tightly bound quartz, material comparable to the Fontainebleau sandstone. Psammite sandstone adheres poorly and will easily disaggregate under very light pressure. He mentioned its structural tolerance:

> Egyptian sandstone is, in general, not very hard and it can often be scratched with a fingernail. The hardness is, at any rate, very uniform throughout each block and so is the breaking strength, which is low but equal throughout. This stone contains neither cavities nor blow holes [holes where a tool can be inserted].

Practically all of the New Kingdom temples and those built later were made of this psammite sandstone which is so soft that one can scratch it with one's fingernails. This includes the temples of Luxor, Karnak, Edfu, and Esna. Even the more recent temples erected during Egypt's Iron Age, such as the Temple of Dendera built by the Ptolemies (c. 250 BC), are composed of extremely soft stone. De Roziere described this temple:

> One surprising fact is that the stones of the Temple of Dendera, one of the most admirable for the execution of its sculpted ornamentations, are precisely the roughest of all. One finds there several varieties of fine sandstone but, in general, the grain is rather coarse, unequal, and can be disaggregated with a fingernail.

Many New Kingdom and later structures, the famous Abu Simbel Temple for example, were hollowed directly into hills of very soft sandstone, so no heavy lifting or hauling was necessary for construction. After the Aswan Dam was constructed, the Abu Simbel Temple was moved in its entirety by a team sponsored by the United Nations (1964–1966) to avoid inundation by Lake Nasser. The operation was far more difficult than anticipated because of the weakness of the sandstone, which is so fragile that it was necessary to cut very deep into the cliff to obtain a mass strong enough to withstand the move from the edge of the lake to the top of the hill. De Roziere commented on the ease with which this material is carved:

> From Philae to Dendera, a distance of about fifty leagues in which the most important and best preserved edifices of ancient Egypt are found, nearly all are made of sandstone. Even though limestone mountains reign over the two sites of the Thebaid in more than three-fifths of this area, hardly any ruins made of limestone are found, and the few that exist are the least significant. That alone is proof enough of the preference shown by the Egyptian architects for sandstone over all of the several fine varieties of limestone found in their country. . . . But what must have, above all, met their approval was the extreme ease with which it could be chiseled, its docility, if I may use the term, to yield in every sense to the tool and to receive on its different faces the numerous figures and reliefs with which Egyptian architects felt compelled to decorate all the walls of these great edifices.

Because the limestone of the Theban landscape is hard, it was not used during the New Kingdom. Instead, a soft grade of limestone found at Tura, devoid of fossil shells, was employed. This limestone is unlike that used for the core blocks of Old Kingdom pyramids, which is relatively hard and difficult to carve because it contains large fossil shells. The French Egyptologist Gaston Maspero (1846–1916) described the type of soft limestone used for the New Kingdom temples of Memphis:

> The Tura quarries enjoyed the privilege of furnishing choice material for the royal architects. Nowhere else could such white limestone be seen, so soft for carving, so perfect to receive and preserve all of the finesse of a bas-relief.

The casing blocks of the Great Pyramid and the Step Pyramid at Saqqara, reputed to come from Tura, are very much harder than the soft Tura limestone used even in today's restorations. It seems logical that soft materials, such as psammite sandstone and this very soft limestone to which Maspero refers, should have been used during the Old Kingdom when only modest stone or soft copper tools were available, but the opposite occurred.

Furthermore, unlike the Old Kingdom workmen, those of the New Kingdom and later periods rarely used large building units. A few obelisks and colossal statues are exceptional cases. Only the lintels and architraves of some New Kingdom and later temples have lengths comparable to those of the more ancient temples, but those of the later ones were less massive. The temples of Karnak are characterized by huge pylons, but all were made of small blocks.

The front pylon of the Temple of Dendera has a width of 113 meters (370 feet), a thickness of 15 meters (49 feet), and a height of 42 meters (138 feet). The first pylon of the Temple of Luxor, built by Ramses II, is a more modest 27 meters (88.5 feet) high, with each of its towers 30 meters (98 feet) in width. Although their dimensions are impressive, these giant monuments composed of small stone blocks cannot compare to the superstructures of the Old Kingdom, where monolithic beams in late pyramids weigh eighty tons and the Valley Temple of the Second Pyramid of Giza exhibits blocks weighing at least 500 tons.

Most of the colossal statues built during the New Kingdom and later, the remains of the great obelisks built by Theban and Greek rulers, those made during the later periods which were transported to Rome, during the Roman occupation, and Paris, London, and New York during the nineteenth century, were cut from a type of granite known as oriental red granite or pink syenite, a material relatively easy to carve. It cannot be scratched with one's fingernails like psammite sandstone, but it will easily disaggregate when hit with a pointed instrument.

There has been great confusion over this material. Pink syenite has two principal components: large, elongated, pink to brick-red feldspar crystals that are truncated at the corners, and extremely soft black mica. This type of mica has a hardness of 2.5, according to Mohs' scale, which is the same as plaster, and it makes an ideal point of attack for a tool. The pink feldspar crystals are also fragile, making this variety of granite easy to carve. However, since the inception of Egyptology, pink syenite has been confused with harder types of granite because its soft mica has been mistaken for an amphibole that requires a tempered steel tool to be sculpted. The main reason for the confusion is that today the word syenite indicates a hard hornblende, whereas in literature written before the nineteenth century the word syenite was used to describe soft granite from Syene (Aswan).

Most syenite monuments are found in northern Egypt, mostly in the Delta, and were erected during the Late and Ptolemaic periods. They have been discovered in Bahbeht, Canope, and the greatest accumulation is found in the Ptolemaic capital of Alexandria, where the entire land is scattered with the ruins of syenite statues, walls, and obelisks.

The overview permits assessment of the paradoxical and dramatic contrast. The pyramids of the Old Kingdom consisted essentially of fossil shell limestone, a heterogeneous material very difficult to cut precisely. Temples dating to the end of the Eighteenth Dynasty (1400 BC) are found over the entire face of Egypt. They were made of very soft white limestone, even when constructed in entirely granitic regions in southern Egypt. After the Eighteenth Dynasty, the use of soft limestone eventually gave way to soft sandstone. The sandstone of Silsilis, in southern Egypt, was used to build the New Kingdom temples of Karnak, Luxor, and Edfu; it is homogeneous, soft, and easy to sculpt. Therein lies the great technological paradox of Egypt: at a time when tools were made of stone and copper, a tremendous amount of hard varieties of stone were used in monuments, but when bronze and iron were introduced, only the very softest stone material was used. There is more than ample evidence to support the existence of two different masonry methods used in different epochs and yielding very different results.

CHAPTER 4

The False Proofs of Egyptology

EVEN THOUGH THE TRADITIONAL EXPLANATION OF PYRA-mid construction is illogical and remains unproven, it has been accepted as a matter of faith, reinforced and protected by the sheer weight of scholarly opinion. What proof has Egyptology offered to support the accepted theory? Logistical studies are generally used as proof even though they are highly speculative and prove nothing. The great efforts made over a long time to explain construction problems in no way mean that basic theoretical assumptions are correct, especially since problems remain unresolved, despite the numerous studies, and important facts remain unconsidered. Despite the efforts of experts, the construction method is still a matter of legitimate debate.

If logistical reports are used as proof of construction, they constitute false proof. There are six additional false proofs. The following explains why each one is either erroneous or open to interpretation.

1. Quarried Blocks

There are a few blocks in a trench on the north side of the Second Pyramid of Giza, and Egyptologists use them as evidence to support the traditional carving and hoisting theory. The blocks are relatively small, 3×2.5meters (3.28×2.75 yards) wide and 0.3 meters (1 foot) high. The northern vertical face of this quarry bears inscriptions and a large cartouche containing the name of the New Kingdom pharaoh, Ramses II (1298–1235 BC), who demolished numerous monuments to obtain ready-made blocks for his own constructions. The inscriptions honor Mey, a chief architect of Ramses II, who, according to the inscriptions, removed casing blocks from the Second Pyramid and dismantled a temple of the complex. This occurred 1,400 years after the pyramid was built. There are no other inscriptions by which to date the quarry.

Ramses II and other pharaohs took a number of ready-made blocks from various pyramids, but they were incapable of producing a monument or any combination of monuments equivalent in volume to the Great Pyramid. This holds true even though Ramses II used enormous wealth and manpower endlessly to rob ready-made blocks from existing monuments over his sixty-five year reign.

The pattern of chisel marks also in the trench near the pyramid have been dated to the time of Ramses II. It is relevant to consider what has been determined historically about Egypt's quarry methods. Klemm and his wife made a complete dating of the sandstone quarries of Gebel el-Silsila and presented a paper at the Second International Congress of Egyptologists in 1979. Their study dated the various quarry methods used historically in Egypt. The following is an abstract of their paper:

> Most quarries were dated to well-defined historical periods with the aid of chisel marks, block technique, inscriptions, and pottery sherds. The most anciently quarried areas are at the northern edges of Gebel el-Silsila. These were quarried prior to the New Kingdom, perhaps in the Middle Kingdom. The chisel marks of this period are irregularly oriented **[Figure 5].** The northern part of Gebel el-Silsila was exploited during the New Kingdom, in about

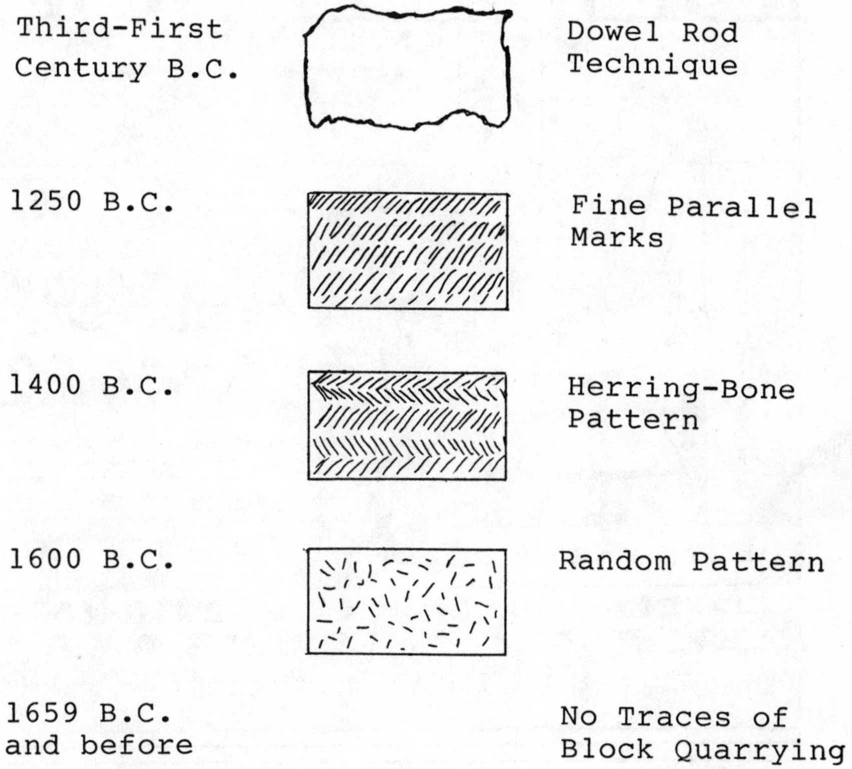

Third-First Century B.C.		Dowel Rod Technique
1250 B.C.		Fine Parallel Marks
1400 B.C.		Herring-Bone Pattern
1600 B.C.		Random Pattern
1659 B.C. and before		No Traces of Block Quarrying

FIGURE 5. *Block Techniques.*

the Eighteenth Dynasty, and chisel marks form a herringbone pattern. In the Nineteenth Dynasty Ramses II introduced a fine parallel pattern that still prevailed when the Ptolemies exploited large quarries at the site. At the southern end of Gebel el-Silsila are the Roman quarry sites. No chisel marks of the previous types are found, but only wedge marks made by wooden dowels.

The Egyptians carefully cut stone from quarries, continually refining their chisel strokes because during the Middle and New Kingdoms the quarry was considered to be the eternal body of the god Amun. Treating Amun's body haphazardly was an act of sacrilege, so quarrying was piously conducted to remove

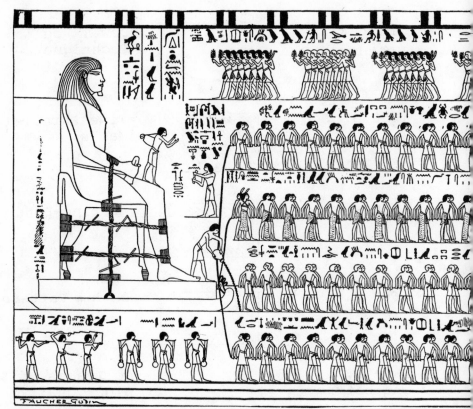

FIGURE 6. *Detail from tomb of Djehutihotip depicts transport of a colossal statue.*

blocks in finished form. The Egyptian method of quarrying would not have been efficient for constructing the Great Pyramid.

On the southern end of Gebel el-Silsila, only the traces of wooden dowels appear. Dowels were inserted into the quarry and wetted with water, so that when the wood swelled, the stone cracked. This method is frequently shown in books depicting pyramid construction, but the Klemms' dating shows that this primitive method was never used by the Egyptians. It was exclusively a Roman technique dating to the Roman occupation of Egypt.

If this crude Roman method would have been used for pyramid construction, as is advocated, the amount of general debris at Giza would be staggering, including countless millions of unusable cracked blocks. Before the Klemms' presentation, it was assumed that because doweling is a primitive quarrying method it is also the oldest. One sees that the blocks in the trench near the Second Pyramid of Giza cannot be used as evidence to support the accepted theory.

Although the Klemms did not date limestone quarries, a general dating of quarrying in Egypt is established nevertheless. The implications are profound. From 27 BC to AD 379, the Romans quarried stone with wooden dowels. From 332 to 1250 BC, fine, parallel chisel strokes were used in Egyptian quarries. In 1400 BC Egyptians were making herringbone chisel patterns when cutting. During 1600 BC, they cut stone using random strokes, and before that time, there is no trace of block quarrying at all. How did the Egyptians remove stone in more ancient times for pyramid construction?

2. The Transport of the Statue of Djehutihotep

A Twelfth Dynasty (1800 BC) bas-relief from the tomb of Djehutihotep depicts the transport of the colossal statue of this ruler of Hermopolis. It was produced about 800 years after the construction of the Great Pyramid, yet it is used as evidence to support the traditional theory of pyramid construction.

The colossus no longer exists, but it stood 6.50 meters (21.32 feet) high and weighed about sixty tons according to what can be determined from inscriptions. The bas-relief depicts the colossus being hauled on a sledge to which it was solidly attached with thick cords. Protective bands can be seen under cables at the corners of the statue. In four lines, 172 men are pulling the colossus. Three workers carrying a liquid, presumably water, are shown. A worker is pouring the liquid in front of the sledge to ease its movement over the surface of Nile silt. Adams remarked about the bas-relief:

> The existence of a document of this order (and there exist others both in Egypt and Mesopotamia) allows us to throw into the wastepaper basket, without hesitation, all of the fantastic propositions too often made about the transport of the ancient Egyptian megaliths.*

Is this method applicable for constructing the Great Pyramid? We know that sixty tons easily can be hauled over a flat terrain. An experiment led by Henri Chevrier, a French architect, showed that 25 kilograms (55 pounds) of force are exerted to pull 150 kilograms (330 pounds), indicating that 400 men were required to pull the colossus (60 tons or 132,000 pounds divided by 330 pounds). In other words, each man would be required to pull only one-sixth of the load (150/25 = 6). Using the system for an average six-ton block from the Great Pyramid on flat ground would require only forty men. But the same operation on a ramp would be extremely complex.

The noted French Egyptologist Jean-Philippe Lauer suggests that inclined ramps of 3:1 and 4:1 were used. If this were the case, from 140 to 200 men would have been required to raise one block, and the operation was presumably conducted with men pushing and hoisting the blocks as high as the 450-foot summit of the Great Pyramid. How does this comply with the number of blocks which would have to have been set per day?

According to Herodotus's account, 2.6 million blocks were transported to the foot of the Great Pyramid during a twenty-year period, which is the approximate length of Khufu's reign. The number of blocks moved per year would have been 130,000. This means that an average of 1,400 blocks would have been hauled per day. This would have required 250,000 men making one journey per day, if we allow for a 150-man team per block (1,400 × 150). If the team made two journeys per day, 105,000 men would have been required. Four journeys per day

*Translation from the French from *L'Archeologie devant l'imposture.*

per team would required 52,500 men working together at one time. Yet, it would have been impossible to get the job done. This enormous number of men would have been squeezed together shoulder to shoulder at the work site, an area about the size of a large sports arena.

3. The Clay Ramps

The principle of this wet-silt track could not apply to ramps for pyramid construction. It would create a ridiculous scenario, 52,500 men working in an area the size of a sports complex, with many trodding and sliding in mud while hazardously maneuvering extremely heavy blocks at great heights.

This is not to say that ramps were never used at all. Because pulleys were not known in Egypt until Roman times, the only option archaeological evidence provides for raising blocks is ramps. For the Great Pyramid, it is estimated that any straight-slope ramp would have been a mile long, containing an enormous amount of material. Its great breadth and length would have covered the quarry. Helicoidal ramps have been suggested, but many Egyptologists offer several well-founded arguments against their actual use, including the fact that no wraparound ramp has ever been found.

At Saqqara, a mud ramp was found *in situ* at the pyramid usually attributed to Pharaoh Semkhemkhet of the Third Dynasty. But this small pyramid is not composed of large blocks. Carrying small blocks up a ramp was the most sensible and obvious way of producing this type of pyramid, affording a scenario very different from the one just described. Whereas there are remains of ramps at Giza, the tremendous amount of material called for by the standard theory does not exist, and whereas it might be expected that an earthen material would degrade, a small amount of remains nevertheless suggests the use of small ramps of the size useful for climbing the pyramids.

It has been proposed that pyramid blocks were hauled on sledges with wooden rollers attached. No evidence exists to support this hypothesis. The wheel was introduced as a transportation means by the Hyksos when they brought chariots to

Egypt during their takeover at the end of the Middle Kingdom. The oldest surviving document implying the use of the wheel for hauling stone is a bas-relief from the palace of Sennacherib at Nineveh, now in the British Museum. It dates to 750 BC or 2,000 years after the Great Pyramid was built. The Great Pyramid, the most impressive monument of the ancient world, was built before the introduction of the wheel as a means of transportation.

4. The Tura Stele

A stele discovered in the Tura quarries is attributed to the Eighteenth Dynasty pharaoh Amosis (1580–1558 BC). The stele itself disappeared during the nineteenth century, and only a sketch remains **(Figure 7)**. The sketch shows a stone block placed on a sledge being pulled by oxen. Although the wheel had been introduced in Egypt by this time, this bas-relief indicates that it was still not being used for hauling stone.

Pharaoh Amosis opened the Tura quarries to obtain soft stone for the temple of the god Ptah of Memphis. The Tura stele is not acceptable as evidence to support the traditional theory of pyramid construction because it was produced almost 1,000 years after the Great Pyramid was built.

The Tura stele and the other documents used to support the traditional theory are the product of a society fostering different technology from that of its ancestors. Any long and successful civilization is bound to have emerging and declining technologies. Although archaeologists refrain from wild conjecture, there are vague admissions that some advanced technique was known to the builders of the Great Pyramids. According to Edwards:

> Cheops, who may have been a megalomaniac, could never, during a reign of about twenty-three years, have erected a building of the size and durability of the Great Pyramid if technical advances had not enabled his masons to handle stones of very considerable weight and dimensions.

FIGURE 7. *Tura detail.*

Edwards implies that a clever method was used, but historians, with few exceptions, view ancient civilizations as though they were technologically inferior to our own in every respect. Many factors contributed to the general destruction of Egyptian technological information. During periods of anarchy, the Egyptians destroyed much of it themselves, and, too, Egypt suffered invasion by the Ethiopians, Assyrians, Persians, Romans, Nubians, and Mohammedans. The information lost when fire completely destroyed the great library of Alexandria by the end of the third century was also devastating. The Mohammedans viewed Egypt's wondrous architectural achievements as deeds of the devil and exploited blocks for their own buildings, ravaging tombs in search of treasure wherever possible. The Napoleonic expedition inspired a frenzy of interest by antique dealers, and many precious artifacts were removed during the 1900s. An untold number of relics were damaged or destroyed during their exploits as gunpowder and battering rams were used to open tombs. Numerous written records became rubble and statues were fragmented, their remains divided among different museums.

All contribute to the fact that scientific knowledge has not been transmitted flawlessly from antiquity to our time. One has only to read Herodotus's *Melpomene* to realize that it was proved long before this historian's time that the earth is round. Yet this fact had to be painstakingly rediscovered in more modern times.

A modern superiority complex prevails in scholarly literature despite the weight of evidence of a great forgotten technology used for pyramid construction. This ancient science is explored in the coming chapters and highlights the technological differences between the Old and New Kingdoms.

5. The Bas-Relief of Rekhmire
The wall paintings in the New Kingdom tomb of the official Rekhmire (1400 BC) are famous for their illustrations of the period's technology. One painting shows blocks being carved with bronze tools. This painting was produced 1,300 years after the construction of the Great Pyramid, and, therefore, is not relevant.

6. The Bas-Relief of Unas
A bas-relief on the wall of the causeway approaching the pyramid of pharaoh Unas (2356–2323 BC) of the Fifth Dynasty is the last of the false proofs. The bas-relief depicts the fact that Unas dismantled a temple in the pyramid complex of his predecessor, Djedkara-Isesi, and reused the blocks for his own pyramid. The bas-relief shows a boat transporting huge temple columns along the Nile River to the Unas pyramid complex. About two miles separate the two pyramids. I observed these columns among the ruins. Instead of being monolithic as depicted in the bas-relief, they consist of units held together by tongue and groove joints, and the units weigh no more than a half ton each.

This bas-relief is used to make a sweeping generalization about pyramid construction. It is used to explain that casing blocks were transported from across the Nile and that granite blocks came from 400 miles upstream at Aswan. It will become

FIGURE 8. *A bas-relief appearing on wall of causeway to the pyramid of Unas dates to about 2200 B.C.*

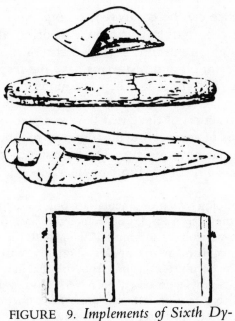

FIGURE 9. *Implements of Sixth Dynasty are typical of Old Kingdom tools.*

clear that this bas-relief was made during a period which was critical for the technology used to build the Great Pyramids. The fact that Unas reused pyramid blocks has nothing to do with how those blocks were originally produced and placed in Djedkara-Isesi's pyramid. The false proofs of Egyptology will soon appear as transparent as Egyptian royal linen.

Egyptian history is viewed by scholars mostly from a New Kingdom–Theban perspective as a result of the numerous documents that have survived from the New Kingdom capital of Thebes. The more ancient capital of Memphis has not been excavated effectively, limiting information about the most important urban center of the ancient world before the prominence of Thebes.

Scholars have sufficient information only to speculate about the culture of the Pyramid Age. Scientific data and archaeological evidence can be compared to empty urns into which scholars pour the elixir of their own theories, attitudes, and beliefs. Although an interpretation of test results and data may be required, scientists and historians have the responsibility of maintaining a critical spirit when encountering irreconcilable flaws of theory. Certainly, the lingering problems associated with the construction of the Great Pyramids and other incredible ancient feats of engineering are too great to ignore. In recent years the enigmas have given rise to fantastic theories. Adams commented on some of the most popular:

> On the chronology of monumental art one sees, throughout the planet, that the first examples of architecture are often megalithic edifices, or even isolated megaliths. Then, with the appearance of iron, this megalithism disappears suddenly with few exceptions. . . . The occultists conclude from this that in bygone epochs, a mysterious knowledge based on a very advanced science, but known only to a few initiates, allowed the extraction, transport, and placement of huge stones. Generally, such propositions are accompanied by a notorious "aging" of the edifice under consideration. Sometimes the Atlanteans and their teaching tradition are of definitive help, but the most effective aid in all circumstances is extraterrestrial. . . . Another proposition, or even affirmation, has recently been added to the others: it is the simplest, the most naive, and also the oldest, giants.

Though these various theories are fun and intriguing, they offer no definitive solution. The secret science speculated upon is never specifically identified, and baffling ultramodern technology, such as antigravity machines and antediluvian Atlantian crystal generators, never address all of the anomalies we have explored. The fantasy theories are based on conjecture as opposed to actual archaeological evidence, and both the fanciful and traditional theories will continue to thrive until the actual solution being presented here is firmly established. Let us now explore Egypt's fabulous Stone Age science used to build the Great Pyramids—lost but now recovered.

CHAPTER 5

The Solution

THE GREAT PYRAMIDS REFLECT A TECHNOLOGY OF THE AN-
cient world that yields a sophisticated product or result but has
no relationship to what we think of today as advanced or high
technology. To visit the Pyramid Age would be to enter a world
in which our objective, secular view of science does not exist.
Anciently in Egypt, science and religion were part of one body
of knowledge, and the priests were responsible for fostering and
preserving that knowledge. Particular arts and sciences were
attributed to particular gods. Ptah was the god of craftsmen,
and Khnum, the Divine Potter, was a god worshipped by the
pharaohs of the Pyramid Age. As will be further discussed, it
was Khnum to whom the technology in question was attributed. Thoth was the god of writing, and the knowledge of
Khnum was written in the Books of Thoth.

We know that the ancient priest-scientists of Heliopolis fostered the sciences of engineering, mathematics, and astronomy,
and that all played a role in pyramid construction, but the
science most germane to pyramid construction is overlooked.
The mystery science has nothing to do with the classical physics
of electricity, heat, optics, or mechanics, or anything in com-

mon with the quantum physics—atomic, nuclear, or solid state. The science that made pyramids possible was chemistry or, more precisely, its forerunner, alchemy. Just how were stone monuments built with ancient chemistry?

Alchemy evokes images of medieval pursuits in mysticism and magic. Old alchemical notebooks depict vain searches for the ever-illusive Philosopher's Stone, reputed to be empowered to transform base metals into gold and provide an elixir of eternal youth. As will be discussed, the legendary Philosopher's Stone represents the last misinterpreted vestiges of the alchemical science that flourished during the Pyramid Age and was known in Egypt more than 6,000 years ago.

Although medieval alchemy was accompanied by esoteric teachings, because it derived from an era that united science and religion, technically alchemy encompasses historical chemical developments. The word alchemy is the source of the modern word chemistry, the latter appearing about 250 years ago. There were great alchemical achievements during antiquity.

One can appreciate the ingenuity of the researchers of antiquity who first extracted copper from an ore of malachite, malachite having no metallic appearance whatsoever. This great alchemical discovery elevated Stone Age man to the Chalcolithic period. For some time historians thought that the melting point of copper, 1,083° C [1,981° F], was reached with great difficulty by using a hand bellows. Then it became apparent that the task was probably accomplished in an easier way, through chemistry.

Temperatures can be raised with energy released during exothermic (heat-producing) chemical reactions. Copper and lead are commonly located in close proximity, and lead played a fundamental role in primeval copper extraction. Lead can be oxidized easily with the aid of a hand bellows. A mixture of copper ore (malachite) and lead ore (galena) heated in a hearth to only 700° C (1,292° F) automatically reaches a temperature, through a heat-producing chemical reaction, that is close to that required for extracting copper. The addition of a flux, which in Egypt was a native salt called natron (sodium carbonate), lowered the fusion point sufficiently for copper extraction. Silver can be smelted similarly.

Egyptian alchemists developed vibrant blue enamel in prehistoric times at about 3800 BC. The discovery was a by-product of copper smelting. Appendix 1 discusses that, contrary to popular belief, enamel production was no accident. Instead, an experimenter mixed a powder of chrysocolla with natron and applied a flame. The result was hard, glossy blue enamel that was then melted and applied to beads and pebbles.

The ancient Egyptians are well known for using minerals such as chrysocolla and lapis lazuli to produce enamels, which for them were imitations of these minerals or stones. They had a word for such products, *ari-kat,* meaning man-made or synthetic. They sought to imitate stones because the highest spiritual influence was attributed to stone. The early priests learned to identify rocks and minerals and classified them according to the spiritual beliefs. In Egyptian mythology carnelian and other red stones represented the blood of Isis, a goddess of fertility. Lapis lazuli was associated with daybreak. Chrysocolla was associated with what was called the "First Time" event of Creation. It is not surprising to find that minerals and rocks had divine properties in a world where all of nature was revered.

All available stones, both nonprecious and semiprecious, possessed sacred, eternal qualities. It must have been known from ancestral lore that even though all living things perish, even trees, the imposing rocks and cliffs stood eternally. Almost everything was depicted symbolically and stone was symbolic of the eternal realm. Knowing this, one can understand why stone materials were devoted exclusively to religious monuments and sacred funerary paraphernalia. These were intended to survive for eternity, whereas earthly dwellings, even royal palaces, were composed of perishable sun-dried mud brick that need to last only a lifetime.

When the Egyptian alchemists developed glassmaking during the New Kingdom, it was to carry on the old religious tradition of making synthetic stones. This age-old tradition reveals the very heart of the remarkable alchemical invention germane to the riddle of pyramid construction: the priests of Khnum had long been adept at the art of making extraordinary cements. Cement found in various parts of the courses of the Great Pyramid is about 4,500 years old, yet it is still in good condition. This ancient mortar is far superior to cements used in construction today. The modern portland cement used to repair ancient Egyptian monuments has cracked and degraded in only about fifty years.

If the ancient Egyptians had the ability to produce exceptionally high-quality cement, what prevented them from adding fossil shells to their cement to produce high-quality limestone concrete? The answer is that nothing prevented them. I will demonstrate that the pyramid blocks are not natural stone; the blocks are actually exceptionally high-quality limestone concrete—synthetic stone—cast directly in place. The blocks consist of about ninety to ninety-five percent limestone rubble and five to ten percent cement. They are imitations of natural limestone, made in the age-old religious tradition of alchemical stonemaking. No stone cutting or heavy hauling or hoisting was ever required for pyramid construction.

So that there will be no doubt about what gives me the authority to make this rather astounding claim, I will explain my background as it relates to this research. I am a research scientist specializing in low-temperature mineral synthesis. In 1972 I founded the private research company CORDI (Coordination and Development of Innovation), and, in 1979, the Geopolymer Institute, both in France. At the Geopolymer Institute I founded a new branch of chemistry that I named geopolymerization. I currently have more than twenty-five international patents for geopolymeric products and processes. My products are made in the United States and Europe by large manufacturers. The products have many diverse applications.

Geopolymeric products range from advanced materials to simple, yet highly sophisticated cements. The geopolymeric cements are made with inorganic chemical reactions in which alumina and silica materials are integrated to form synthetic zeolites, secondary rock-forming minerals. There is no way of distinguishing a synthetic zeolite from a natural one. And geopolymeric cements are chemically comparable to the natural cements that bind such stones as sandstone, puddingstone, and fossil-shell limestone.

Geopolymers are revolutionary for the concrete industry. Any type of rock aggregate can be used, and concrete made with the geopolymeric binder is practically indistinguishable from natural stone. Geologists unfamiliar with the technical possibilities afforded by geopolymerization have scrutinized geopolymeric concrete and have mistaken it for natural stone. This is unprecedented technology; no tremendous heat or pressure is required to produce this synthetic stone. Geopolymeric concrete sets rapidly at room temperatures to form synthetic stone, beautiful in appearance and abundant with unprecedented properties.

To develop a new branch of chemistry is one thing, but to apply that chemistry to ancient history is quite another. How did I learn that the pyramid stone is also geopolymeric? Any theory must be feasible; then, there must be evidence; and ultimately, hard scientific proof is required. All mysteries associated with pyramid construction must be resolved.

Advanced technology plays no part in the production of geopolymers. This is the most basic prerequisite if the theory is to be feasible. An individual of the Stone Age could produce geopolymers if he or she astutely applied the knowledge that comes from intelligent, repeated observation and experimentation with substances found in the environment. Only theoretical knowledge about mineral elements, how to distinguish them and how they can be chemically manipulated, must be acquired. Knowing this, I studied the ecology of Egypt to learn whether or not the necessary material was available for the production of a geopolymeric binder.

I found that some suitable ingredients were available in quantities of millions of tons. Mud from the Nile River contains alumina and is well suited for low-temperature mineral synthesis. The natron salt is extraordinarily abundant in the deserts and salt lakes. Natron reacts with lime and water to produce caustic soda, the main ingredient for alchemically making stone. An abundance of lime would have been available by calcining limestone in simple hearths. In ancient times, the Sinai mines were rich in deposits of turquoise and chrysocolla, needed for the production of synthetic zeolites. The mines also contained the arsenic minerals of olivenite and scorodite, needed to produce rapid hydraulic setting in large concrete blocks.

These same elements were used by the Egyptians in other processes. Nile silt was used for making sun-dried mud bricks and various minerals were used to make enamels. Natron was a sacred product used not only for flux, but also for mummification and deification rites. The following excerpts from the Pyramid Texts, found on the walls of the burial chamber of the Fifth Dynasty pyramid of Unas, show the sacred value of natron:

> Thou purifiest thyself, Horus is purified: One pastil of natron
> Thou purifiest thyself, Seth is purified: One pastil of natron
> Thou purifiest thyself, Thoth is purified: One pastil of natron
> Thou purifiest thyself, God is purified: One pastil of natron
> Thou purifiest thyself, that thou rest thyself among them:
> One pastil of natron
> Thy mouth is like that of the milk calf on the day of his birth:
> Five pastils of natron from the north, at Stpt.

The mouth of the newborn milk calf was considered to be clean because the calf had never eaten; and Stpt, a place where natron was gathered, is now called Wadi el-Natron.

Many of the same elements applicable for alchemical stone-making later played a role in glassmaking. By studying the ecology and the ancient products and documents of the Egyptians, I was able to trace the basic alchemical inventions that led to the development of the pyramid stone. These inventions are discussed chronologically in some detail in Appendix 1.

A fascinating view of the pyramids never imagined in modern times emerges. These alchemical discoveries address an exotic facet of pyramid construction. Next, we will explore feasibility.

CHAPTER 6

The Feasibility of the Theory

WITH CHEMISTRY, THE TASK OF PYRAMID CONSTRUCTION was easily accomplished with the tools of the Pyramid Age. With no carving or block hoisting required, the implements needed were simply those used to lay sun-dried mud bricks: a hoe to scrape up fossil-shell limestone, a basket to transport ingredients, a trough in which to prepare ingredients, a ladder, a square, a plumb line, a level, a builder's trowel, and wooden molds.

These tools were found in the Sixth Dynasty pyramid of Pharaoh Pepi II. Because the molds found are only small scale models, there is no way of determining whether or not they were intended for mud bricks or large stone blocks. Pepi II's pyramid was made of both.

Whereas precision cutting about 2.5 million nummulitic limestone blocks for the Great Pyramid with copper tools would be a formidable chore, copper implements are suitable for sawing and planing tree trunks into planks for molds. The

FIGURE 10. *Pyramids of the Fourth Dynasty were constructed of concrete materials transported in containers (A), then poured into molds (B), casting blocks directly in place.*

ancient Egyptians excelled in carpentry and were the inventors of plywood. According to the *Dictionaire des Techniques Archaeologiques:*

> Carpentry appeared in Egypt at the end of the pre-Dynastic period, around 3500 BC, when copper tools were sufficiently developed to enable them to be used in woodworking. Throughout all epochs, the Egyptian carpenter was a remarkable craftsman. He invented all manners of preparing wood joints and made them with skill: dowelling, mortices and tenons, dovetails, glueing, veneering, and marquetry. Wood being scarce in his country, he was the inventor of plywood. In a sarcophagus made during the Third Dynasty [around 2650 BC] there was actually a fragment of plywood found

FIGURE 11. *Mastaba from the tomb of Ti, about 2550 B.C., shows carpenters sawing planks and preparing mortices.*

which was made from six layers of wood, each about four milli-meters (0.15 inch) thick, held together by small flat rectangular tenons and tiny round dowels. Where two pieces had to be joined side-by-side, their edges were chamfered so as to unite exactly. The grain direction in successive layers is alternated, as in modern plywood, to provide greater strength and to avoid warping.

As early as the First Dynasty (3200 BC), carpenters assembled planks with perfect right angles. They made round dowels of ivory or wood. The flat rectangular wooden dowel appeared during the Fourth Dynasty. A wall painting from this period illustrates the use of copper saws and the preparation of mor-tices and tenons using copper chisels. The exquisite furniture placed in the tomb of Pharaoh Khufu's mother, Queen Hetep-Heres, exemplifies how cleverly carpenters prepared dovetails and mortices and tenons. The magnificent funerary boat of Khufu, mentioned earlier, is another example of remarkable craftsmanship.

The Palermo Stone, fragmentary remains of royal annals, indicates that Sneferu, of the Fourth Dynasty, assigned a fleet of ships to import cedar from Lebanon. The trees of Egypt are not hardwood and do not yield planks of the appropriate dimen-sions for molds. Egypt began to import cypress, cedar, and juniper from Lebanon as early as the pre-dynastic epoch. One variety of juniper reaches a height of 20 meters (21.8 yards), excellent for making molds which must measure from 1 to 1.5 meters (1.09 to 1.64 yards) wide.

Once set up, the molds were waterproofed from the inside with a thick layer of the cement itself. The cement became part of the block and can be seen at the bottom of blocks in the Great Pyramid. Wooden braces were suitable for stabilizing packed molds. Oil makes a suitable mold release, and Herodotus re-ported that the builders of the Great Pyramid smelled of rancid oil.

Because wood was so scarce, the remains of large wooden molds no longer exist. There is, however, a bas-relief that may depict a large stone block being cast. Wall paintings from the tomb of the Eighteenth Dynasty official Rekhmire (1400 BC),

A. *Lepsius recreation suggests workmen are preparing a stack of bricks.*

B. *Newberry recreation suggests a stack of bricks.*

C. *Tournus photograph of original painting does not clearly define a stack of bricks.*

FIGURE 12. *Fresco of brick workshop from tomb of Rekhmire.*

are precise illustrations of the technology of the New Kingdom. Although alchemical stonemaking is primarily Old Kingdom technology, it was used during the New Kingdom on a smaller scale.

A brick workshop is depicted in one of the paintings. One block appears too large to have been made of mud, because a mud brick would crack to pieces at the size depicted. Copies of the bas-relief were painted during the nineteenth century by K. R. Lepsius and P. E. Newberry. A comparison with the original shows that their reproductions were modified to clarify the theme. The reproductions enhanced the large block to make it appear to be a stack of small bricks. This destroyed the theme if indeed the production of a large stone was intended. Because both types of materials were made using similar implements, and there is nothing to indicate that the large block was mud brick instead of stone, the original painting is certainly open to interpretation.

The molds would have been easily disassembled so that one or more faces of a block could be used as a partial mold for casting the next block, producing the close fit. One of the characteristics of geopolymeric concrete is that there is no appreciable shrinkage, and blocks do not fuse when cast directly against each other. Although it would have been impossible to achieve the close fit (as close as 0.002 inch) of the 115,000 casing stones originally on the Great Pyramid with primitive tools, such joints are easily achieved when casting geopolymeric concrete.

Once cast, within hours or even less, depending on the formula (minutes using today's formulas), a block hardened. The mold was removed for reuse while a block was still relatively soft. A covering of reeds or palm leaves was probably applied to the blocks, affording an optimum amount of ventilation. This was required to harden (carbonate) the lime and protect the blocks from becoming brittle from evaporation. When the covering was removed, the blocks continued to harden in the sunlight, the heat accelerating setting.

As statues and sarcophagi were produced, finishing touches

would have been made with copper tools during the early stages of setting. I observed marks on core masonry of the Great Pyramid unlike those made with a chisel. Some appear to be impressions made by reeds. I also noticed long, sweeping impressions that fan out exactly like a palm leaf. Using a microscope, I was clearly able to see wood-grain impressions on a sample from the ascending passageway of the Great Pyramid.

It would be impossible for such an enormous cement industry to have left no traces of its existence, but those traces would never be recognized by anyone unaware of this technology. The most obvious traces are the tremendous quantities of minerals excavated from the Sinai mines, blue minerals such as turquoise and chrysocolla, generically known as mafkat during the Old Kingdom. Egyptologists are well aware of the industrial quantities of mafkat mined in the Sinai, but they cannot account for its consumption in such enormous quantities.

The mining expeditions of the pharaohs correspond exactly with the construction of the pyramids. Pyramid-building pharaohs are depicted in large reliefs in the cliff faces at the Sinai mines, where they are shown protecting mineral deposits from invading bedouins. There is no doubt about what was sought. Expeditions led by the archaeologist Beno Rothenberg (1967–1972), from Tel-Aviv Israel, demonstrate that mineral veins containing turquoise and chrysocolla had been primitively excavated, whereas veins of copper carbonate ore were left unexcavated.

The most basic product to any cement industry is lime. To produce lime, limestone or dolomite was calcined in kilns. No distinction was made between limestone, dolomite, and magnesite, each a white stone yielding different limes and, therefore, different qualities of cement. It is well established archaeologically that the production of lime itself is the oldest industrial process of mankind, dating back at least 10,000 years. Lime mortar in the ruins of Jericho, in the Jordan valley, is still intact after 9,000 years.

Herodotus reported that canals once connected the Great Pyramid to the Nile River. Egyptologists suggest that if these

FIGURE 13. *Fifth Dynasty stele on wall of Sinai mines shows the pharoah Sahure symbolically smiting an intruder.*

canals existed at the site, they were used to transport casing blocks from Tura, across the river. How would a canal serve the cement industry? A canal makes an ideal reaction basin for the on-site production of enormous quantities of cement.

I can envision two methods for the on-site production of the cement. One would entail placing suitable quantities of natron and lime in a dry canal. Nile mud (clay + silt) and water could have easily been captured in the canal during the annual flood period. The water dissolved the natron and put the lime in suspension, forming caustic soda. Caustic soda reacts with Nile mud, sixty percent alumina, to produce a triple aluminate of sodium, calcium, and magnesium. When the water evaporated, an activated substance would remain. The addition of siliceous minerals and another quantity of natron and lime produced a silico-aluminate, resulting in a basic geopolymeric cement. Other products were added, and, if necessary, the material could be stored.

Another method is even easier and is possible due to the nature of the Giza limestone. The limestone of Giza contains three or four percent of kaolinite, an aluminous silicate clay. The kaolinitic limestone requires only the addition of lime, natron, and water for a geopolymeric reaction to occur.

The vast amount of limestone rubble required to make pyramid blocks was easily obtained. Water, probably brought as close as possible by canal, was used to flood the bedrock of Giza to saturate it for easy disaggregation. The limestone of Giza becomes so extremely soft when saturated that it can be broken easily into chunks when wooden sticks are inserted. The body of the Great Sphinx was sculpted as muddy limestone rubble was scooped into baskets for use in pyramid blocks. Men wading in wet, muddy limestone while working in the desert heat makes more sense than men banging away at quarries in a hot, dusty desert, as called for by the accepted theory. By agglomerating stone, a better building material resulted because the blocks of the Great Pyramid are more strongly adhered than is the natural bedrock.

The landscape is also scattered with considerable quantities of loose shells, camites, strombites, turbinites, helicites, and especially nummulites. In ancient times there were hills of loose shells at Giza. The Greek geographer Strabo (64 BC) observed them:

> We cannot allow ourselves to remain silent on one thing that we saw at the pyramids, namely, the heaps of small stone chips in front of

these monuments. There we find pieces which, from their shape and size, resemble lentils. Sometimes they even look like half-threshed seeds. It is claimed that they are the petrified remains of the food of the workers but this is most unlikely, for we too have a hill at home set in the middle of a plain which is filled with small calcareous tuffs similar to lentils.

The more loose material naturally present, the less rubble excavation required. Loose material remaining at the site today is incorrectly assumed to be debris from stonecutting.

Agglomerating stone is far, far easier than cutting and hoisting massive blocks. To imagine the difficulty of building a pyramid by way of the accepted theory, one need only see how difficult it is to destroy even a small pyramid. It is much easier to destroy than to create almost anything, and Abd el-Latif (AD 1161–1231), a physician of Baghdad, described the difficulty encountered by a team that set out to destroy the Third Pyramid of Giza, which is only seven percent the size of the Great Pyramid:

> When Melic Alaziz Othman Ben Yussuf succeeded his father, he allowed himself to be persuaded by several persons of his court, people devoid of common sense, to demolish certain pyramids. They started with the red pyramid, which is the third of the Great Pyramids and the least considerable. The sultan sent his diggers, miners, and quarrymen, under the command of several of the principal officers and emirs of his court, and gave them the order to destroy it.

> To carry out their orders they set up a camp near the pyramid. There they assembled a large number of workers and housed them at great expense. They stayed for eight entire months with everyone doing his allotted task, removing, day after day with the expenditure of all his force, one or two stones. Some would push from the top with wedges and levers while others pulled from the bottom with cords and ropes. When one of the stones eventually fell it made an appalling noise, which could be heard from a great distance and shook the ground and made the mountains tremble.

> In falling, it became embedded in the sand and pulling it out required great effort. They forced in wedges, thus splitting the

stones into several pieces, then they loaded each piece onto a chariot and pulled it on foot to the mountain a short distance away where it was discarded.

After having camped for a long time and using all of their money and strength, their resolution and courage diminished daily. They were shamefully obligated to abandon their work. Far from obtaining the success for which they had hoped, all that they did was damage the pyramid and demonstrate their weakness and lack of power. This occurred in the year 593 [AD 1196]. Today, if one looks at the stones that were discarded, he has the impression that the pyramid must have been completely destroyed. But if one glances at the pyramid itself, he sees that it has undergone no degradation and that just on one side part of the casing stone has become detached.

Casting pyramid blocks *in situ* greatly simplified matters of logistics, enabling the construction of the Great Pyramid without doubling or tripling the life span of the pharaohs. Instead of 100,000 workers per year at Giza as called for by the accepted theory, as few as 1,400 workers could carry enough material to build the Great Pyramid in twenty years based on the following calculation: In Cambodia, during the Khmer revolution in 1976, men each carried about 3 cubic meters (3.9 cubic yards) per day to construct dams. One man, therefore, in one day can carry enough material to produce a block weighing from four to six tons. This would provide for 1,400 blocks set per day, the number reported by Herodotus. The number of men required, of course, depended on how many days were worked, which might depend on how many religious holidays were celebrated. Assuming that each man carried one basket per hour and worked about three months a year, or perhaps 100 days, the maximum number of carriers needed for a twenty-year period were 2,352, for fifteen years, 3,136 workers; and for ten years, 4,704 workers. Assuming that each excavator was attended by three carriers and one stone caster, then three carriers represented five men at work. This would place between 1,000 and 3,000 men on the work site during a three-month work period per year, or 400 to 1,000 during a ten-month-per-year work period, in order to complete the Great Pyramid in fifteen to twenty years.

Men easily could have carried one 22.5 kilogram (50-pound) basket every fifteen minutes to the base of the pyramid, one basket every thirty minutes to the middle, and one basket to the top of the pyramid on a ramp every hour. If a basket contained 0.3 cubic meter (0.039 cubic yard), then per day each man could have carried: one basket in fifteen minutes for a total of 1.42 cubic meters (1.87 cubic pards) or one basket every thirty minutes for a total of 0.71 cubic meter (0.94 cubic yard) or one basket per sixty minutes for a total of 0.36 cubic meter (0.47 cubic yard).

Table I. Number of Carriers Required to Build the Great Pyramid (~2.6 Million Blocks)

Construction Period	Four Blocks/Day Carrier	Two Blocks/Day Carrier	One Block/Day Carrier
Twenty Years			
300 days/year	196	392	784
200 days/year	294	588	1,176
100 days/year	588	1,176	2,352
Fifteen Years			
300 days/year	260	520	1,040
200 days/year	392	784	1,568
100 days/year	784	1,568	3,136
Ten Years			
300 days/year	392	784	1,568
200 days/year	588	1176	2,352
100 days/year	1,176	2,352	4,704

Additional workers were required for mining, transporting and crushing minerals, gathering natron, oil, wood, and other necessary products, preparing ingredients, digging canals, carrying water, making tools and molds, providing food and other personal needs, and performing miscellaneous chores. This might raise the total of men required by an additional few hundred. Total figures allow for freedom to maneuver at the work site and are considerably more reasonable than the 100,000 men per year at the site called for by the standard theory. The casting theory is quite feasible and easily settles problems of logistics.

CHAPTER 7

The Hard
Scientific Proof

THOUGH I AM THE FIRST TO REPRODUCE THE SYNTHETIC
pyramid stone and apply the technology to the construction
theory, another French chemist, Henry le Chatelier (1850–
1936), was the first to discover that the ancient Egyptians produced man-made stone. Le Chatelier was also a metallurgist and
ceramist. He worked with newly developed micrographic techniques, glass slides, thin section analysis, and photography in
combination with the microscope. He was the first to examine
enameled funerary statuettes from Egypt's Thinite epoch (c.
3000 BC) with these techniques and saw them as they had never
been seen before.

As Le Chatelier studied enameled funerary statuettes, he
found that his observation methods enabled him to notice that
the enamel was not a coating applied to the surface of the
statuettes. Instead, the enamel was the result of minerals which
migrated from within the stone itself. He cut thin sections with
a diamond-tipped saw and observed a gradually increasing con-

centration of minerals that had migrated to or near the surface of the stone to form enamel. The process is like that which occurs with Egyptian faience, a self-glazing ceramic. Le Chatelier was astonished to realize that the statuettes were man-made stone.

He and his colleagues tried in vain to duplicate the process. The method that produced the statuettes is one of my chemical discoveries discussed in Appendix 1. Le Chatelier's research took place in the early 1900s and his revelation should have raised debate about other stone artifacts, especially the pyramids with their numerous enigmatic features.

Academics, however, are not necessarily innovators. And scholars involved with the soft sciences, such as history, may not necessarily be scientific minded. In fact, during my presentation at the Second International Congress of Egyptologists, I used le Chatelier's work to make the Egyptologists who were present aware that science had already shown that the Egyptians produced man-made stone. Acknowledging that, they were still unwilling to concede that the pyramid stone might be man-made.

It was not until some years after I devised my theory that I analyzed actual ancient geopolymer. In 1981, Liliane Courtois of the Center for Archaeological Research, in Paris, and I carried out an X-ray chemical analysis on fragments of lime vessels from Tel-Ramad, Syria, dating from 6000 BC. The vessels were made of a white stony lime material. In other words, they are classified as being made primarily of lime. We made a presentation at the Twenty-First International Symposium on Archaeometry, held at the Brookhaven National Laboratory in New York. We reported that the samples contain up to forty-one percent of analcime (analcite), a zeolite that is easy to produce. This high amount of zeolitic material is not found in the raw material from which the vases were made and could only be the result of geopolymerization. The fact is that synthetic zeolites had been produced 8,000 years ago in the Middle East. In modern times they were first produced by an English scientist named Barrer in the 1950s.

Knowing that it would be impossible to prove my theory without samples of pyramid stone, in 1982 I made an appointment to visit Jean-Philippe Lauer at his home in Paris. Lauer, now over eighty-five years old, is eminent among European Egyptologists. He spent fifty-six years of his career restoring the pyramid of Zoser. He has his own conservative views on pyramid construction based on more than fifty years of study, and his attitude about my research is reserved. In a letter I received before I visited him, he said, "I defy you to prove that the pyramid stone is synthetic."

That, of course, was my intent. During our visit, he gave me samples from the pyramids of Khufu and Teti. The sample from Teti came from an outer casing block and the one from the Great Pyramid came from the ascending passageway.

I had X-ray chemical analysis performed on the samples by two different laboratories to be sure that there would be no analytical discrepancies. I presented a paper on the test results at the International Congress of Egyptologists held that same year in Toronto. At the congress, Lauer and I each made separate presentations about our theories of pyramid construction. Despite knowing that I was making a presentation using his samples, Lauer did not attend my presentation because he did not take my theory seriously. *The Toronto Star* newspaper covered the congress and published Lauer's following response to my research (September 7, 1982): "There are many ridiculous surveys, not stupid, but impossible. Not many are serious."

X-ray chemical analysis detects bulk chemical composition. These tests undoubtedly show that Lauer's samples are manmade. The samples contain mineral elements highly uncommon in natural limestone, and these foreign minerals can take part in the production of a geopolymeric binder.

The sample from the Teti pyramid is lighter in density than the sample from Khufu's pyramid (the Great Pyramid). The Teti sample is weak and extremely weathered, and it lacks one of the minerals found in the sample from the Great Pyramid. The samples contain some phosphate minerals, one of which was identified as brushite, which is thought to represent an organic material occurring in bird droppings, bone, and teeth, but it would be rare to find brushite in natural limestone.

The presence of such organic materials in the pyramid stone affords new possibilities for a better understanding of ancient culture. If bird droppings were a source of the brushite, this might explain a function of the large place known as Ostrich Farm, which was not far from Giza. It is well known that in ancient Egypt, bird droppings, urine, and animal dung were added to straw and mud to increase the cohesiveness of mud brick.

If bone were a source of brushite, this could shed new light on the mysterious sacrificial rites of antiquity. The sacred animals would have been slaughtered and burned on the sacrificial altars, their bones calcined to ashes. The ashes would have been powdered and used as an ingredient of the religious monument. The vestiges of this alchemical knowledge may have influenced customs and inspired mythology and legends of later times. The Medusa myth, for instance, concerns humans turned to stone. The Romans, well known for the durable pozzuolanic cement still intact in Roman ruins, occupied Egypt and apparently absorbed certain alchemical knowledge. One legend recounts that 1,000 animals were sacrificed during the construction of the Roman Colosseum. Roman cement, which I have reproduced, is a remarkable ancient product. A late president of the American Concrete Institute (ACI) had on his desk a sample of Roman concrete that had been underwater for more than 2,000 years in the harbor of Port Pozzuoli in Italy. Recent underwater explorations have revealed the exceptionally high quality of the concrete used to build Caesarea, the monumental seaport city of ancient Judea built in the First Century by King Herod.

The pyramid samples also contain a mineral known as opal CT, a siliceous material. I had a debate about this with Michael S. Tite, Head of the Museum Laboratory at the British Museum. Tite was the coordinator of the Archaeometry '84 Symposium, held at the Smithsonian Institution in Washington, DC, in 1984. As coordinator, he had the advantage of prior review of my presentation. He took advantage of this and submitted a piece of a casing block exhibited at the British Museum to chemical analysis at the museum laboratory.

After my presentation, he arose and told the symposium, "All of the features that they [his analytical team] saw can be explained on the basis of natural origin, and there is really no need to introduce this hypothesis of reconstituted stone." Like anyone unfamiliar with geopolymerization, Tite saw nothing unusual in the mineral composition.

I met with Tite in London shortly thereafter to have a closer look at his test results. His charts showed practically the same peaks as the charts produced by my analysis, indicating a comparable mineralogical makeup in our samples. I presented my official rebuttal to Tite at the Science in Egyptology Symposium, held in England at the Manchester Museum in June 1984. Whereas a geological explanation for the presence of opal CT is valid, the presence of opal CT (detected by X-ray diffraction or microscopy) could also imply the addition of silicate materials during stone manufacture. The presence of opal CT in the pyramid stone might result from an addition of ashes from burnt offerings of such siliceous materials as cereal husks, straw, and certain types of reeds.

To my knowledge, the only other researcher who performed a comparative chemical analysis on stone from Egyptian quarries and pyramid stone is Klemm, whose project was described previously. Thanks to help from colleagues, especially Hisham Gaber, a geology graduate of Ain Shams University in Cairo, I obtained samples from the quarries of Tura and Mokhatam in the Arabian mountains, where it is believed that the casing blocks originated. Gaber collected more than thirty samples from various sites. X-ray diffraction and microscopical analyses of the quarry samples indicates that they are pure calcite, sometimes containing a trace of dolomite. None of the quarry samples contains any of the unusual minerals found in the pyramid samples.

Although the quarry samples do not match the pyramid stone, a sample of stone I made with geopolymeric cement and fine limestone is mineralogically comparable to the latter, producing similar peaks on the X-ray charts. Researchers who previously performed chemical analysis on pyramid stone never suspected anything out of the ordinary even though their samples contain elements uncommon in natural limestone. A case in point is a project mentioned in Chapter 1, the joint research venture carried out by Ain Shams University and SRI International. G. E. Brown, a geologist at Stanford University, was unable to palentologically classify casing-block samples devoid of classifiable fossils, which enable petrographic comparison. Consequently, he could draw only tentative conclusions about the origin of the casing blocks. Because it is not easy to match blocks which appear incomparable mineralogically with the natural limestone of Egypt, one begins to see how the use of man-made stone settles the outstanding scientific dilemmas.

Another issue settled is the controversy raised by Klemm's geochemical study. Klemm created quite a debate with geologists when he compared trace elements from twenty core blocks of the Great Pyramid with those of his quarry samples and determined that the pyramid blocks had been quarried from sites all over Egypt. If Klemm's data are correct, his conclusion that the stones were quarried from all over Egypt does not necessarily follow. Not only does it make for insurmountable logistical problems, but the apparently conflicting geological and geochemical studies uphold my findings. Minerals were mined for the cement from various sites, and fossil shells were gathered for the building blocks at Giza. The geological and geochemical reports contain no inaccurate data but were misinterpreted because the basic premise of pyramid construction on which most scientists rely is incorrect. Applying the standard theory ensures that the conflict will remain forever unresolved, even when the best modern equipment and well-trained scientists are used.

Some Egyptologists criticize my findings because I obtained only two small samples of pyramid stone for analysis. However, the samples analyzed by Klemm (which came from the rough core blocks), Brown, and Tite can serve further to confirm my test results. In 1984 I submitted a research proposal to the Egyptian Antiquities Organization in Cairo requesting permission to sample the core blocks of the Great Pyramid. The permission was denied. The following excerpts are from their letter to me, translated from French:

Cairo, December 16, 1984
Dear Sir:
We are answering your letter from October 15, 1984, and I have the duty of informing you that the Permanent Committee of the Egyptian Antiquities Organization, during their meeting on December 6, 1984, regrets not responding favorably to your proposal concerning the authorization for analyzing the stones of the pyramids, the Sphinx, and the quarries. The decision is because your hypothesis represents only a private point of view which has no analogy with archaeological or geological facts.
Sincerely yours,
The President of the Egyptian Antiquities Organization

Even if geopolymeric concrete is as strong and beautiful as natural stone, some telltale signs of its artificial nature must

FIGURE 14. *Drawing from* Description de l'Egypte *shows jumbled shells in pyramid core blocks.*

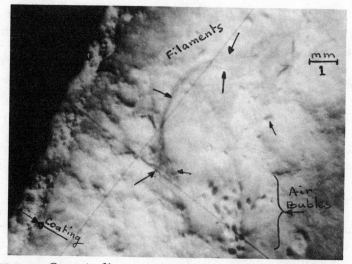

FIGURE 15. *Organic fibers, air bubbles, and an artificial red coating are visible on a sample stone from the ascending passageway of the Great Pyramid.*

exist. The signs would depend on the variety of stone imitated. For instance, nummulitic limestone is comprised of the skeletal remains of foraminifers that accumulate over millions of years to form sedimentary layers of bedrock. The fossil shells lie horizontally or flat in the bedrock. Jomard and de Roziere, however, described the rough building blocks of the Great Pyramid as being composed of shells that are in disarray:

> The main variety of limestone in the Great Pyramid is almost solely formed of an accumulation of nummulites, which are disk-like fossil shells of various sizes that seem to be arranged in all orientations.

As in any concrete, the aggregates are for the most part jumbled, in this case devoid of sedimentary layering.

In addition to the jumbled shells and chemical makeup, the pyramid stone demonstrates other telltale physical features. Scattered through Lauer's samples are numerous air bubbles. The bubbles are not round, but oval, like those that occur during the manipulation of clay. The broken surfaces have a clay-matrix look. This can often be observed with the naked eye on the broken surface of casing blocks.

I noticed a small dark streak just beneath the surface of a broken part of the sample from the Great Pyramid. The streak is visible because it is close to the surface. I contracted three different laboratories to identify this particle. All three laboratories reported that the streak could be nothing other than a small bundle of two or three organic fibers, possibly hair. The fibers are unlikely to be algal filaments occurring naturally, since algae are mainly calcite-forming and not easily preserved. The presence of organic fibers could instead result from the accidental incorporation of fragments of hair rope or the deliberate incorporation of animal remains from ritual sacrifices. The fibers are flat, like human arm hair, but they may not necessarily be of human origin. The bundle is surrounded by clusters of air bubbles. Hair has never been discovered in 50-million-year-old rocks. The limestone would have formed under the ocean 50 million years ago during the Middle Eocene geological epoch. Whereas fur-bearing mammals on the ocean floor among the foraminifers 50 million years ago creates an impossible scenario, hair from animals or the arms of workers probably commonly fell into the stone-making slurry during pyramid construction. Organic fibers were not found in the quarry samples.

The sample from the Great Pyramid provided by Lauer is topped with a white coating overlaid with a brownish-red surface coloration. Such coloration appears also on a few remaining outer casing blocks of this pyramid and varies from brownish red to greyish black. There has been long debate about whether the coloration is a type of paint or a patina, the latter resulting gradually from desert weather conditions.

Attempting to show that the casing block coloration of the Khufu and Khafra pyramids is a paint, Andre Pochan, in 1934, analyzed the coloration appearing on these pyramids. His tests revealed the presence of minerals highly uncommon in limestone, leading him to conclude that the coloration could not be a patina because that would require a migration of minerals from within the stone itself. He therefore proposed that some type of hard, siliceous binder was applied and painted over with a pigment of red ochre.

A. Lucas accepted the validity of Pochan's chemical analysis but disputed the presence of a deliberate coating. Lucas maintained that the coloration is a patina. Lauer and K. L. Gauri, of the Stone Conservation Laboratory of the University of Louisville, in Kentucky, also maintain that the coloration is a patina. Pochan and Lauer hotly debated the issue for twenty years. Lauer's opinion carries great weight among peers, and he had the last word on the subject because he outlived Pochan. The chemistry of geopolymerization serves to settle this issue as well.

Because Pochan had already analyzed the red coloration, I analyzed only the underlying white coating appearing on the sample from the Great Pyramid. I submitted Lauer's sample to two different laboratories employing experts with diverse backgrounds in geology and mineralogy. Combining our expertise, I was amazed to find a tremendously complex geopolymeric chemical system in the white coating. Its principal ingredients are two calcium phosphates, brushite and crystalline hydroxyapatite, both found in bone, and a zeolite called ZK-20. The coating is pure geopolymeric cement. It is the key to the composition of the pyramid stone. This binder is infinitely more sophisticated than the simple gypsum and lime cement by which scholars have characterized Egyptian cement technology. Indeed, the binder is even more sophisticated than I had expected.

Even though Pochan did not understand the chemistry involved, he was nevertheless correct in his surmise that the red coloration is synthetic. As he knew, the minerals opined to have migrated are highly uncommon in natural limestone. In any case, the amount of minerals present in the stone is too small to form a patina. Additionally, the minerals in the red coloration, like those in the white coating, are insoluble and, therefore, could not have migrated, nor could minerals have migrated through the white coating to form a red coloration. Furthermore, the sample I analyzed exhibiting the red coloration came from the pyramid's interior where it was unaffected by weathering. Finally, using a microscope, I observed two cracks in the red coating of this sample. One crack is deep and exposes white limestone, making it much more recent than the coating. The other crack is ancient, and it is filled with the red coloration. The color was obviously painted on because it filled the crack. The coating and coloration are truly remarkable alchemical products, showing no blistering or other appreciable deterioration after about 4,500 years.

Geologists who have analyzed the pyramid blocks have recognized no known adhesives holding the stone together. Not realizing that the unusual minerals in the stone comprise the binder, they have not recognized the stone as synthetic. Likewise, researchers recognize no known chemical composition to justify a man-made coating and coloration on the stone. A report that typifies the reaction of geologists to this material is amusing. A geologist was commissioned by the owners of a collection of limestone artifacts from ancient Egypt to prove them to be natural stone because museum authenticators interested in the collection detected that the stone was artificial. They opined that the pieces must, therefore, be fakes. Trying to prove the natural origin of the limestone, the geologist claimed that perhaps some extraterrestrial system, far in advance of our own, might possess the technology required for producing such stone, but lacking proof of that, we of the earth must consider the stone to be of natural origin.

There is a historical account that supports the presence of paint on the Great Pyramid, and it also mentions remarkable pyramid cement. The following remarks were made by Abd el-Latif:

These pyramids are built of large stones, ten to twenty cubits [16.6–33 feet] in length by a thickness of two to three cubits [20–30 inches] and a similar width. What is worthy of the greatest admiration is the extreme precision with which the stones have been dressed and laid one over the other. Their foundations are so well leveled that one cannot plunge a needle or a hair between any two stones. They are cemented by mortar which forms a layer the thickness of a sheet of paper. I do not know what this mortar is made of; it is totally unknown to me. The stones are covered with writings in ancient characters whose meaning today I do not know and nowhere in all of Egypt have I met anyone who, even by hearsay, is able to interpret them. The inscriptions are so numerous that if one were to copy on paper merely those on the surface of the two pyramids, ten thousand pages would be filled.

Even though the paper-thin cement would afford no appreciable cohesive power for adhering one block to another, it is assumed that the builders, nevertheless, applied a thin coating of what is assumed to be ordinary lime-gypsum plaster. But Abd el-Latif's account shows that the Arabs, who were producing lime-gypsum plaster and lime mortar more than 3,000 years after the Great Pyramid was built, found the thin cement completely unfamiliar and quite impressive. Paper-thin mortar is a by-product of geopolymerization that forms when there is excess water in the slurry. The weight of aggregates squeezes watery cement to the surfaces, where it sets to form a skin. We may never learn much more about the colored hieroglyphs cited above. Abd el-Latif's report was made shortly before the earthquake of AD 1301. Cairo was destroyed, and most of the outer casing blocks were stripped to rebuild the city.

That the pyramid stone is synthetic has eluded several individuals who might have recognized it. It never occurred to Jomard and de Roziere that the pyramid stone was a concrete when they observed the jumbled shells in 1801. Only poor-quality cement was produced after the fall of the Roman Empire in AD 476. Portland cement was invented only in 1824. It was not manufactured until the 1830s.

Pochan recognized the coloration on the pyramid blocks as synthetic because it contains minerals uncommon in limestone. It follows that had he analyzed the pyramid stone as well, he would also have recognized it as synthetic, especially if he had considered the work of le Chatelier. And in 1974, the revelation eluded researchers of SRI International. Their team attempted to locate hidden chambers in the Great Pyramids of Giza. The project failed, however, because the pyramid stone contains so much moisture that the electromagnetic waves would not transmit, and were instead absorbed by the stone. This was unexpected because the natural limestone bedrock at Giza is relatively dry.

Only concrete would be full of moisture. The moisture content encountered by SRI International alone would convince any professional of the concrete industry that the pyramid stone is some kind of concrete. Today's newly built concrete structures are internally moist. The moisture in the pyramid stone is probably the result of the migration of ground water. It is common for concrete structures to absorb ground water in desert environments. Additionally, the Great Pyramids are so massive and were built so rapidly that blocks that were not exposed to air for any appreciable time never fully dried. That the pyramid stone must be a concrete never occurred to the researchers at SRI International.

CHAPTER 8

The Proof at Giza

TO FURTHER DEMONSTRATE THAT THE PYRAMID STONE IS synthetic, I conducted a study at Giza in 1984. A complete survey of the geological strata of the Giza plateau has never been conducted because the site is completely filled with tombs and sand. I surveyed all of the exposed strata in the bedrock, and I made a comparative study between the exposed strata and thousands of blocks in the pyramids and those in the temples at Giza.

The variation in quality of blocks composing the Giza pyramids is striking. Certain blocks are unweathered whereas the majority have become extremely eroded by wind, rain, and the sunlight; the latter is most severe from the south and west. The effects of erosion are most obvious on a very rough layer that forms the top portion of all of the pyramid blocks. This top area, generally from twenty to 30 centimeters (7.87–8.81 inches) thick, is weaker, lighter in density, and more affected by erosion than the rest of the stone. This is because the blocks were produced in the same way that plaster is prepared, as follows:

Aggregates were poured directly into a mold that was partially filled with water and binder. As the mixture combined with the water, the heaviest materials settled to the bottom. Air

FIGURE 16. *Blocks on the west face of Khafra's pyramid exhibit sponge-like upper portions.*

FIGURE 17. *Block fallen from southwest corner of Khafra's pyramid has three lift lines (B-bottom; T-top).*

FIGURE 18. *Arrow points out thick mortar used to seal bottom of mold for block on south face of Khafra's pyramid.*

FIGURE 19. *Davidovits examines transition between bedrock base and pyramid blocks. (A) Fossil shells correspond to the natural sedimentary layering in the bedrock portion of the base. (B) Pyramid blocks cast on bedrock have well-fitted joints. In lighter top portion jumbled and broken fossil shells are visible. (C) Separation between bedrock and pyramid blocks.*

bubbles and excess watery binder rose to the top, producing a lighter, weaker matrix. The top layer also exhibits the fewest number of fossil shells, which were not as crowded within the dense slurry and were therefore depositionally oriented horizontally. No mixing was required to produce the concrete, and precise measurements afforded perfectly level tiers.

The top layer is so rough and riddled with holes that the blocks look like sponges. My first impression was that they resemble geopolymeric foam, a product that I have developed. Gaber accompanied me in my survey, and his professors from the geology department of Ain Shams University commented that the numerous holes in the top portion result from fossil shells having been stripped away by erosion. I explained that although erosion caused the deterioration, it did so because the top layer is more susceptible than is the denser bottom layer.

Furthermore, I observed that blocks on the west side of Khafra's pyramid were protected from weathering. Until about 100 years ago, the first several tiers on the west side were buried in sand. Because erosion occurred after the sand was cleared, the blocks on the west side are relatively unweathered. However, even these unweathered blocks exhibit the light, weak top layer, which, therefore, cannot be attributed to weathering.

All blocks composing the pyramids at Giza, those of Khufu, Khafra, Menkure (Mycerinus in Greek), and the mile-long causeway from Menkure's pyramid to the Nile bear the weak top layer. In contrast, a comparison of the cast blocks and the bedrock demonstrates obvious differences.

To form a level base on the incline of the Giza plateau, five steps on the west side of the pyramid of Khafra were shaped *in situ* from natural bedrock. There are no individual blocks in these bedrock steps, and therefore, shaping them did not involve the arduous labor required to cut perfectly fitting blocks. The transition between the natural bedrock steps and the manmade blocks appears near the middle of the north and south sides of the base of the pyramid. Above are about 2 million individual blocks. At the base, blocks were cast directly on bedrock, which is quite homogeneous in density when cut within a given geological stratum or series thereof. The jumbled shells in the pyramid blocks reported by Jomard and de Roziere are apparent. The nummulites in the bedrock steps are oriented horizontally, characteristic of natural sedimentary layering.

If the pyramid blocks were natural limestone, the unnatural density pattern could be explained only if two adjacent strata of different quality had been included in the cut, the lower of a better quality than the upper. That the pyramid blocks were cast explains why the rough top layer is always about the same size regardless of the height of a block. It would be ridiculous to suppose that quarries exhibiting this unusual feature could have been identified and used to the degree that is exhibited in the pyramids.

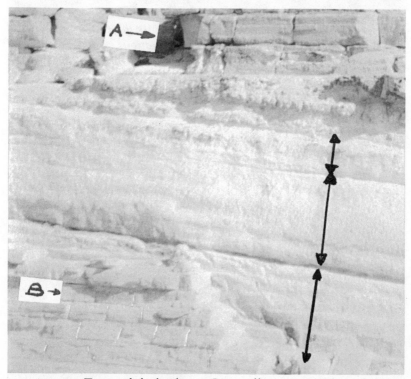

FIGURE 20. *Exposed bedrock at Giza allows comparison between heights of pyramid blocks (A and B) and the divisions of geological strata (arrows).*

101

FIGURE 21. *Second Pyramid of Giza exhibits three different types of joints. A and B are carved modern restorations. C is an original agglomerated stone joint. D is a joint in which thick mortar was applied during construction.*

FIGURE 22. *Blocks in Khafra's mortuary temple have wavy lift lines characteristic of construction interruptions during casting.*

FIGURE 23. *Enormouns blocks in the mortuary temple of Khafra exhibit lightweight, weathered top portions characteristic of concrete.*

FIGURE 24. *Chunk of stone incorporated into block is visible in Khafra's pyramid.*

With few exceptions, the pyramid blocks contain no type of strata. If the blocks were quarried, it would have required that they be extracted to avoid cutting along the division between strata because the blocks are smaller than the strata in the bedrock. Incongruence with regard to strata is opposite to what is advocated by Egyptologists. They assume that the blocks were easy to cut because advantage was taken of natural divisions in the bedrock.

Occasionally, a stratum (lift line) can be observed in very large pyramid blocks. When one does appear, however, it is not as high as the divisions of strata found on the Giza plateau. The divisions of strata in the bedrock near the pyramid of Khafra are about 4.5 meters (5 yards) apart, much greater than the heights of the pyramid blocks.

In the pyramids of Khufu, Khafra, and Menkure, a thick, pink gypsum mortar was used to fill cracks and level imperfect blocks and also to cement a minority of rough trapezoidal-shaped core blocks to neighboring blocks. The mortar was applied to a thickness of up to 20 millimeters (0.78 inch) beneath the base of the trapezoidal blocks. These blocks are positioned with their widest area upward. The mortar was applied to be thickest at the bottom, with that thickness gradually decreasing as it neared the top of the blocks. Practically no mortar is visible at their top edges, because this area is very small. The presence of this thick mortar indicates that these particular blocks were moved into place, as opposed to having been cast *in situ*.

That these trapezoidal blocks are bound by mortar does not invalidate the agglomerated stone theory because the blocks represent only a small minority. Instead, the blocks provide insight into the plan by which the pyramids were constructed. The blocks were probably cast near by and placed during the final construction phase to plug passageways that had remained open to provide ventilation and allow ingress and egress of materials.

I closely examined blocks in the mortuary temple, valley temple, and the temple of the Sphinx in Khafra's complex, and the mortuary temple in Menkure's complex. Walls protected from weathering are smooth and light grey. Large surface areas of blocks composing walls that have been attacked by weather expose the same density variations as appear in the pyramid blocks. Blocks in the temples in Khafra's complex are enormous. They stand approximately 2 to 3 meters (6 to 10 feet) high and, as mentioned, weigh up to 500 tons apiece. The weathered faces of the largest of these blocks exhibit two or three wavy, irregular strata. These are smaller than the divisions of strata in the Giza plateau. The geologists I encountered from Ain Shams University opined that the strata proves that the stones are natural. They were unaware that most types of concrete can also exhibit strata, known as lift lines.

Like those exhibited in the largest pyramid blocks, these lift lines can be explained by the method used to produce the blocks. If the large temple blocks are natural, they would have to have been quarried from close by, because their great size would make them almost impossible to move by primitive means. To cast blocks of such enormous size might require three days. After the workers quit for the day, the unfinished block hardened. As it set, a surface (lift line) formed. The process was repeated daily until the block was complete. The lift lines are visible now that the outer block has been destroyed by weathering. In addition, the strata in the bedrock are horizontal, whereas the wavy lift lines are characteristic of material dumped into a mold.

The planed surfaces and sharp, geometrical angles of the blocks of these temple walls compare exactly with those of modern walls made of concrete blocks. It is strikingly obvious that the northern face of the valley temple in Khafra's complex is a wall of gigantic geopolymeric concrete blocks, formed of parallelepipeds with perfect right angles.

The block quality is excellent. The core blocks of the pyramids, though of better quality than the bedrock body of the Sphinx, do not compare with the fine quality of the temple blocks. The difference can be explained only by the quality of the stonemaking formula itself.

Aside from evidence from the chemical analysis of pyramid stone, geologists find the most compelling evidence for cast in place pyramid stones to be gross features such as the chunks of stone incorporated into the pyramid blocks **(Figure 24)**, the wavy lift lines **(Figure 22)**, the density differences between the pyramid and quarry stone **(Figure 22)**, and the jumbled nature of the fossil shells in the pyramid stone **(Figures 24, 22)**. The apparent absence of sedimentary stratification in the pyramid stones is also powerful geological evidence. Additionally, the quarry rocks contain cracks, ranging from microscopic to several inches in width. These cracks are filled with secondary calcite. Similar cracks were not observed in the pyramid blocks and are thought not to be present.

Petrie reported his examinations of the Giza quarries in *Pyramids and Temples of Giza*:

> It has always been assumed that only the finer stone, used for the casing and passages, was brought from the eastern cliffs, and that the bulk of the masonry was quarried in the neighborhood. But no quarryings exist on the western side adequate to have yielded the bulk of either of the greater pyramids; and the limestone of the western hills is different in character from that of the pyramid masonry, which resembles the qualities usually quarried on the eastern shore. It seems, therefore, that the whole of the stones were quarried in the cliffs of Turra and Masara, and brought across to the selected site. . . . I have repeatedly examined the edge of the desert from Abu Roash to Dahshur, and walked over all the district behind the Pyramids for several miles in each direction; some very slight quarrying just behind the barracks at the Second Pyramid is all that I have seen, beyond mere tomb excavations.

Petrie's survey of the quarries shows that millions of blocks were not quarried anywhere near the Great Pyramids of Giza. Yet, geologists demonstrate that the fossils in the pyramid originally come from Giza, and not from Tura or Masara as Petrie assumed.

The pyramid of Menkure has an exceptional history. Most of its casing blocks, now disappeared, were limestone. Those appearing on the lower quarter of the pyramid are made of carved granite. Some of the blocks are irregularly shaped, typical of carved blocks. Menkure's pyramid probably fell victim to the New Kingdom pharaoh, Ramses II, who routinely used pyramid casing blocks to build or restore temples consecrated to his god, Amun.

The pyramid of Menkure was stripped starting at the bottom, but only one-third was denuded. A subsequent ruler restored the pyramid with carved syenite granite from Aswan, a material which commonly was carved during the New Kingdom. As opposed to supporting the traditional theory of construction, the carved blocks contribute to my theorem. Their appearance clearly demonstrates the difference between carved and cast blocks because carved blocks always exhibit tool marks whereas cast blocks do not.

The head of the Sphinx may be agglomerated stone. I have no data to support this supposition because my request to remove samples was denied. The smooth stone of the head is harder than the body stone and it does not match any of the Giza bedrock. It is assumed that the stone does not match because all such harder stone was quarried away when the Sphinx was sculpted. This would be true if the entire Sphinx, not just the body, were sculpted. A huge crack, however, has developed under the chin, which may represent the point where the head was joined to the bedrock body.

Ancient repairs with lime gypsum mortar caused no damage to the Sphinx and a protective coating formed, which is in my opinion a result of geopolymerization. However, salts leaching from the modern mortar used in repairs have caused the stone to decay. This shows that ancient Egyptian lime-gypsum mortar does not have the same chemical makeup as modern lime-gypsum mortar. The modern material consists exclusively of hydrated calcium sulfate, whereas the ancient mortar is based on a silico-aluminate, a result of geopolymerization. I have observed well-preserved, hard lime-gypsum mortar on some ancient Egyptian monuments and lime-gypsum that is completely disaggregated on others. The disaggregated mortar is modern, and because the modern mortar has deteriorated, it is assumed that lime-gypsum mortar does not endure.

At Saqqara and Giza I found geological layers of well-crystallized gypsum sandwiched between layers of limestone and aluminous clay. When a combination of these three materials is calcined and combined with natron, a geopolymeric lime-gypsum cement results, which sets rapidly and resists erosion. Such cement was used for patching and sealing in most of the pyramids. This is the thick mortar used to set the trapezoidal blocks, previously described, and it is in good condition after thousands of years. However, because it sets rapidly, it does not allow sufficient time for casting and, therefore, is unsuitable for producing limestone concrete. This explains why gypsum is not a component of the geopolymeric binder described previously.

Much of the restoration by Lauer on the pyramid of Zoser was made with portland cement concrete. Those repairs of thirty years ago have cracked and, consequently, had to be replaced with carved limestone. The geopolymeric material would be ideal for a lasting restoration of monuments.

It has been one of my goals not only to offer materials for monument repair, but also to show Egypt how to make unsurpassed building materials with local natural resources for more urgent needs. The poverty of Cairo is heart rending. Some Egyptians are so desperate for housing that they have taken up residence in ancient tombs; others have no dwelling. Poor living conditions and severe overcrowding have caused civil unrest and rioting in recent years; many people are living below the level of their ancestors of thousands of years.

During this study at Giza, I photographed the south and west faces of the pyramid of Khafra below the top thirty levels. The uniformity of lengths of the blocks of Khafra's pyramid show that the use of agglomerated stone is the only viable system of pyramid construction. The heights of the pyramid blocks are more variable than the lengths. This would not call for more molds; the desired height could be achieved by marking the molds at a certain level and by filling them to that point. This system accounts for the dramatic fluctuations relative to the Great Pyramid that Goyon could not correctly explain.

FIGURE 25. *Restoration detail of Zoser's pyramid shows (A) original casing stones over 4,500 years old, and (B) cracked blocks made of portland cement-based concrete less than 50 years old.*

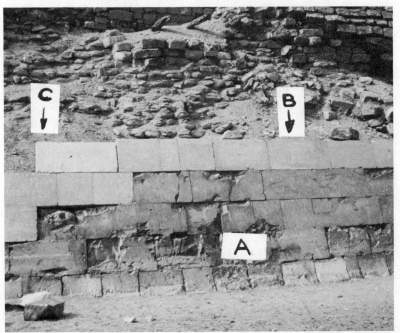

FIGURE 26. *Another detail shows (A) original casing blocks, (B) portland cement-based concrete block, (C) block carved from soft white limestone of Tura during recent restorations.*

109

FIGURE 27. *Basilica in Saint Quentin, France, survived the old city after World War I.*

Staggering the block heights also produces tremendous stability. This type of structural design was used in cathedrals built in northern France and Germany during the Gothic period between the twelfth and fifteenth centuries. They are capable of withstanding an impressive amount of shock. In my home town of Saint Quentin the thirteenth century basilica made this way remains standing although the city was destroyed by bombs in the battle of Somme during World War I (1914–1918). Likewise, the old city hall, similarly constructed, is still standing. In Cologne, West Germany, one such cathedral stood alone above the ruins of the city in World War II. The Great Pyramid was unscathed by the earthquake of 1301 that devastated Cairo.

One of the main purposes of my study at Giza was to determine whether the lengths of individual blocks might recur and, if so, to what degree. A high degree of uniform lengths corroborates the principle of blocks cast in molds. Almost all 2,000 blocks I photographed in Khafra's pyramid conform to ten uniform lengths. The various lengths are set in different patterns throughout the twenty-two steps. That only ten dimensions exist indicates that all twenty-two steps were produced with molds of only five sizes because some blocks were cast with their lengths perpendicular to the plane of the pyramid face.

That the longest blocks are always the same length is extremely strong evidence in favor of the use of cast stone. It shows that each block was produced according to the exact, immediate specifications of the architect during construction. Long blocks always appear directly above or beneath blocks that are short in length, making the construction plan apparent.

Any dimension required could be determined quickly by the architect because it would be relative to the length of the block in the tier directly below. It is simple to determine the length needed when blocks are all produced from molds of the same few sizes. Anyone, however, attempting to explain the preparation and use of blocks of such highly uniform dimensions based on the carving hypothesis would be unable to do so. Blocks could never have been cut, stored, and selected on the scale required.

The south and west faces of Khafra's pyramid are a mirror image of each other, indicating that the entire intricate design is three dimensional. Successive tiers are made of the same pattern, whereas others are made of different, interrelated patterns. Certain tiers have patterns that are almost the same as those of neighboring tiers. The patterns of other tiers are opposite to those surrounding them. All blocks were cast according to an uncanny master plan of patterns that eliminated the formation of vertical joints, which would cause weak points. The pyramid resembles an intricate three-dimensional puzzle that was effectively formulated to create an incredibly strong, stable super-structure.

CHAPTER 9

The Birth of Masonry

THE ROLE OF THE HISTORIAN IS TO EXPLAIN WHY EVENTS occur as they do. Many important facets of history have eluded historians as a result of lost knowledge about the alchemical stonemaking technology. Now that the old science is recovered, one is beckoned to reexamine several issues. New light is shed on the developments that led to construction of the first pyramid. One can recognize reasons for the rise and decline of pyramid building. These have been improperly understood as have critical periods of instability and decline in the Egyptian civilization. Then there is the question of how such an important technology could have been lost. If the old science really did exist, there must be some historical traces. An exploration of these issues sheds new light on many aspects of history. The historical remnants provide additional, powerful proof and significantly deepen our understanding.

The oldest known remains of high-quality cement are found in the ruins of Jericho in the Jordan valley. They date from 9,000 years ago. We know that white lime vessels, based on the synthesis of zeolites, were produced in Tel-Ramad, Syria, 8,000 years ago. Mortar from this era has also survived from Catal-Hujuk, Turkey. The existence of these ancient products suggests that the earliest stonemaking technology migrated into Egypt.

Settlers attracted by the fertile valley arrived with various animals, plants, traditions, skills, materials, and processes. Hard stone vessels first appeared in pre-dynastic Egypt at about 3800 BC. Later, approximately 30,000 hard stone vessels were placed in the first pyramid, the Third Dynasty Step Pyramid at Saqqara. Many of the vessels were handed down from ancestry.

Stone vessels were sacred funerary objects, probably offering vessels. Pottery, whether made of stone or clay, symbolized the god Khnum, the Divine Potter. When hieroglyphic writing was invented, Khnum was represented by the vase symbol. Although unrecognized by Egyptologists, because they have been unaware of its existence, alchemical stonemaking was attributed to Khnum. Egyptology classifies Khnum as a significant early god. But the profound influence of Khnum's religious tradition is vastly underrated.

Khnum is one of the most ancient prehistoric Egyptian gods. Since remote times he possessed many attributes. Like all other Egyptian gods, he was identified with the Sun god, but notably he was regarded as one of the creators of the universe. As the Divine Potter, he was the ultimate technocrat. Khnum was depicted as the Nile god of the annual floods whose out-stretched hands caused the waters to increase. The Nile floods were believed to originate from a sacred cavern beneath the island of Abu (first town), now known as Elephantine, the major center of Khnum worship. Over the eons the annual inundations gradually converted a narrow strip of about 600 miles of coast into rich land, unparalleled for farming.

Khnum's influence grew steadily in early epochs, but diminished after the Twelfth Dynasty and made a resurgence in the Eighteenth Dynasty. Khnum was usually depicted in human form with the head of a flat-horned ram. He was also depicted with four ram heads on a human body, which according to

FIGURE 28. *Detail of bas-relief from temple of Khnum at Elephantine.*

FIGURE 29. *On the royal cartouche of Khufu, the vase is the phonetic sign for "khnumu" and the ram indicates the god Khnum.*

Egyptologist Karl H. Brugsch represented fire, air, earth, and water. The flat-horned ram was not native to Egypt and may have been introduced from the East, suggesting that the technology for making hard stone vessels was brought to Egypt by migratory shepherds whose national symbol was the flat-horned ram.

During antiquity it was customary to depict profession or tribal identity symbolically. In the ancient custom, men of truly great accomplishment were deified, and great principles of nature and science were attributed reverence and honor through divine personification. Other symbols of the shepherd were not personified but became part of the ceremonial vestments of the god king. Throughout pharaonic times the king's royal garb always included the crook and incense-gum collecting flail of the shepherd. The symbols were clearly associated with divine political influence.

The most ancient mythology of the Old Kingdom recounts that the Divine Potter created other gods, divine kings, and mortals on his potter's plate. Khnum used different materials depending on whether the being created was divine or mortal. Divine beings were depicted with materials indicative of the eternal realm. Gods were often depicted in gold with hair of lapis lazuli. The funerary statue of the pharaoh, representing his *ka* (ethereal body), was made of stone. The divine spirit was incarnated in the eternal material of stone.

The mortal man was made of the reddish-brown mud of the Nile River, and man was always depicted in reddish brown on bas-reliefs. The perishable mortal body was destroyed by aging and death. Only with an offering of Khnum's sacred alchemical product, the natron salt, could immortality be imparted at death. If a man was sinful, he knew that his body was subject to being thrown into the river. The sinful would not attain immortality through the seventy-day mummification ritual using natron.

Natron never lost its sacred value. In the Talmud, natron symbolized the Torah (the Law). In Leviticus 2:13 of the Bible, natron was the salt of the covenant between God and the people:

FIGURE 30. *Khnum fashions a pharoah and the ka (spiritual body) on his
potter's wheel.*

And every oblation of thy meat offering shalt thou season with salt;
neither shalt thou suffer the salt of the covenant of thy God to be
lacking from thy meat offering: with all thine offerings thou shalt
offer salt.

The salt mentioned in this verse is not sodium chloride or
potassium nitrate, but natron. Proof of this can be derived from
information provided in Proverbs 25:20:

As he that taketh away a garment in cold weather, and as vinegar
upon nitre [salt], so is he that singeth songs to an heavy heart.

An adverse effect is implied in the verse. If one places vinegar
on natron (sodium carbonate), the natron disintegrates, leaving

a sodium acetate solution. If vinegar is put onto potassium nitrate or sodium chloride there is no disintegration.

The remotely ancient tradition of Khnum is historically outstanding, for it has prevailed in some form throughout the written history of mankind. Thousands of years after the pyramids were built, Khnum was worshipped by the Gnostics, a semi-Christian sect. What is not widely recognized is that the Bible still preserves the age-old religious tradition characteristic of Khnum. A passage from an Egyptian creation legend by Khnum follows:

> The mud of the Nile, heated to excess by the Sun, fermented and generated, without seeds, the races of men and animals.

Passages of the Bible leave no doubt about the belief in the concept of the Divine Potter. Genesis 2:7 mentions the material used to make man, the same type of substance used by Khnum:

> And the Lord God formed man of the dust of the ground, and breathed into his nostrils the breath of life; and man became a living soul.

The Hebrew verb used in the verse to signify deity is *ysr,* the root of *yoser,* which means potter. Further, the tradition can be shown by Job 33:6, where Elihu reminds his elders that he is entitled to speak in their presence:

> I am your equal as far as God is concerned; I, too, have been pinched off from clay.

The tradition of the Divine Potter can be further observed in Isaiah 29:16:

> What perversity is this! Is the potter no better than the clay? Can something that was made say of its maker, "He did not make me"? Or a pot say of the potter, "He is a fool"?

and Isaiah 64:7:

> And yet, Yahweh, you are our Father; we the clay, you the potter, we are all the work of your hand.

FIGURE 31. *Stone vessels found in the Step Pyramid of Zoser at Saqqara.*

The Genesis authors described Creation within the framework of their knowledge, revered information handed down from remote ancestry. Assyriology has been studied widely in relation to the Old Testament, whereas the Egyptian influence has been mostly disregarded.

Although I have not performed an analysis of the hard stone vessels of Khnum, these items exhibit characteristic features of synthetic stone. To explain the vessels, Egyptologists assert that a vesselmaker spent perhaps as much as his entire life making one vessel. But the design features of some of the vessels indicate that time was not the critical factor. Very hard stone materials, basalt, metamorphic schist, and diorite were being used to make the vessels at about the prehistoric epoch when copper was first smelted. The smooth surfaces, absent of tool marks, the vases with long, narrow necks and wide, rounded bellies and interiors and exteriors that perfectly correspond—features unexplainable by any known tooling method—are characteristic of a molded or modeled material. The methods afforded by geopolymerization, a slurry or rock aggregates poured into a mold or a pliable mixture fashioned on a potter's wheel, are truly the only viable means by which to explain the features of

119

these otherwise enigmatic vases. The following are remarks made by Kurt Lange after he studied fragments of stone vessels that he found in the sand and talus near the Step Pyramid at Saqqara:

> This noble and translucid material is of exceptional hardness. . . . They are made of a perfectly homogeneous material, dense, polished, and glossy. . . . At once robust and fragile, of unequalled finesse and elegance of shape, they are of supreme perfection. The internal face is covered with a microscopic network of tiny grooves so regular that only an ultramodern potter's wheel of precision could have produced them. To see the grooves one needs a magnifying glass and good lighting. . . . Obviously, the equipment used must have been some kind of potter's wheel. But how could such a hard material be worked? . . . the plates on which earthenware pots were made with such regularity of form had only just been invented, and it is hard to believe that it was this tool, doubtless still extremely primitive, which was used in the fabrication of the hardest and most perfect bowls ever made.

One can envision the production of the earliest stone vessels. The sacred alchemical products were first gathered. Natron saturated numerous lakes and was also found in large deposits in numerous desert regions. A natron lake was easily identified from other salt lakes because natron absorbs coloring from organic matter, leaving the water surface covered with a brown film. The peculiar taste of the water is also characteristic. Small white, unsoiled masses of pure natron were carefully removed from the tips of encrusted reed stalks growing above the water's surface. It is characteristic for the salt to crystalize more than an inch above the tips.

Another product was lime, acquired by calcining limestone or dolomite. Two of the earliest products of humankind are lime and bread. And the lime supply for stonemaking may have been a by-product of breadmaking in a soft, chalky limestone hearth. The Nile valley was blessed with produce of all kinds, but bread was a staple—the national food. The main crops were winter and summer wheat and six-row barley. After agriculture was introduced in the Faiyum region during neolithic times, the lifestyle of the inhabitants of the Nile Valley gradually transformed from hunter-gatherer to farmer. Bread consumption increased over the epochs with expanded irrigation. Late records indicate that the Greeks dubbed the Egyptians *artophagoi*, the bread-eaters.

With the pharaohs involved in increasing agricultural yield, one can appreciate the precarious position of the high priests responsible for oracles and interpreting the pharaohs' dreams. The size of the pharaohs' monuments may well have depended on the predictability of the Nile. Enormous quantities of lime from breadmaking in hearths, made of or containing limestone or dolomite, automatically would have been available for stonemaking during plenteous years. Soda (natron) ritually added to bread dough to make unleavened bread during remote antiquity, would have placed all of the required elements (lime, natron, and water) in close proximity for the invention of one of the primary ingredients of stone making, caustic soda.

The Nile yielded sacred water for the process. Egyptian cosmogony asserted that the Nile water was the original abode of the gods from which sprang the forces of light and darkness. The Egyptian name for the Nile was Hapu, and the Nile god Hapu was identified with the cosmogonic gods. Hapu took the form of Khnum during the inundation, when an annual solemn, festival was celebrated to rejoice the rise of the waters.

Many types of rock aggregates, considered by the Egyptians to be withered or injured rocks, were available. Examples are flint, slate, steatite, diorite, alabaster, quartzite, limestone, dolomite, granite, basalt, and sandstone. Precious gems, such as diamond, ruby, and sapphire, were unknown. Semiprecious varieties acquired by mining or trade included lapis lazuli, amethyst, carnelian, red jasper, peridot, amazonite, garnet, quartz, serpentine, breccia, agate, calcite, chalcedony, and feldspar.

In addition, the blue minerals required for geopolymerization, generically known as mafkat during the more ancient periods, are included in **Table II.** The first mining operations in the Sinai Peninsula were primitive. Mineral deposits were attacked with pointed flint implements. Sandstone masses were removed and crushed with harder stones to free mafkat nodules. Even though turquoise and chrysocolla look similar, the Egyptians made a distinction between the two. The following are the remarks of a miner from the time of Pharaoh Ammenemes III:

> I found that it was difficult to determine the right color when the desert is hot in the summer. The hills burn . . . and the colors fluctuate . . . during the severe summer season the color is not right.

Chrysocolla dehydrates in the hot desert sun, becoming whitish on the surface. Heating a sample with a flame would also have enabled a distinction because chrysocolla causes a flame to turn green.

Nile silt was probably an ingredient of the earliest vessels. Silt was the traditional material for Khnum's mortal processes, and perhaps a union between the divine and mortal was symbolized through stonemaking.

Table II. The Mafkat Minerals

Mineral	Composition	Color
malachite	copper carbonate, hydrated	bright green
azurite	copper carbonate, hydrated	light/dark blue
chalcanthite	copper sulfate, hydrated	sky blue
antlerite	basic copper sulfate	light/dark green
linarite	basic sulfate of lead and copper	deep blue
olivenite	basic copper arsenate	avocado green
libethenite	copper phosphate, hydrated	olive green
turquoise	basic phosphate of aluminium and copper, hydrated	sky blue/green
chrysocolla	copper silicate, hydrated	sky blue/green
scorodite	iron arsenate, hydrated	light green/blue
lazulite	basic phosphate of iron and magnesium	bright/dull blue

Another substance was not vital to the chemistry but may have been added because it symbolized the highest spiritual essence. The product was gold, the metal of the Sun. During my analyses, I found flecks of gold dust in Lauer's sample from the Great Pyramid. It is possible that the gold did not occur naturally and was instead ritually added. Divine eternal qualities were attributed to gold. In addition to its beauty and association with the Sun god, gold does not rust or tarnish and can be worked indefinitely without becoming brittle or damaged. Even though gold was probably always an item of exchange, anciently its value was purely sacred. A monetary value gradually manifested. Some experts believe that the Egyptians never minted state gold coins until the Greek occupation or after 332 BC.

The practices of the first vesselmakers are lost in prehistory, and writing and a standard system of weights and measures was not adopted by 3800 BC. We can, therefore, only conjecture about a recipe for making a stone vessel of that period:

THE ETERNAL VESSEL OF KHNUM

1   heqat natron
1½   heqat calcined limestone
2   hin Nile water
2   heqat powder of mafkat
3   heqat Nile silt
5   heqat eternal rock particles
Ceremonial quantity of gold dust

Combine the sacred natron with lime powder scraped from the hearth and blend them in a wooden bowl with blessed water to form the caustic substance. Obtain mafkat which turns white on the surface during summer and which produces a green color of fire when you burn it. Powder the mafkat by crushing it with hard rocks and add it to the caustic substance. When the mafkat has been consumed, add fine silt such as Khnum uses to make perishable creatures. Recite prayers every day until the liquid has the consistency of honey, then add the injured, eternal aggregates (the limbs of Neter [God]), and the golden particles (the spirit of Neter), to incarnate His Divine Presence.

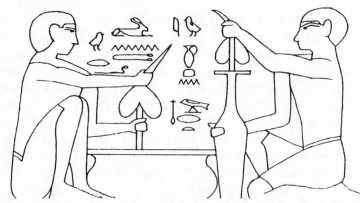

FIGURE 32. *Bas-relief from the tomb of Merah shows the hollowing out of Egyptian alabaster (CaCo₃) vases by a liquid in a skin or bladder.*

> Protect your hands with oil and knead the material. Then fashion the vessel on your turning plates. Tear strips of linen and coat them with bitumen. Wind the strips around the outside of the vessel. Line the inside and carefully pack it. Allow the vessel to remain overnight. It will gain strength. When the vessel is strong, unwind the linen. Cover the vessel loosely with a linen cloth so that it can breathe. Remove the cloth when the vessel attains eternal life. Rejoice that Khnum's living vessel may endure forever!

Although the ritual is speculative, the chemistry is based on reactions that surely were known. An analysis of stone pottery may prove that the early binders were far more sophisticated. A process involving turquoise and allowing objects to harden in air-tight molds was introduced at about 3000 BC and is described in Appendix 1. Methods used to make vases with narrow necks and rounded bellies were innovated on for making glass vases in the Eighteenth Dynasty at about 1350 BC.

A bas-relief from the Sixth Dynasty tomb of Merah, at Saqqara, is interpreted by Egyptologists to depict workmen drilling out stone vessels **(Figure 32)**. In 1982, I presented a different interpretation at the 22nd Symposium of Archaeometry, held at the University of Bradford, in Bradford, United Kingdom. The vessels shown were made of Egyptian alabaster, a calcium carbonate stone. Alabaster vases made as shown were not carved or agglomerated. Instead, they were made by bio-tooling, that is, using an acidic liquid such as vinegar, citric or oxalic acid, or a combination of acidic liquids, to act upon the alabaster (calcium carbonate)

It is obvious the vase makers are not drilling. Rather they are squeezing an acidic liquid, stored in a sewn animal skin or a bladder, through a tube. I have measured the efficiency of using acidic liquids of the type just mentioned on Egyptian alabaster in my laboratory and found it greater than that of abrasion methods. Unlike abrasion and carving methods, using acidic liquids produces a smooth finish.

From primitive beginnings, Khnum's alchemical stonemaking technology advanced beyond pottery to produce the world's most impressive architecture. The earliest burial places were pits where funerary gifts were placed for use in the afterlife. Buried bodies were naturally preserved in the warm, dry sand of the desert necropolises. Mastabas represent the next phase of tomb construction. These are rectangular mud-brick structures, named mastabas from the Arabic word for bench used to describe their shape.

Stone material began to appear in the mastabas erected at Abydos and Saqqara during the Archaic period. These tombs have been badly plundered and only enough material remains to establish a tenuous history of this period. The remains suggest a constant evolution of mastaba design and an increased magnificence of furnishings. The early royal mastabas of the First Dynasty consisted of a large covered underground chamber surrounded at ground level by a wall. As the dynasty progressed, the tombs acquired additional storerooms and an access stairway. Large wooden beams and linings were incorporated into the tombs of the pharaohs. Sealed in the tombs were funerary offerings of food, precious articles of copper and gold, and various commemorative items. The tombs also included a vast array of alchemically made vessels in various beautiful shapes and hard stone materials.

An artifact from a First Dynasty cenotaph indicates that the precious mafkat deposits were jealously guarded. An ivory label of Den, the fifth king of the First Dynasty, depicts him symbolically smiting a bedouin in the Sinai.

A dramatic architectural advance appeared by the end of the Second Dynasty. The mastabas were reinforced with stone floors, lintels, jambs, and walls. The inner walls of the central chamber of the tomb of Khasekhemwy, the last king of the Second Dynasty, were lined with limestone.

No chemical analysis of stone from a mastaba has been made. It was technically feasible to carve stone for the mastabas, because the magnitude of work required for pyramid construction is not approached. According to tradition, however, this stone would be agglomerated and may represent the next phase in the progression of stonemaking technology. The stonemaking formula in use at this time was not practical for large scale building operations because a proportionally great amount of mafkat was required. The next major technological innovation would revolutionize tomb construction and have dramatic impact on the course of history.

CHAPTER 10

The Invention of Stone Buildings

KHASEKHEMWY LEFT NO MALE HEIR TO THE THRONE, AND the Third Dynasty pharaoh first to rule was Zanakht. He was followed by Neterikhet (Zoser). Pharaoh Zoser's architect, Imhotep, was responsible for the construction of the first pyramid. Before discussing this accomplishment, we will review what little relevant information has survived about this intriguing historical personality. Imhotep left an unforgettable legacy. Historically, the lives of few men are celebrated for 3,000 years, but Imhotep was renowned from the height of his achievements, at about 2700 BC, into the Greco-Roman period. Imhotep was so highly honored as a physician and sage that he came to be counted among the gods. He was deified in Egypt 2,000 years after his death, when he was appropriated by the Greeks, who called him Imuthes and identified him with the god Asclepius, son of Apollo, their great sage and legendary discoverer of medicine.

FIGURE 33. *Statue of Imhotep.*

Imhotep wrote the earliest "wisdom literature," venerated maxim, which regrettably has not survived, and Egypt considered him as the greatest of scribes. This presiding genius of King Zoser's reign was the first great national hero of Egypt. During King Zoser's reign, Imhotep was the second most eminent man in Egypt, and this is registered in stone. On the base of a statue of King Zoser, excavated at the Step Pyramid, the name and titles of Imhotep are listed in an equal place of honor as those of the king. Imhotep had many titles, Chancellor of the

King of Lower Egypt, the First after the King of Upper Egypt, Administrator of the Great Palace, Physician, Hereditary Noble, High Priest of Anu (On or Heliopolis), Chief Architect for Pharaoh Zoser, and, interestingly, Sculptor, and Maker of Stone Vessels.

The titles confirm the records of the Greco-Egyptian historian Manetho, written in Greek 2,400 years later, during the early Ptolemaic era in the third century BC. Manetho was one of the last high priests of Heliopolis. Part of his text describing Imhotep was translated in AD 340 by the ecclesiastic historian Eusebius to read, "the inventor of the art of building with hewn stone." This refers to the construction of the first pyramid. In fact, Eusebius's translation is incorrect. The Greek words Manetho used, *xestos* (xeston) *lithon,* do not mean hewn stone: they mean polished stone. The words describe stone with a beautiful, smooth surface, a feature characteristic of fine, agglomerated casing stone so smooth that it reflects the Sun. These words were also used in the Greek texts of Herodotus and

FIGURE 34. *Step pyramid of Zoser was the world's first building made entirely of stone.*

Sextus Julius Africanus (third century). It is impossible for translators accurately to translate texts while lacking vital technical knowledge. Similar errors of translation have been made throughout history, and more examples will be provided.

Imhotep was regarded as the son of a woman named Khradu'ankh and the god Ptah of Memphis. The title Hereditary Noble indicates aristocratic parentage. His career would have begun when he was a boy trained by a master scribe. With his parents among the elite, lessons would have begun around the age of twelve. Because priests were among the literate of Egypt, he may have received scribal training by entering the priesthood. His title, High Priest of Heliopolis, was traditionally attained on two conditions. A man either succeeded his father in the priesthood, or he was personally appointed to office by the king because of some great deed. The position of high priest was attained after extensive training in the arts and sciences—reading, writing, engineering, arithmetic, geometry, the measurement of space, the calculation of time by rising and setting stars, and astronomy. The Heliopolitan priests became guardians of the sacred knowledge, and their reputation for being the wise men of the country sustained even into the Late period.

Their religious ideologies and sciences were heavily applied to the construction of tombs and other sacred architecture. A magnificent solar temple oriented by the heavenly bodies was erected during the reign of Zoser to mark the most sacred place in Heliopolis. The city was the holy sanctuary of Egypt, the ground itself religiously symbolic. The site for Heliopolis had been chosen at a location in the apex of the Delta where the inundating Nile waters first began to recede. There the earth, fertilized by the arrival of silt and nurtured by the Sun, received the first renewed life of the agricultural year. This ground represented rebirth and Creation.

Located about twenty miles north of Memphis, the town is estimated to have measured $1,200 \times 800$ meters. It became the capital of the thirteenth Lower Egyptian nome or district. No precise archaeological history of the city has been established.

So it is unknown when ground was first broken for construction. The city is considered to have been founded during prehistory, and it had a very impressive life span. It flourished in the Pyramid Age and still remained an important center when Herodotus visited Egypt in the fifth century BC. Tradition holds that the Holy Family found asylum in Heliopolis during the flight into Egypt. Today, all of the temples and buildings of Heliopolis have vanished and the abandoned site has been incorporated into a suburb of eastern Cairo. Only a single standing obelisk, erected for a jubilee of Pharaoh Sesostris I (1971–1926 BC), remains amid empty fields.

When King Zoser was enthroned, he no doubt expected to be buried in a mud-brick mastaba similar to that of his predecessors. The site for his tomb was selected at Saqqara, south of Memphis. Design plans and calculations for orienting the monument were being made. At this point, the subsequent history of the construction of the first pyramid must be revised based on my discoveries.

Minerals were being excavated to produce stone, presumably for lining interior walls and floors. King Zoser's workmen enscribed a stele in the sandstone cliffs of the mines of Wadi Maghara in the Sinai to commemorate the construction of the monument. Some time before actual construction got underway, Imhotep made an important discovery. Certain titles of his Chief Architect, Sculptor, and Maker of Stone Vessels profile prerequisite skills for building a monument with alchemically made stone. He would have applied himself to producing a mastaba which would last forever. Like the pride in a great nation, the pride intrinsic to a monument would be its longevity.

Khnum's clergy apparently amalgamated its alchemical science with that of the Heliopolitan priests when stone was first made for use in architecture. Imhotep perhaps specialized in materials processing or alchemy. His aim may have been to strengthen the sun-dried Nile silt bricks used for mastabas. Any attempts made by Imhotep or others to fire bricks made of silt from the Nile River would have been futile. The Nile silt

131

contains no silico-aluminates, the components required for producing good, fired bricks at temperatures that they were capable of achieving. They would not even come close to the required temperatures of 1,300 to 1,500° C (2,400 to 2,700° F). Ordinary clay had been fired for pottery since pre-dynastic times by using fluxes to lower firing temperature, but this fired material was impractical for construction purposes.

Imhotep added water to the yellow limestone of Saqqara. This material contains aluminous clay, which is released in water, yielding a muddy limestone. Water eases disaggregation, making the limestone ideal for stonemaking, and the clay itself produces a dramatic result in combination with caustic soda. Using aluminous clay, the required amount of mafkat, the material of the process most difficult to obtain, was eliminated for building the pyramid. Mafkat was required only for stones of high quality, such as the protective casing stones. By reducing the amount of mafkat required, Imhotep's simple innovation permitted the enormous leap from small-scale funerary applications to the massive scale of the pyramids.

Small mud-brick molds were filled, as they had been for countless generations, to produce the pharaoh's mastaba. But for the first time, the mud-brick molds were being filled with limestone concrete materials. The new stone bricks, several inches long, were dried in the sun, demolded, and transported to the construction site; these early bricks were not cast in place. The alchemically made stone bricks were used to produce a huge, square mastaba with its sides oriented to cardinal points. The burial chamber was underground. The mastaba was covered with small casing bricks of smooth, alchemically made limestone, and the sacred monument was considered to be complete.

Some time passed, and the stone bricks showed no sign of cracking. The pharaoh no doubt soon desired to make additional use of the new building material. Imhotep drew up plans to enlarge the mastaba. First, ten feet of fine, agglomerated limestone were applied on each of its sides. Then, a more elaborate plan was devised. A twenty-five foot extension on its

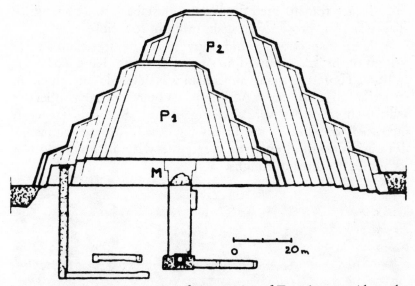

FIGURE 35. *Successive stages of construction of Zoser's pyramid are the mastaba(M) and elaborations on the design (P1 and P2).*

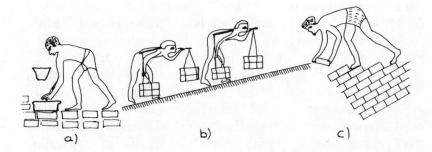

FIGURE 36. *To construct Third Dynasty pyramids, worker (A) made limestone bricks in wooden molds, (B) transported the bricks to the construction site, and (C) built the pyramid in inclined layers.*

eastern face transformed the square mastaba into a rectangular shape, and the project was again brought to a close.

A later inspection would show that the stone under the weight of the mass showed no sign of cracking. King Zoser and Imhotep conferred again, and a plan was devised to heighten the structure to two tiers. Additional subterranean chambers, a shaft, and corridors were also dug. As the size of the structure increased, the size of the bricks increased. We are witness to dramatic design alterations inevitable with all revolutionary technological breakthroughs.

FIGURE 37. *Limestone bricks of Zoser's pyramid are rounded like molded bricks.*

The more extraordinary their architectural wonder became, the more they built upon it. The amount of stone that could be made would have appeared endless. A transformation into a four-tiered structure was followed by another construction phase in which the final form of a six-tiered pyramid, sixty meters (198 feet) high emerged. Its design included internal walls and inclined stone layers to provide great stability. With great skill and ingenuity, Imhotep incorporated all of the engineering and artistic methods the nation had derived from countless decades of building with wood, bundles of reeds and stalks, and sun-dried silt brick.

The final outcome was an extraordinary funerary complex. The Heliopolitan religious doctrine profoundly influenced its architectural form and the symbolism of its motifs. The design theme incorporated mythology which preserved and amalgamated Egypt's most ancient and cherished cosmological beliefs. Heliopolitan theology taught that in the beginning, a primordial megalith, known as the Ben Ben (benben), arose out of the waters of Chaos. The benben represented the hill or mound upon which Creation began. The benben has been interpreted to symbolize dense, primeval physical substance or matter. The Creator appeared on the benben in human form, as Atum, the personification of the Sun, or in the form of Bennu, the phoenix of light. Out of elemental chaos the Creator separated the darkness from the waters. The Creator formed a trinity after having created himself and Shu, the god of air, and Tefnut, the goddess of moisture. Tefnut and Shu procreated Geb, the earth, and Nut, the heavens. Four other deities were created, and all of the gods together made up the Heliopolitan Enneade. In later times, the Greek philosopher Empedocles (c. 495–435 BC) recognized in the primordial Egyptian gods personifications of air, water, earth, and fire. Empedocles, and alchemists of later eras, held that these were the indestructible elements that composed all matter.

James Henry Breasted (1886–1935), founder of the Oriental Institute at the University of Chicago, first recognized that the pyramids themselves are representations of the benben. After the first Heliopolitan temple was built, Egypt had adopted the ideology that the benben, or stone symbolic of the Sun god, was located beneath the temple.

The theogonic theme appears in subterranean chambers of King Zoser's pyramid. Special chambers are lined with blue ceramic tiles in patterns depicting the primeval reed marsh from which vegetable life first emerged. Blue was the color symbolic of the Creator, and the blue glaze on the tiles imitated chrysocolla, the mafkat mineral indicative of Creation. With the exception of this monumental first pyramid, the artistic theme depicting the events of Creation was preserved only in the holy of holies of the great Sun temples.

In a specially designed room a life-size stone statue of Zoser seated upon his throne represented his eternally reigning spirit or *ka*. When this statue was found by archaeologists, it was intact except for damage to the eyes and surrounding facial area. The eyes were probably made of semiprecious gems, which would most likely have been pillaged when the tomb was plundered. Certain stone statues of the Old Kingdom now in the Louvre and the Cairo Museum are greatly admired for their inlaid eyes, a technique offering extraordinary realism and easily afforded by using alchemically made stone. Other rooms held the 30,000 stone vessels of Khnum, agglomerated using aggregates of schist, breccia, granite, diorite, and various other stones.

Surrounding the pyramid, a wall with clean architectural lines, originally more than thirty feet high, encloses more than a square-mile area. A characteristic of the smooth stone, encasing the wall and now mostly removed, is that it appears to be polished. The wall protects an elegant entrance colonnade, great courts, large buildings, a mortuary temple, and ceremonial altars and shrines. The enclosed area is virtually an entire town. The design character of the enclosure wall resembles contemporary architecture, and did, in fact, influence a style of twentieth-century architecture. European architects visiting Saqqara earlier in the century found the enclosure wall a refreshing, appealing diversion from ornate Victorian architecture. They left with the inspiration for a style of architecture that we now consider modern and take for granted.

It was the pride of Egypt. Zoser's funerary complex, with its towering pyramid and exquisite artistry, was unprecedented in the history of the world. Throughout Egyptian history the time of Imhotep was looked on as an age of great wisdom. Like the First Time event of Creation, as it was called, and the founding or amalgamation of the Egyptian nation by the first pharaoh, King Menes, the construction of the Step Pyramid was viewed as another first time event of great importance.

CHAPTER 11

It Is Written in Hieroglyphs

WRITTEN TEXTS OF PYRAMID CONSTRUCTION MUST HAVE existed. The legacy of and events surrounding these monuments were far too important to have been unrecorded. Surviving documents from the Old Kingdom (c. 2705–2250 BC) are limited in number and extent, and Egyptologists have long claimed that no ancient Egyptian record from any period describes how the pyramids were built. Their error is that they seek records of stone cutting, hauling, and hoisting. They do not have the pertinent texts that would be required for making their historical deductions about pyramid construction.

Unaware of the technology used, Egyptologists have misunderstood the meaning of Egyptian writings that document pyramid construction—writings that concur with my findings. A pertinent document was enscribed on a rock, called the Famine Stele, discovered on the island of Sehel, near Elephantin, by Charles Wilbour in 1889. Egyptologists are divided on its authenticity, but insist the document is a copy of Old

Kingdom texts made by priests of Khnum in about 200 BC. The texts date to the reign of the pharoah Zoser, 2,500 years earlier.

During 200 BC, foreign kings ruled Egypt. In 332 BC, the king of Macedon, Alexander the Great, led an allied Greek army into Egypt. Having endured centuries of oppressive foreign domination, Egypt welcomed Alexander as the deliverer. Egypt had been ruled by Libya, Sudan, Assyria, Nubia, and Persia, and only managed to regain a brief reestablishment of native power when the Greek army advanced. Alexander sacrificed to Egyptian gods and ceremoniously received the double crown of the pharaohs, acquiring the title "Son of the Sun."

In the winter of 332–31 BC, Alexander founded the capital city of Alexandria in northern Egypt along the Mediterranean Sea at the western edge of the Nile delta. After his death, Egypt was ruled by his subordinates, who laid the basis for the Ptolemaic dynasty. Under Ptolemaic kings, Alexandria rapidly became the main religious and intellectual center of Jewish and Hellenistic culture. Even though Greek interests dominated, there was no desire to eradicate Egyptian culture. The Macedonian people held the utmost regard for the Egyptians. They admiringly traced their own architectural heritage and religion to Egypt. Numerous Egyptian deities were identified with Greek gods.

Under Hellenistic cultural dominion Egyptian cities became known by Greek names. The holy city of the Sun cult, Anu, became known as Heliopolis, the city of the Sun. A town called Khmun (the City of Eight) became known as Hermopolis, the city of the Greek god Hermes. The Greeks identified the Egyptian god Djehuti, or Thoth as he was called in Greek, with Hermes. The town of Khmun acquired its name from the Ogdoad, four pairs of primeval gods that presided in the waters of Chaos, namely, Darkness, Invisibility, Secret, and Eternity. By historic times, Thoth had absorbed and replaced these gods. Thoth became the personification of divine wisdom, the scribe of the gods who protected learning and literature. Egyptian texts called him Lord of Divine Books, Scribe of the Company of Gods, and Lord of Divine Speech.

Alexandria possessed two celebrated royal libraries, and Hermopolis also maintained a great library, containing treasured literature preserved by the virtues of Thoth. It was this library that preserved a document from the time of King Zoser that recorded Imhotep's revelation.

The Famine Stele was produced during the reign of King Ptolemy V Epiphanes (205–182 BC). This king was enthroned at the age of five, and his reign was characterized by the loss of foreign territory, revolts in the Nile delta, and general civil and political upheavals. His decree inscribed on the famous Rosetta stone, produced in 196 BC, indicates that in this political setting native Egyptians were gaining more control over their domestic affairs. Taxes and debts were remitted and temples received benefactions.

The political climate was appropriate for the clergy of Khnum to resolve a matter of growing concern to them: Greek troops stationed in the region near the first cataract paid great tribute to the goddess Isis. Greeks at all levels, soldiers, commanders, and the king himself especially venerated this goddess. The king's father, Ptolemy IV, was so devoted to Isis that he made the title Beloved of Isis part of his royal name. An old temple of Isis at Philea, built during the Saite period (664–525 BC), was torn down by Ptolemy II (285–246 BC) and replaced with an extravagant, costly temple. Territories of Nubia, south of the border, were dedicated to Isis, and additional elaborate offerings made her cult the wealthiest in southern Egypt.

The region Isis occupied was the primary seat of Khnum worship since remotely ancient times. It encompassed the entire cataract region, including the island of Elephantine, Philea, Sehel, Esna, and Aswan. Elephantine, the sanctuary of Khnum, is located in the middle of the river, and the island represented the official southernmost border throughout most of the nation's history. Elephantine served as a garrison because of its location directly below the first cataract, a natural defensive barrier, and also as an entrepot for imports entering Egypt by ship from the south.

The importance of the island of the southern frontier varied after the Middle Kingdom (2035–1668 BC), depending on what territory Egypt controlled. Khnum's influence was vastly diminished before the Ptolemaic period, long after the pyramids were built. Khnum's temples suffered a great deal of damage over the centuries at the hands of invaders entering from the south. And Khnum's delapidated temples sorely contrasted with the exquisite new temple of Isis. This, coupled with the loss of Nubian territory to Isis, meant that Khnum's cult was rapidly being displaced by that of Isis.

An opportunity apparently presented itself for Khnum's clergy to confront the king with the matter. The Rosetta stone informs us that in the eighth year of the reign of Ptolemy V, the Nile produced an extraordinary inundation of all of the plains. This created famine by diminishing the productive farm land temporarily. Khnum symbolized the Nile, and his clergy administered matters concerning its aberrant flooding. A nilometer leading from the bank to the low water level, with calibrated steps to measure the rise of flood water, still remains on Elephantine.

The priests visited the Hermopolitan library probably around 190 BC. There they referenced old texts to demonstrate how Nile aberrations had been remedied in the past. Even though there were many famines in Egyptian history, they sought records dating to the time of Pharaoh Zoser and Imhotep. These records showed generous offerings to Khnum for ending a famine, and the priests were able to demonstrate to the king that their cult had more than 2,500 years of experience in effectively dealing with abnormalities of the Nile.

The accounts they referenced had been preserved for 2,500 years despite episodes of civil war and invasion. They produced from the records a dramatic historical story, animating Khnum, as was customary with Egyptian gods, in an episode with King Zoser. For this they used a written message sent to Elephantine by King Zoser, identifying his pleas for an eight-year famine to end. They sought to show that the territory given to Isis had been dedicated to Khnum by King Zoser himself. Not only did the priests have the data to produce a stele serving as a territorial

FIGURE 38. *Famine Stele on Sehel, near Elephantine.*

marker, but they could demonstrate the prosperity provided for Egypt by their cult's careful management of the Nile over the ages. Their records also served to remind the Greek administration of the great legacy that Khnum's alchemical technology had given Egypt.

They reproduced inscriptions on a rock, now called the Famine Stele, which stands on the large island of Sehel, 3 kilometers (1.8 miles) south of Elephantine. Sehel, treasured for its mineral deposits, was the traditional abode of the goddess Anunkis, Khnum's daughter. When the stele was viewed by the king and his ministers, its authenticity and authority were honored. The Greeks revered Zoser as an exceptionally great king, who, along with Imhotep, was considered to be one of the founders of Egyptian culture. An earlier king, Ptolemy II, had established the worship of Imhotep as a deity in the upper level of the temple of Deir el-Bahari, located on the West Bank almost directly opposite Karnak. Still standing are remains of a temple dedicated to Imhotep on the island of Sehel built by Ptolemy V at about 186 BC.

It appears that the priests had advised the king well with regard to the Nile. The wise management of the destructive flood turned it into a blessing. The Rosetta stone relates that King Ptolemy V spared no expense in erecting a dam to direct an overflow of the Nile to proper channels. In doing this, he created an abundant crop yield and earned the title Savior of Egypt. The king also drew up a new decree to provide benefactions for Khnum's temples. Khnum was given all rights of sovereignty up to a distance of twenty miles of Elephantine,

FIGURE 39. *Upper portion of columns 12 to 21 (read from right to left) on the Famine Stele.*

which included lost portions of Nubia. All who fished or hunted within this territory were required to pay a fee. The quarries of Sehel and Aswan could be exploited only by consent of Khnum's priests. Boats would pay duty on imports, such as metals or wood entering Egypt along the Nile from the south.

The Famine Stele contains other major elements having nothing to do with territorial rights or famine. Actually, the stele might be better named Khnum's Alchemical Stele, for it holds the key to the method of manufacturing man-made stone. Of about 2,600 hieroglyphs making up the inscriptions, about 650 or approximately one-third pertain to rocks and mineral ores and their processing.

Some Egyptologists believe that the relevant inscriptions on the Famine Stele were derived from authentic documents dating from Pharaoh Zoser's reign (2630–2611 BC), that were enhanced by Khnum's priests during the Ptolemaic period. The Famine Stele consists of five chapters, made up of thirty-two columns of hieroglyphs written from right to left: columns 1 to 4, The Description of the Famine; Columns 4 to 6,★ The Visit to the Library of Hermopolis; Columns 8 to 18, The Revelations of Imhotep; Columns 18 to 22, The Dream of Pharaoh Zoser; Columns 22 to 32, The Royal Decree.

Three main characters are featured in the account written on the stele, Khnum, Pharaoh Zoser, and Imhotep. Vital passages relative to making man-made stone for construction purposes are found in columns 6 to 22: In columns 11 to 18, Imhotep describes the rocks and mineral ores of the Elephantine region to Zoser. Columns 18 to 20 describe a dream of Pharaoh Zoser, in which Khnum gives the mineral ores to Zoser to build his sacred monument. A pyramid cannot be built with mineral ores unless one uses the minerals to produce a binder for agglomerating stone. Limestone (transliterated *ainr hedj*), the predominant variety of stone found in the pyramids, is not found on the list. Sandstone *(Ainr rwdt),* the primary material used to build temples between 1500 BC and Roman times, is not listed,

---

★Column 7 is not relevant, so it is omitted.

nor is Aswan granite *(mat)*, the preferable building material of the Ptolemaic period, especially at Alexandria.

The hieroglyphic names of several minerals on the list have never been translated. Other words are of dubious translation. Their correct translation is vital to the meaning of the stele. I refer to the latter as key words, and they are related to rocks and minerals or their synthesis. Based on my own archaeological discoveries and knowledge of mineralogy and chemistry, I have started an in-depth study to decipher as many of the untranslated and mistranslated terms as possible.

I have produced a new translation of the stele, presented here. It combines my research with the standard translations made by Egyptologists Karl Brugsch (1891), W. Pleyte (1891), Jacques Morgan (1894), Kurt Sethe (1901), and Paul Barguet (1953). Barguet's translation reflects the most up-to-date knowledge of Egyptology. The only fairly recent study of the stele was made by S. Aufere in 1984. The only improvement the latter may provide is a possible translation of one semiprecious variety of stone. The key words I studied follow:

Ari-Kat

The first is an adjective which is transliterated into English as *ari-kat*. *Ari,* when associated with minerals is a verb that means to work with, fashion, create, form, or beget. The second part of the work, *kat,* means man. *Ari-kat* means the work done by man. In other words, *ari-kat* means man–made, processed, or synthetic. A general example of its use is the designation of imitation lapis lazuli. The word appears in columns 13, 19, and 20. In columns 13 and 19, it describes the process of mineral ores for pyramid building. In column 20 it refers to Khnum creating mankind.

Rwdt

Another key word appears in column 11 and is transliterated *rwdt*. Barguet translated this word to mean hard stone. J. R. Harris, in *Lexicographical Studies in Ancient Egyptian Minerals,* discussed *rwdt* in some detail and stated: "In any event, there can be little doubt that *rwdt* is a term indicating hard stone in general, though which stone would fall into the category it is difficult to say, especially in view of the reference to alabaster as *rwdt*."

Alabaster is very soft stone. *Rwdt,* however, generally refers to the monumental sandstone of southern Egypt. This is the soft stone discussed in Chapter 3 used to build the temples of Karnak, Luxor, Edfu, Dendera, and Abu-Simbel—the stone material so soft that it can be scratched with one's fingernails. This type of stone is eight times as soft as Aswan granite, and *rwdt* therefore could not indicate hard stone.

Rwdt, however, also means to germinate or grow. A causative verb form, *s-rwdt,* means to make solid or tie strongly. *Rwdt* also describes aggregates or pebbles of sandstone, quartzite, and granite. These varieties of stone result from the natural solid-ification of aggregates. Sand, for instance, reconstitutes into sandstone in nature. *Rwdt* could therefore indicate aggregates that can be naturally or otherwise cemented into stone and could be the determinative for agglomerated stone.

Ain

The word transliterated *ainr* simply means natural, solid stone. Most types of stone used for construction are referred to as *ainr.* When the "r" is omitted from *ainr* to produce *ain,* the word has a slightly different meaning. Ain is a generic word for stone, simply used to set it apart from other materials such as wood or metal. The generic word *ain* appears in column 15 to describe the various rocks and mineral varieties, whereas *ainr* or solid stone block does not appear in the Famine Stele at all.

Tesh

The composite word, *rwdt uteshui,* appears at the end of column 11. Barguet translates the word to mean "hard stone from the quarries." He notes, however, that his translation may be doubtful because of the peculiar way in which the word is written. I have shown that *rwdt* could not mean hard stone.

145

The root word *tesh* also appears in two stone materials listed in column 15. Barguet transliterates this root as *sheti*. *Tesh* has the general meaning of crush, separate, or split. The word *betesh* indicates the action of dissolving or disaggregation. *Tesh*, therefore, describes a stone that has been crushed, disaggregated, or split, meaning an aggregate such as would be required for making synthetic stone. The compound word *rwdt uteshui* could refer to the raw material, crushed, disaggregated, or naturally weathered natural stone. If this assumption is correct, the stony materials *(ain)* listed in column 15 were in a loose form or easy to disaggregate. In column 15 two names contain the root *tesh*, whereas four names do not. As discussed later, however, the two stones (*mthay* and *bekhen*) belong to the category of disaggregated materials.

Mthay

Mthay appears to contain the word *mat,* which means granite. Harris agrees with Barguet when he notes that it is strange that granite is not otherwise mentioned in the Famine Stele. They expected to find stone suitable for construction. Furthermore, granite and sandstone are the most common stone varieties found in the Aswan region.

It is likely that this remarkable form of writing alters the word *mat* (granite). Except for the peculiar hieroglyphic orthography that occurs in the Famine Stele, granite is always written in a standard way, namely, a sickle, which indicates the sound "me," accompanied by various adjectives.

Instead of the sickle, in columns 15 a denuded bird appears, devoid of feathers or wings. This way of writing "me" also appears in the word *mut,* meaning to kill himself. A similar word, *meth,* means to die. And *mat* or granite is often written with the ideogram for heart of life, suggesting the notion of living granite. Assuming that the scribe wanted to indicate that the desirable granite chosen must be weathered, loosely bound, or disaggregated, he would have emphasized the idea of dying or withered granite.

Bekhen

The stone called *bekhen* has also been named in inscriptions at Wadi el-Hammamat, located in the desert southwest of Aswan. *Bekhen* is considered to be one of several possibilities, black basalt, diorite, sandy schist, porphyry, graywacke, or psammite. The inscriptions at Wadi el-Hammamat indicate that quarrying *bekhen* was carried out in a primitive fashion. The boulders chosen were pushed off a cliff and thereby split into numerous chunks. This would indicate that this hard stone was, after all, crushed in smaller aggregates, as would be required for agglomeration.

Aat

According to Harris a word transliterated *aat* refers to mineral ores. *Aat* appears in columns 11 and 19. In column 19, one really appreciates the exceptional value of this text. It speaks of the actual processing of mineral ores, which were being used for the very first time for building a pyramid and temples. Verse 19, quoting Khnum, reads, "I give you rare ore after rare ore . . . never before has anyone processed them [to make stone] in order to build the temples of the gods. . . ."

Khnem, Khem

This hieroglyph opens several areas of discussion. None of the aforementioned translators have offered a phonetic value for the hieroglyphic symbol or ideogram depicted. The symbol signifies odor, but not a pleasant scent such as that of perfume. Instead, it depicts substances that give off an odor, efflux, or emanation which is not offensive; the word, therefore, does not imply stench. At times the symbol is found in combination with the symbol for pleasure or pride.

Brugsch suggests that the ideogram signifies an unguent, whereas Barguet did not attempt to translate it. Instead, he remained cautious and stated that it indicated, "products connected with those cited in column 11," that is, mineral ores.

One area of discussion this ideogram raises is etymological. It may seem incredible to find that our modern word for chemistry was derived from a root word associated with Khnum. Certain hieroglyphic words variously transliterated as *khnem, shemm,* and *shnem,* include this ideogram. This would indicate that the word is associated with or is one of Khnum's odorous products. The base khnem or khem became alchemy through language corruption, for example: Greek, chymeia; Arabic, al-kimiya; Middle Latin, alchemia; Old French, Alchimie; English: alchemy, chemistry.

Some etymologists hold that the word "alchemy" originated from the ancient name for Egypt, Kemit, which means black earth. Others maintain that the root is the Hebrew word for Sun, Chemesch. I propose that the original root of the word "alchemy" is *khem* or *Khnum.* The corruption in Greek could have produced *khemy* or *chemy;* the name of the pharaoh for whom the Great Pyramid was built, Khnum-Khufu, was altered in Greek to Cheops and also Chemis. It appears that the ancient Greek, Assyrian, Hebrew, and Aramaic scholars used similar phonetic values to indicate the sacred alchemical knowledge of Khnum. The modern word chemistry can be traced to the Egyptian root word for chemistry or chemical processes.

The ideogram for Khnem is the key for deciphering certain minerals found on the stele. I suggest that the symbol could depict a bladder containing urine, which would give off an odor as opposed to the pleasant scent of perfume. My assumption is that the symbol signifies chemical odors specifically. Most chemical products have a particular odor with which chemists are familiar. According to columns 11 and 12, the odorous products are the mineral ores used for building the pyramid and temples.

It has not been considered that the ancient Egyptians used some of the same methods we use today for classifying and determining the chemical composition of minerals. We know that since prehistoric times the Egyptians heated minerals for enamel production. Today, the blowpipe is used to detect various phenomena that occur during heating. Some minerals melt and give the flame a color, such as violet for potassium and yellow for sodium. Some types of minerals break up, whereas others shed flakes, and still others swell and emit bubbles. Some, such as arsenic minerals and sulfides produce irritating fumes. My examination of the Famine Stele reveals that then, just as today, the names of certain minerals were derived from their chemical composition. When mineral ores are to be deciphered, it is when odor, color, taste, and other chemical determinatives are considered that we comply with their means of classification.

The English words for stones, derived from Greek and Latin, can usually be traced to the root word for their color or general appearance. For instance, ruby comes from the Latin word *rebeus,* which is akin to the Latin word *ruber,* meaning red. But this was not the main criterion for naming rocks and minerals in ancient Egypt. Barguet, for example, was unsuccessful in deciphering the hieroglyphic names of rocks and minerals on the Famine Stele by comparing them with the hieroglyphic words for colors. Because the Egyptians generally did not classify rocks and minerals by color, the majority of their hieroglyphic names have no contemporary equivalent.

Determinative mineralogy was never before applied to deciphering the Famine Stele. Perhaps the main reason for this is that the large-scale chemical uses of minerals was unknown. Even today, Egypt's primary mafkat mineral used for pyramid construction, chrysocolla, has no major industrial use. Turquoise has only an ornamental value. The arsenic minerals, olivenite (arsenate of copper) and scorodite (arsenate of iron), are listed in guides to rocks and minerals as being of interest only to mineralogists and collectors. In ancient Egypt these minerals, blended with copper ores, were used to produce the well-known copper with a high arsenic content. Olivenite and scorodite could also have been used to produce rapid hydraulic setting, needed for large pyramid blocks. Although arsenates are not similarly used in modern geopolymers, arsenic chemical wastes act as a catalyst when combined with geopolymers, environmentally safe containment of chemical wastes being one of the applications of geopolymers.

Scorodite is an arsenic mineral that when heated gives off a strong odor of onion or garlic, and there is historical testimony indicating the use of arsenic minerals in pyramid construction. In his book titled *Euterpe,* the Greek historian, Herodotus (c. 485–425 BC), reported what Egyptian guides told him about the method of constructing the Great Pyramid. Egyptologists use Herodotus's account to support the standard theory of pyramid construction, and his full account will be more fully examined in the next chapter. One passage reads:

> On the pyramid is shown an inscription in Egyptian characters of how much was spent on radishes, onions, and garlic for the workmen. The person interpreting the inscriptions, as I remember well, told me this amounted to 1,600 talents of silver.

Today, 1600 talents of silver represents approximately $100 million in U.S. currency, a colossal sum for feeding radish, onion, and garlic to workers. Herodotus was surprised by the large sum for such a limited variety of food. In light of Khnum's chemistry, the legendary implication becomes clear: The sum of $100 million represents the cost of mining arsenic minerals for constructing the Great Pyramid.

The Famine Stele also supports the fact that the ancient Egyptians used arsenic minerals for pyramid construction. The stele lists garlic, onion, and radish stones.

Hedsh

For the mineral ore that smells like onions when heated, the word is *hedsh* (also *uteshi*). Barguet provides no translation. Harris says the meaning remains inconclusive. Brugsch thinks the word means white. According to E. A. Wallis Budge's hieroglyphic dictionary, *hedsh* means onion. But the translation of onion for a stone has puzzled Egyptologists and they have, therefore, avoided translation. The *hedsh* stone could be a mineral ore that gives off a white fume which smells like onion when heated.

Tem

Similarly, the words *tutem* and *taam,* containing the root *tem,* are thought to mean garlic. An ore listed in column 16, *tem-ikr,* could indicate a mineral that gives off the odor of garlic. The last two letters, "kr," mean weak. This, therefore, could qualify the word to mean the mineral that gives off a weak smell of garlic.

Kau

Kau (also *ka-t*) means radish. An ore in column 16, *ka-y,* could indicate an ore that smells like radishes when heated.

Based on the key words discussed, the following is my translation of the relevant passages of the Famine Stele. The English transliterations are provided for rocks and minerals which remain untranslated. Small parts of the stele are missing because they contain no relevant information. Those portions are here filled in with ellipses, and on the hieroglyphic **chart** with diagonal lines. The new translation clearly depicts mineral processing for fabricating pyramid stone.

The Revelation of Imhotep

(Column 11) On the east side (of Elephantine) are numerous mountains containing all of the ores, all of the crushed (disaggregated) stones (aggregates) suitable for agglomeration, all of the products (Column 12) people are seeking for building the temples of the gods of the North and South, the stables for the sacred animals, the pyramid of the king, and the statues to be erected in the temples and the sanctuaries. Moreover, all of these chemical products are in front of Khnum and surrounding him. . . . (Column 13) . . . in the middle of the river is a wonderful place where on both sides people are processing the ores. . . . (Column 14) . . . learn the names of the gods which are in the temple of Khnum. . . . (Column 15) Learn the names of the stone materials which are to be found eastward, upstream of Elephantine: *bekhen, mtay* (dead or weathered granite), *mhtbtb, regs, hedsh* (disaggregated onion stone), . . . *prdn,* . . .

THE PYRAMIDS

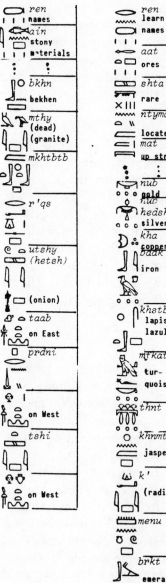

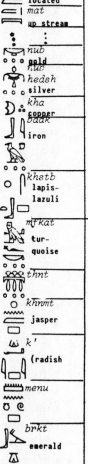

COL. 11.

un	they are
khat	numerous
tutu	mountains
m gerg-fa	in the side
tut	East
ger	to found
aat	ores
neb	all
rwdt uteshui	crushed stones (weathered aggregates)
khet	products

COL. 12

neb hehi sen	all are seeking
khus	to build
neterhet	temples god
neb	all
n sunut	from South
hanut	North
nti	for

(12)

aam	animals
neter	sacred
her	and
aa	pyramid
nti	for
sutin	king
hena	with
khente	statues
neb aha	all erected
sen	they
het neterhet	in temples
her	and
tat	sanctuaries
ra	more
ger	over
tu	products (chemicals)
sen	they
ab	are found
er	
kheft	in front
n	
khnum	of khnum
n teb	and around him
fa-teb	

COL. 15.

ren	names
ain	stony materials
bkhn	bekhen
mthy	(dead) (granite)
mkhtbtb	
r'qs	
utshy	(hetsh)
	(onion)
taab	on East
prdni	
	on West
tshi	
	on West

COL. 16.

ren	learn
	names
aat	ores
shta	rare
ntymat	located
mat	up stream
nub	gold
nub	
hedsh	silver
kha	copper
baak	iron
khstb	lapis-lazuli
mfkat	tur-quoise
thnt	
khnmt	jasper
k'	(radish
menu	
brkt	emerald

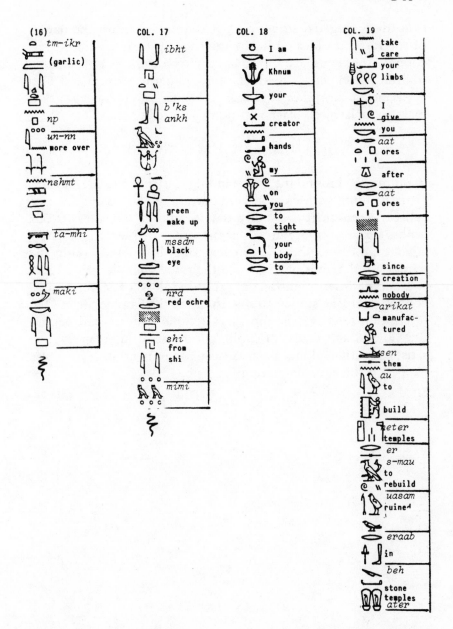

FIGURE 40. *The Famine Stele. Davidovits translation of columns 11, 12, 15, 16, 17, 18, and 19.*

153

teshi (disaggregated stone). . . . (Column 16) Learn the names of the rare ores located in the quarries upstream: gold, silver, copper, iron, lapis lazuli, turquoise, chrysocolla, red jasper, *ka-y* (radish stone), *mnu, esmerald, tem-ikr* (garlic stone), and also *neshemnet, ta-mehy, heaget* (Column 17), *ibehet, bekes-ankh,* green makup (malachite), black antimony, and red ochre. . . .

The Dream of Pharaoh Zoser

(Column 18) I found the god standing. He spoke to me, saying, "I am Khnum, your creator. I am putting my hands upon you in order to strengthen your body, to (Column 19) take care of your limbs. I give you rare ore after rare ore. . . . Never before has anyone processed them (to make stone) in order to build the temples of the gods or to rebuild the ruined temples. . . ."

Building inscriptions relating to the Colossi of Memnon also contain language similar to that found in the Famine Stele. One inscription refers to the mortuary temple which stood behind the Colossi and reads, "Behold, the heart of his majesty was satisfied with making a very great monument such as never happened since the beginning."

CHAPTER 12

It Is Written in Greek

NOT TO BE OVERLOOKED IS THE CLASSICAL HISTORICAL AC-
count of pyramid construction, the well-known account of
Herodotus. His account reflects beliefs popular in Egypt during
the fifth century BC, which Egyptologists assume have no significant bearing on the actual method of pyramid construction.
In any case, they agree that it complies fully with the standard
carving and hoisting theory. But does it?

Herodotus was a remarkable and reliable historian, a unique
figure of antiquity. He is called the Father of History for producing the first comprehensive attempt at historical narrative
based on scientific inquiry. His work marks the beginning of the
Western approach to historical reporting. His writing shows
superb analytical skills; it is anecdotal, charming, and entertain-
ing.

Born in Asia Minor around 485 BC, he began seventeen years
of extensive travel in the ancient world while in his twenties.
The journey for which he is most well known is a four-month

stay in Egypt, which he recounts in his entire second book of
The History. One summer, sometime after 460 BC, Herodotus
arrived in the western Delta at the town of Canope, Egypt. He
visited several renowned sites and encountered many people
until his departure from Pelusuim in the eastern Delta before the
following winter.

He was captivated by Egypt's wondrous monuments and
geography. He reported what he learned of these and of history,
arts, folklore, customs, and beliefs. During his visit to
Memphis, he discussed the construction of the Great Pyramids
with local guides. Herodotus's work has been translated several
times since AD 1450 from the old Ionic Greek, with each trans-
lator attempting to improve on the precise meaning of the text.
The relevant portion of his report of their account is presented
below. I have emphasized certain words and phrases vital to the
true method of pyramid construction. The account begins:

> Now, they told me, that to the death of Rhampsinitus there was a
> perfect distribution of justice, and that all of Egypt was in a high
> state of prosperity. But that Cheops, the next king to reign,
> brought the people absolute misery. First he shut all the temples,
> and forbade the offering of sacrifice. Then he ordered all of the
> Egyptians to work for him. Some were appointed to *drag stone from
> the quarries* in the Arabian mountains to the Nile. Others he ordered
> to *receive the stones* which were transported in boats across the river,
> and *drag them* to the hills called the Libyan.

The group of emphasized words refers to the transportation of
stone. As opposed to stone blocks, this description could just as
well relate to the hauling of stone rubble. The limestone material used for the casing blocks was most likely hauled from
quarries in the Arabian mountains. The quote continues:

> And they worked in gangs of 100,000 men, each gang working for
> three months. For ten years the people were afflicted with toil in
> order to make the road for the *conveyance of stone*. This work, in my
> opinion, was not much less than that of the pyramid itself; for the
> road is five stades [3,021 feet] in length, and its width ten orgyae [60

feet], and its height, where it is the highest, eight orgyae [48 feet]; and it is built of *polished* stone and is covered with *engravings* of animals.

Again, a reference to hauling stone may just as well relate to the hauling of rubble. Above, and again in the next portion provided below, the word polished appears to describe smooth stone bearing no tool marks. This is the same word, *xeston,* used about 200 years later by Manetho to describe pyramid stone. As discussed in Chapter 10, this word does not mean hewn. Herodotus's account never states that the pyramid blocks were carved.

Another word above is translated engraved. Engraving is assumed by Herodotus, who does not understand the construction method. Just the same, inscriptions or impressions do not require carving. Assuming agglomeration, hieroglyphic figures were impressed in objects such as the Colossi of Memnon and monolithic sarcophagi by the mold. Herodotus continues:

> As I said, ten years went into the making of this road, including the underground chambers on the mound upon which the pyramid stands. These the king made as a burial place for himself. These last were built on a sort of island made by *introducing water by canals from the Nile.* Twenty years were spent erecting the pyramid itself. It is a square, each face is eight plethra [820 feet], and the height is the same; it is built entirely of *polished* stones, and jointed with the greatest exactness; none of the stones are less than thirty feet.

Again, we see a reference to the beautiful, polished stones. There is also mention of canals extending from the Nile to the site. As mentioned in Chapter 6, on-site canals would be necessary for introducing water onto the Giza plateau for disaggregating the limestone and for the production of enormous quantities of cement. Mythology also supports the existence of on-site canals. According to mythology, the pyramids would be connected to the Nile so that the spirit of the pharaoh could travel in his boat each night to the underworld.

Residues of cement production have long since vanished. There is, however, another historical account that implies that the river was let in through a canal to dissolve salts, as would be necessary for cement production. This comes from *Historical Library,* by Diodorus Siculus (21 BC), a later Greek historian visiting the pyramids:

> And the most remarkable part of the account is that, though the surrounding land consists of nothing but sand, not a trace remains either of ramps or the dressing of stones, so that they do not appear to have been made by the slow hand of man but instead look like a sudden creation, as though they had been made by a god and set down bodily in the sand. Some Egyptians make a marvel out of these matters, saying that in as much as ramps were made with salt and saltpeter, when the river was let it dissolved them and completely effaced them without the intervention of man's hand.

Herodotus continues. . . .

> This pyramid was built thus; in the form of steps, which some call crosae, and others call bomides. After preparing the foundation, they raised stones by using *machines made of short planks of wood,* which raised the stones from the ground to the first range of steps. On this range there was another *machine* which received the stone upon arrival. Another *machine* advanced the stone on the second step. Either there were as many *machines* as steps, or there was really only one, and portable, to reach each range in succession whenever they wished to raise the stone higher. I am telling both possibilities because both were mentioned.

When researchers introduce designs for wooden machines, which they propose might have been used for hoisting pyramid blocks, their concepts do not comply with the archaeological record. No evidence of any such wooden machinery from the Pyramid Age has ever been found by archaeologists. There was certainly no focus during the late Stone Age on the invention of machinery as we think of it—structures consisting of a framework and fixed and moving parts.

Herodotus's firsthand reporting nevertheless led to speculation about the existence of tripods and pulleys during the Old

Kingdom, but archaeologists are satisfied that these implements were not introduced in Egypt until Roman times, after 30 BC. This contradiction between the firsthand report and the archaeological record produces a dilemma. The solution, however, is simple.

The wooden machines cited were wooden molds. The quote reads in the following manner when the word "machine" is changed to read "mold."

> This pyramid was built thus; in the form of steps, which some call crosae, and others call bomides. After preparing the foundation, they raised the other stones by using *molds made of short planks of wood,* which raised the stones from the ground to the first range of steps. On this range there was another *mold* which received the stone [rubble] upon arrival. Another *mold* advanced the stone on the second step. Either there were as many *molds* as steps, or there was really only one, and portable, to reach each range in succession whenever they wished to raise the stone higher. I am telling both possibilities because both were mentioned.

The slight language distortion that converted *molds* to *machines* shows how difficult it can be to interpret even very simple technical words when knowledge has been lost. A mold can be considered as an apparatus or device. The Greek word, *mechane,* used by Herodotus, is a general term indicating something contrived, invented, or fabricated. Because the word is nonspecific, a gross generalization, what is left to the imagination produces a conceptual distortion, and unfamiliarity with the actual construction method bears on the way translators interpreted and therefore translated the text.

Not only does Herodotus's account not support stone cutting, it also does not imply that blocks were hoisted up the pyramid. What exists is a description complying with piling a pyramid tier by tier. The account never states that blocks were raised via ramps or from the ground by machine directly to great heights. The account continues:

> The highest parts of it, therefore, were first finished, and afterwards they completed the parts next following. Last of all they finished

159

the parts on the ground, and those that were the lowest. On the pyramid is shown an inscription in Egyptian characters of how much was spent on *radishes, onions,* and *garlic* for the workmen. The person interpreting the inscription, as I well remember, told me this amounted to 1,600 talents of silver. And if this be true, how much more was probably expended in iron tools, in bread, and in clothing for the workers, since they took the time that I have mentioned to build this edifice without even counting, in my opinion, the time for quarrying the stones, their transportation, and the construction of subterranean chambers, which were without doubt considerable.

Herodotus, who liked to calculate problems, had trouble believing that the pyramid had been built in twenty years. But more interestingly, without appropriate scientific insight, the reference to onion and garlic is absolutely absurd. It appeared, for instance, so ridiculous to the noted Egyptologists Budge and Gaston Maspero, that they thought Herodotus was deceived by the interpreter. Budge commented in *The Mummy* that the inscriptions were pure invention. We now know, however, that chemical odors, such as those resembling garlic, comply with Khnum's alchemical processes. Knowing this, we recognize that this passage is something truly precious. It is a piece of genuine news preserved from the time of the completion of the Great Pyramid.

Herodotus's comments about other costs clearly indicate that he did not understand the chemical sense of the inscriptions. Nor does it seem that he was made to appreciate why this relevant information was provided. It was certainly considered to be a primary part of the guides' explanation, lending a clue that they may have understood something about the construction method. If they did not understand, they certainly knew that the inscriptions were relevant.

It is not difficult to understand why the guides would be ineffective in communicating the construction method to Herodotus if they understood it. There seems to have been no suitable Greek word to describe such stone, the closest word being *polished (xeston).* Communicating the notion of man-made stone and stone otherwise prepared or manipulated by man could easily be misunderstood, especially when conversing with a traveler unfamiliar with the technology through an interpreter.

Different possibilities emerge regarding Herodotus's quote. One is that the guides thought they were adequately communicating the method of pyramid construction. The interpreter may have distorted the account in translation. More probably, the guides related only distorted legendary information. Whatever the case, modern translators have inadvertently obscured the text by misinterpreting some key words. Preconceived ideas about pyramid construction played a significant role in the translations of the text into modern languages.

Although the account contains some misinformation, we also find that, paragraph by paragraph, it is riddled with clues of the actual construction method—relevant clues that could not be present otherwise. The amount and relevance of the clues can be no accident, nor can these clues be ignored. This leads to the standard interpretation of the account coming into serious question. When stripped of distortion, a clearer account emerges. Instead of supporting the standard theory, this account must be taken as historical documentation supporting my findings.

CHAPTER 13

It Is Written in Latin

WHEN DID THE LAST VESTIGES OF THE TECHNOLOGY DISAP-
pear and why? The answer to these questions remains elusive.
Existing alchemical knowledge can still be pinpointed to a time
shortly after the death of Jesus Christ. A description is found in
the ancient science encyclopedia written by Pliny the Elder (AD
23–79), the Roman naturalist. Pliny's account is not legendary
or written esoterically; it clearly describes the salient features of
the technology. But Pliny's description has not been understood
by modern science, because to recognize what is written, one
must have the appropriate knowledge.

Pliny became one of the authorities on science and its history
for the Middle Ages, making a profound impact on the intellectual development of western Europe. He had established a new
type of scientific literature—the encyclopedia. He was the first
to collect old, diversified material of science and pseudoscience
and methodically and expertly assemble it. The resulting encyclopedia of *Natural History*, consisting of thirty-seven books, is

163

HISTOIRE NATURELLE

DE PLINE

TRADUCTION NOUVELLE

PAR M. AJASSON DE GRANDSAGNE

ANNOTÉE

PAR MM. BEUDANT, BRONGNIART, G. CUVIER,
DAUNOU, ÉMERIC DAVID, DESCURET, DOÉ, E. DOLO, DUSGATE,
FÉE, L. FOUCHÉ, FOURIER, GUIBOURT, ÉLOI JOHANNEAU,
LACROIX, LAFOSSE, LEMERCIER, LETRONNE, LOUIS LISKENNE,
L. MARCUS, MONGÈS,
C. L. F. PANCKOUCKE, VALENTIN PARISOT,
QUATREMÈRE DE QUINCY, P. ROBERT, ROBIQUET,
H. THIBAUD, THUROT, VALENCIENNES, HIPP. VERGNE.

TOME TREIZIÈME.

PARIS

C. L. F. PANCKOUCKE

MEMBRE DE L'ORDRE ROYAL DE LA LÉGION D'HONNEUR
ÉDITEUR, RUE DES POITEVINS, Nº 14

M DCCC XXXII.

impressive in its scope. It covers botany, zoology, geography, anthropology, cosmology, astronomy, and mineralogy. During the Middle Ages, lessons in his work often substituted for a general education, and Pliny's authority remained undiminished for over 1,500 years.

It was not until 1492 that Pliny's authority was first challenged in *Concerning the Errors of Pliny,* by the noted physician and philologist Niccolo Leoniceno. Although Pliny's encyclopedia is today appreciated as one of the monumental literary works of classical antiquity, modern science declares the work useless as science. Be that as it may, if our aim is to understand, appreciate, and indeed attempt to recover the best of the sciences of antiquity, Pliny's encyclopedia is a jewel of science.

To date, the passages related to alchemical stonemaking confuse scholars, resulting in gross errors of translation in Pliny's work. Worse, the salient principles and characteristics of the ancient science being unknown, the translators dismissed Pliny's account as erroneous. De Roziere commented on the problems of translation:

> M. Grosse, author of a German translation of Pliny, highly esteemed by learned people, points out that in the whole of this description the Roman naturalist seems to have done his best to make himself obscure. "Despite my familiarity," he said, "both with Pliny's style and with the meaning he gives to terms, it has been difficult, sometimes even impossible, to translate the passages clearly and exactly." The reason was certainly that he was simply unfamiliar with the substance that Pliny was describing.

One can appreciate the difficulty of literally translating technical material after technical knowledge has been lost, especially for a strictly literary scholar. Except for my translation, all attempts to translate the relevant passages have been futile.

In 1883, the French Academy of Sciences, in order to compare ancient scientific knowledge with that of its day, produced and annotated a French translation of Pliny's encyclopedia. The first half of the nineteenth century produced several important developments. Jean Francois Champollion deciphered Egyptian hieroglyphs, and Georg Friedrich Grotefend deciphered Persian cuneiform. Portland cement was first manufactured, and a complete mineral classification was established. The latter allowed for a comprehensive critique of Pliny's writings on mineralogy by the French Academy of Sciences.

A passage from Book 31 of Pliny's encyclopedia made no sense to the French scholars. But the passage is compelling in its support of the existence of alchemical stonemaking. The passage appears in Latin as follows:

> Nitrariae Aegypti circa Naucratim et Memphim tantum solebant esse, circa Memphim deteriores. Nam et lapidescit ibi in acervis: multique sunt cumuli ea de causa saxei. Faciunt ex his vasa. . . .

Translated into English this passage reads:

> In previous times, Egypt had no outcrops of natron except for those near Naucratis and Memphis, the products of Memphis being reputedly inferior. It is a fact that in accumulations of materials it (natron) petrifies [minerals]. In this way occurs a multitude of heaps [of minerals] which become transformed into real rocks. The Egyptians make vases of it. . . .

This particular passage is simple and straightforward, so there is no error of translation—the Egyptians made real rocks according to Pliny. And the last sentence suggests that Khnum's technology was again being used to produce stone vases. Pliny provides a more detailed description of the manufacture of artificial stone in a segment about vase production. The vases are called murrhine vases. The following is a standard translation of Pliny's description found in Book 37:

> Date of the introduction of the murrhine vases and what they commemorated:

> VII. With this same victory came the introduction to Rome of the murrhine vases. Pompey was the first to dedicate murrhine cups and bowls to Jupiter in the Capitol. These vessels soon passed into daily use, and they were in demand for display and tableware.

Lavish expenditure on these items increased daily: an ex-consul drank from a murrhine vessel for which he paid 70 talents [about $1 million U.S. in 1988] although it held just three pints.

He was so taken with the vessel that he gnawed its edges. The damage actually caused its value to increase, and today no murrhine vessel has a higher price upon it.

The same man squandered vast sums to acquire other articles of this substance, which can be determined by their number, so high that when Nero robbed them from his children for display they filled the private theatre in his gardens beyond the Tiber, a theatre large enough to satisfy even Nero's urge to sing before a full house as he rehearsed for his appearance at Pompey's theatre.

It was at this event that I counted the pieces of a single broken vessel included in the exhibition. It was decided that the pieces, like the remains of Alexander the Great, should be preserved in an urn for display, presumably as a token of the sorrows and misfortune of the age. Before dying, the consul Titus Petronius, in order to spite Nero, had a murrhine bowl, valued at 30 talents [$500,000 U.S.], broken in order to deprive the Emperor's dining table of it. But Nero, as befitted an emperor, surpassed everyone else by paying 100 talents [$1.5 million U.S.] for a single vessel. It is a memorable fact that an emperor, head of the fatherland, should drink at such a high price.

The passage indicates that the precious stone vases were dedicated to Jupiter, the supreme god in Roman mythology. This could reflect a carry-over in religious tradition. It is probable that more anciently alchemically made stone vessels were dedicated to the Sun god of Egypt, Ra in the form of Khnum-Ra. After the Roman conquest, Jupiter was worshipped in Egypt in the form of Jupiter-Amun, Amun being the supreme deity identified with the Sun during the late era. It could be that the word murrhine was derived from the name of Khnum.

The Latin spelling is *murrhinum*. Excluding the "m," the succession of consonants in Latin is: .rrh.n.m, which could be a Latin way of writing .kh.n.m: The letters "kh" are pronounced the same as are "ch" in German and the letter "j" *(jota)* in Spanish, the sound heard in the name Juan. This pronunciation has a guttural sound "rrh." This type of pronunciation or sound would transform the word to *mukhinum,* which is close to the name Khnum.

These vases were truly precious items, either because of sacred tradition or simple technological developments. Adding certain raw materials and heating under certain conditions produces extraordinarily beautiful optical qualities, such as those described next. Clearly, the material described has features that do not comply with those of natural stone. In the relevant passages, emphasis is added.

> VIII. The murrhine vases come to us from the East. They are found there in various little-known places, especially in the kingdom of Parthia. The finest come from Carmania. *They are said to be made of a liquid to which heat gives consistence when covered with earth.* Their dimensions never exceed those of a small display stand. Rarely, their thickness is no more than that of a drinking vessel such as mentioned. They are not very brilliant. They glisten rather than shine. What makes them fetch a high price is the varieties of shades, the veins, as they revolve, vary repeatedly from pink to white, or a combination of the two, the pink becoming firey or the milk-white becoming red as the new shade merges through the vein. Some connoisseurs especially admire the edges of a piece, where the colors are reflected as in the inner part of a rainbow. Others favor thick veins. Any transparency or fading is a flaw. *Also there are the grains and the blisters which, like warts on human bodies, are just beneath the surface. The stone is also appreciated for its odor.*

According to Pliny, these vases were made from a liquid that hardened when heated, a description indicating that the vases could not have been produced by carving natural stone. The mention of blisters and odor could refer only to an artificially produced material. A puzzled committee of scientists from the French Academy of Sciences responded as follows:

> The matter of the murrhine vases was discussed for a long time. According to Scaliger, Mariette, Lagrange, et al., it was porcelain that, in Roman times, was only made at the extremities of the known world (China, Japan, and Formosa), and which, transported at great cost overland through the hands of twenty different people,

must indeed have fetched an enormous price. But porcelain is artificial, and the variety of colors, the play of light on the murrhine surface, the stripes, and the wavy stains of which Pliny speaks, are not traits of porcelain. Moreover, ". . . humorem sub terra calore densari. . . ." [a liquid to which heat gives consistency when covered with earth, i.e., hardens when it is heated in clay] can hardly mean a man-made process analogous to that which transforms kaolin into porcelain. But from his description, the only natural substance with all the features described by Pliny is fluorite.

Despite Pliny's description of a material that could only be man-made, the French scholars decided that the vases had to be made of fluorite, a stone material, with white and pink veins, which must be carved. Their comments continue:

To identify fluorite in the midst of so many heterogeneous substances would have been difficult; to extract it, i.e., to isolate it and purify it, impossible. It was thus necessary to find native pieces of heterogeneous material with as little filler as possible. This was rare. Rarer still were pink crystallized samples, for pink is last in the order of abundance: greenish grey, white, yellow, violet, blue, honey yellow, and pink. It should be remembered that, even today, fine specimens of fluorite are used to make beautiful vases. Recently, fluorite was used to give a matte finish to porcelain statues which had become vitrified during firing.

In this last statement, the scholars were referring to the fact that fluorite is used to produce hydrofluoric acid, vital to ceramic production. Fluorite is dissolved in sulfuric acid to make hydrofluoric acid for attacking glass. An interpretation of Pliny's text by the French Academy of Sciences follows:

For which he paid 70 talents: Such incredible sums (70 talents) are almost beyond belief. Seventy talents equals almost 35,000 sovereigns [\$1 million U.S.] in our money; and we shall be referring to a sum more than four times as great as this a little later—and all this for a vessel meant for the least auspicious applications.

Any transparency or fading are flaws: Semitransparency: this is confirmed below.

The stone is also appreciated for its odor: This is one of the reasons to believe that the murrhine was artificial.

Made of a liquid to which heat gives consistence: It is difficult to understand that heat can cause solidification. Normal experience is that when a solid is heated it melts. Thus, we must consider the possible meanings of the expression, viz: (1) evaporation followed by condensation, binding together of a magma, and still more likely, crystallization, (2) kinds of stalactites or stalagmites (remembering that there does exist a compact variety composed of small lumps bound together).

In the 1830s, the members of the French Academy of Sciences did not know that a liquid could become hard when heated. With organic chemistry not yet developed, the phenomenon was unknown. In keeping with developments in inorganic chemistry in their day, the transformations of the different states of matter as produced by heat could only occur in an immutable manner. When heated, solids become liquids. Liquids become gases. Then, upon cooling, gases become liquids as they condense, and liquids become solids as they crystallize. This fundamental, uniform behavior of all matter constituted immutable natural laws for the members of the distinguished French Academy of Sciences.

Therefore, Pliny's description was nonsense in their opinion. It defied natural laws. Their consensus was, "Beware of Pliny and his fantastical descriptions!" Modern chemistry, of course, has substantiated Pliny's claim that liquids can become solid when heated. Thermosetting plastics harden upon heating. And the chemistry of geopolymerization demonstrates that a colloidal solution of minerals hardens when heated.

However, Pliny's authority in this regard has still not been vindicated. Despite the description that could only indicate the production of artificial stone, fluorite, a natural stone, remains in the translations of Pliny's text.

Every Egyptian hieroglyphic and cuneiform text deciphered during the early 1800s reflects the limitations of the scientific knowledge of that time. For 150 years, the translations of most have not been updated to reflect modern knowledge. This means that ancient texts that may contain descriptions of alchemical stonemaking remain grossly inaccurate.

Pliny is appreciated for his ability to tie together bits of information from scattered sources and arrive at conclusions that often prove to be accurate. He criticized the pharaohs for building such elaborate pyramid tombs but probably gave little thought to the pyramid construction method. Like Pochan and the researchers at SRI International, Pliny also overlooked the construction method. He knew that the murrhine vases were artificial stone, and he knew that, using natron, the Egyptians made "real rock," yet, though he wondered how the Egyptians raised the heavy blocks in the Great Pyramid so high, he never applied his knowledge to pyramid construction.

CHAPTER 14

The Rise of Pyramids

PYRAMID CONSTRUCTION METHODS POSE GREAT QUES-
tions. The work that would be involved using the accepted
method is staggering, even with modern machinery; and with
the construction method eluding historians, reasons for the rise
and decline of pyramid building are misunderstood.

In general, Egyptologists advocate that early pyramid building put an intolerable burden on manpower and the economy,
causing the decline. This explanation fails to address the reason
that pyramid building was not at least attempted during certain
later wealthy dynasties possessing additional territory, masses of
slaves, better tools, and executing prolific building projects.

The reasons for the rise and decline of pyramid construction
crystalize when one considers the developments associated with
the use of cast stone. The developments in construction parallel
those of the modern concrete industry after the introduction of
portland cement; specifically, the first pyramid blocks weighed
only a few pounds. Their size gradually increased over the

FIGURE 41. *Sphinx and the Great Pyramid.*

pyramid-building era to include enormous blocks and support beams weighing up to hundreds of tons apiece. If the pyramids were built of carved blocks, the evolution of pyramid construction would be highly unlikely. An overview clarifies these points.

The Great Pyramid is one of the earliest pyramids. More than seventy pyramids are known, and others may be concealed beneath the desert sands. Any still buried would not be great pyramids, but small, ruined structures. All known pyramids are situated in groups located at several different geographical areas of the necropolis on the West Bank.

The pyramid of Pharaoh Zoser served as a protoype for following Third Dynasty pyramids. Because Third Dynasty history is obscure, with the number and order of reigns still debated, the identification of the pyramids immediately following Zoser's is tenuous. Tentatively among Zoser's Third Dynasty pyramid-building successors were pharaohs Sekhemkhet,

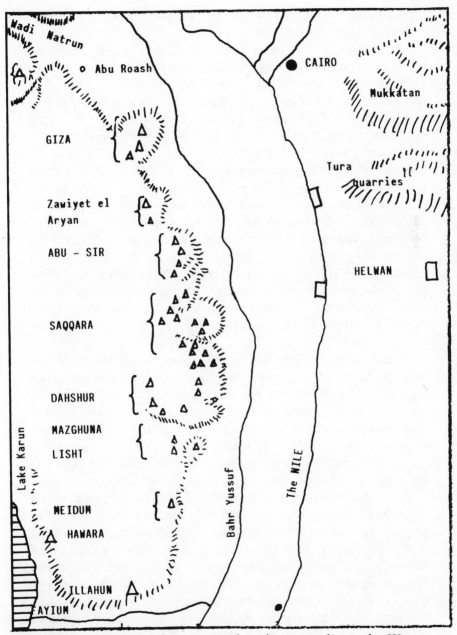

FIGURE 42. *The pyramids are situated in the necropolis on the West Bank of the Nile.*

175

Neb-ka, and Kha-ba. None of these kings reigned long enough to complete his monument.

The pyramid considered second in chronology is attributed to Zoser's successor, Sekhemkhet, who is believed to have reigned from six to eight years. This complex is located at Saqqara near the original pyramid and was planned along a similar design. The intent to build a larger monument is apparent from a larger enclosure. This unfinished monument is in ruins. Only two tiers remain.

One distinctive architectural feature found inside is a door framed by an arch. If this pyramid is correctly dated to the Third Dynasty, the arch would most likely be the earliest ever constructed. Nearby, several Ptolemaic mummies were discovered in the sand. Also discovered were objects dating from the Twenty-sixth Dynasty and later. During the Twenty-sixth Dynasty old traditions were revived. A chamber inside the pyramid, which was first entered during excavation in the 1950s, showed signs of previous entry even though almost 1,000 items of gold jewelry had not been removed from the adjoining passageway.

Construction ramps were found *in situ*. These ramps do not support the hoisting of enormous blocks for the Great Pyramids because the blocks of this structure are small. If this pyramid is correctly dated to the era when stone was agglomerated, the blocks were manufactured near the site in numerous small wooden molds. The blocks were then carried up the ramps and placed to construct the pyramid. It would have been cumbersome and unnecessary to cast these small blocks in place.

Relief drawings on the sandstone cliffs near the Sinai mines show Sekhemkhet smiting the local desert people in order to protect mineral deposits. Rothenberg's expedition examined tool marks and graffiti on cavern walls, enabling a distinction between early and late mining operations. Whereas Middle and New Kingdom dynasties used pointed metal tools, in earlier times mine shafts were produced with pointed flint tools. Rothenberg observed that the mines were most heavily exploited by the end of the Fourth Dynasty. In other words, the mines

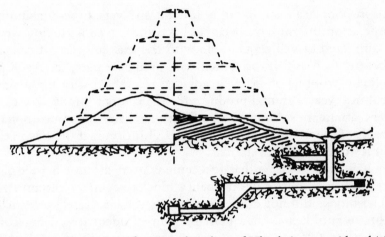

FIGURE 43. *Depiction of projected outline of Kha-ba's pyramid, which was never completed, rises over ruins.*

were heavily exploited by the time the major pyramids were built.

Sandstone masses were removed from the mines by producing a series of holes. This stone was then crushed into sand with harder rocks to free the mafkat nodules. The mafkat itself was most likely transported back to Egypt to be crushed for the cement.

A pyramid located at Zawiet el-Aryan, not far from Giza, is known as the Layer Pyramid and belongs to the first phases of Egyptian architecture. It has not been attributed adequately. Pharaoh Kha-ba's name is found in the nearby cemetery, making him the most likely builder. The Layer Pyramid was poorly constructed and is in a state of ruin. The use of small limestone blocks here still prevails, but they have become somewhat larger. The block quality is inferior and is believed to originate from a quarry to the south. This quarry may well be the origin of the aggregates used to produce blocks for the pyramid. No chemical analysis has been made of these blocks, but their inferior quality could be the result of several factors.

A mining or general work slowdown or the use of inferior minerals are possibilities. If the king was elderly when crowned or in poor health, mining, a difficult and very time-consuming operation, might have been cut back and the construction work completed as well as possible with the least amount of cement before his death. If the cement was used sparingly, the resulting blocks would not be well adhered. If these were poor agricultural years, animal products for the cement might have been less abundant. Another possibility is that the noncarbonate parts of the limestone did not react. This occurs if the clay in the limestone is not aluminous.

It is also possible that the cement used did not harden fast enough to produce good quality blocks beyond a certain size. The blocks did not crack to pieces as the larger size present in this pyramid, and they perhaps seemed adequate during construction. Close observation may have revealed tiny cracks or a poor finish, prompting the Heliopolitan specialists to continue experimenting with the formula.

The objective for Third Dynasty builders was to achieve more rapid setting, yielding larger blocks of better quality. Building with larger units has definite advantages. The architects no doubt realized that large blocks, being difficult to move, provided more protection for the burial chambers. Large units are less likely to be exploited at a later date, and transporting stones is a lot of work that can be eliminated provided the blocks can be cast directly in place. In other words, the larger the building units, the less work involved.

Three other structures built far from Memphis are tentatively grouped into the Third Dynasty. Generally, these show no architectual advance over Pharaoh Zoser's pyramid. These pyramids are small and far inferior except for larger blocks. Third Dynasty pyramids were designed as stepped structures with subterranean tombs. Structural designs varied in the different pyramids as architects experimented with engineering possibilities.

The last Third Dynasty king was Huni, also the last to build a step pyramid. His structure is usually discussed in connection with Fourth Dynasty pyramids because of its controversial history. It seems that Sneferu, the first king of the Fourth Dynasty, performed an experiment on Huni's pyramid. Huni's large step pyramid had been beautifully constructed at Meidum, forty miles south of Memphis. It originally had seven tiers and stood ninety-two meters (304 feet) high. Some of its blocks weigh about 0.25 ton (550 pounds).

When Sneferu was enthroned, he ordered his workmen to increase its height and add additional casing blocks from the base to the summit of Huni's pyramid. This produced the first exquisite, geometrical pyramid. The design was hailed as a great innovation, the inspiration for subsequent pyramids. The newly transformed pyramid, with its smooth finish of casing blocks, reflected brilliant streams of gleaming sunlight and won Sneferu the reputation of solar innovator. Sneferu ushered in the era we call the Pyramid Age.

The technically precise, pure geometric form was the sacred solar symbol of the benben. The word benben came to mean pyramid stone or stone symbolic of the Sun god in the sacred Egyptian hieroglyphic language. A representational benben of pyramidal form was elevated on top of a tall pillar to form an obelisk at the temple in Heliopolis in early times. This benben is assumed to have been a meteorite. To fuel this assumption is Pliny's report in Book II of *Natural History,* suggesting that a meteorite or "stone falling from the Sun," was worshipped at Abydos, in northern Upper Egypt. In keeping, however, with its shape and with religious tradition, the pyramidal benben in Heliopolis would more likely have been alchemically made stone.

At some point in history, Huni's elegant superstructure or Sneferu's mystical architectural form underwent a sudden, cataclysmic demise. Much of its outer masonry crashed to the ground in one tumultuous earth-shaking moment. A huge mound of stone debris resulted. It still surrounds the monument. The site attracts a great deal of attention, with the causes of the incident becoming one of the puzzles of Egyptology.

The generally held theory is that, at an unknown date, key support blocks shifted out of place or were removed. If the latter, the most likely culprit would have been Ramses II, who

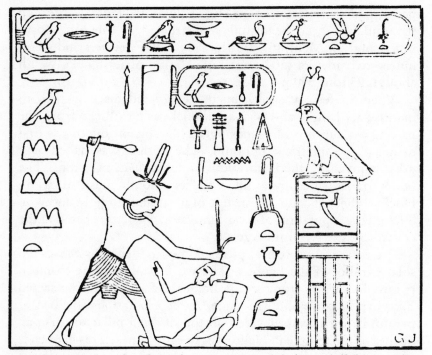

FIGURE 44. *A stele of Sneferu was engraved on a cliff face in the Sinai.*

was notorious for pillaging blocks from pyramds for his own monuments. Other theories accounting for the cataclysm are that the pyramid was disturbed by an earthquake or that there were incompatibilities between the original and the radical new design. Any of these possibilities might have caused a chain reaction, setting off the enormous avalanche that tore away most of the outer masonry. Now, when viewed from afar, the remains have the surreal appearance of a fabulous high tower rising from the midst of an enormous mound.

Sneferu was the most industrious builder in Egyptian history. On the Libyan plateau, six miles south of Saqqara, at Dashur, he constructed two gigantic pyramids. They dominate the sky-line even today. He appropriately named the first the Southern Shining Pyramid, and the second, to the north, the Shining

Pyramid. Today, they are known as the Bent Pyramid (also Rhomboidal, Blunted, and False Pyramid) and the Red Pyramid, respectively. Together they incorporate more stone than the Great Pyramid. Sneferu's workmen produced the monuments during the king's twenty-four year reign, and we have already considered the logistical problems that this creates for engineers.

In addition, the Palermo Stone records that Sneferu built temples throughout Egypt. He is also believed to have constructed the first Valley temples and causeways, as well as the small, subsidiary pyramids found south of parent structures. These types of masonry works adorned his own construction and were also believed to have been added by him to Huni's complex. Sneferu far exceeded other prolific builders of Egyptian history.

The Palermo Stone records that he sent to Lebanon for cedar. He launched a fleet of forty large ships to retrieve enormous beams of cedar at the Lebanon coast, the same sort of mission carried out since early times. We have already considered how this historical event connects with the preparation of molds for pyramid construction. Also relevant is that Sneferu's name is found in the Sinai in large reliefs in the cliffs. As would be expected, he exploited the mines on an enormous scale. The Sinai mines exploited by him were known as Sneferu's mines for 1,000 years.

Sneferu's Bent Pyramid was the first of the truly colossal superstructures. It is well preserved with a tip that is still pointed, and a great many of its casing blocks remain intact. This pyramid is in a restricted entry zone, so I have not examined it personally. Some of the casing blocks on the lower part of the pyramid are reported to be five feet high, a sure sign of casting on the spot, whereas some of the smaller masonry fits together fairly roughly, suggesting the use of precast stone. The heights of blocks range from small to large, providing for stability.

The modern name of Bent Pyramid was inspired by the angle of its slope, which suddenly diminishes on the upper half of the pyramid. Its shape makes it unique among pyramids. The architect radically altered the angle in an attempt to reduce the tremendous amount of stress on the corbeled walls of inner chambers, which, it is believed were already beginning to crack during construction.

It is believed that for this reason Sneferu went on to build the even larger Red Pyramid, so called because of the pink tint of its stones. Here the blocks are huge, with each one cast directly in place. Cummulative alchemical and engineering developments afforded superior strength and design over all previous pyramids. The burial chamber, traditionally underground, was incorporated into the pyramid itself. The heights of the blocks vary from 0.5 meters (1.64 feet) to 1.4 meters (4.6 feet). The Red Pyramid stands 103.36 meters (113 yards) high, and has a square base of 220 × 220 meters (240 × 240 yards). Its dimensions approach those of the Great Pyramid to follow.

Painted limestone statutes of Prince Rahotep and his wife Nofret, the former a son of Sneferu, were found in the cemetery around Huni's pyramid at Meidum. The paint used is a fine alchemical product that maintains its fresh color today. The inlaid eyes are truly exquisite, a technique afforded by agglomerated stone. Eyelids are made of copper, the whites of the eye are quartz, and the corneas are rock crystal. The material composing the irises is of uncertain composition, thought perhaps to be a type of resin. The Fourth Dynasty produced the most remarkable statuary.

Another son of Sneferu was Khnum-Khufu, who built the Great Pyramid. His full name shows his reverence for Khnum. Although today it is called the Great Pyramid, Khufu named his monument The Pyramid which is the Place of the Sunrise and Sunset. The name, inspired by Heliopolitan mythology, depicted the pyramid as the throne of the Sun god Ra during his daily course across the heavens.

Khufu and his pyramid were richly endowed with a royal estate, which had been maintained for thousands of years. During those years a line of priests assigned to Khufu faithfully maintained temples and property and ritually prepared offerings for the deceased god-king. Altars were covered over with offerings of flowers, incense, and food. Monuments that make reference to these priests date to several historical periods spanning thousands of years. They indicate that the tradition was not broken until Ptolemaic times.

This same tradition was upheld by priests of Khufu's father, Sneferu, and also those of his son, Khafra. Like his father, Khufu sponsored numerous building projects. His name appears on monuments throughout Egypt. He excavated for minerals in the Arabian Desert, Nubia, and the Sinai, where he was depicted on the cliffs protecting the mines.

Much of the complex belonging to the Great Pyramid has been destroyed. Only the foundations of the enclosure walls and the mortuary temple remain. The great causeway that Herodotus remarked almost equaled the pyramid in size was practically intact until 100 years ago. Today many large blocks remain to provide an idea of its original size and solidity. Other portions of the complex, such as the Valley Temple, are yet to be excavated. The cemetery surrounding the Great Pyramid is the most extensive, with large, impressive mastabas.

The seventh or eighth in chronology, the Great Pyramid is the largest and represents the peak in engineering design. Never again would Egypt build on this scale. Because of its masterful construction, this monument is the most celebrated of all time. It is little wonder that modern engineers wince at the thought of duplicating this monument, even with the best equipment. The base is 232 meters (253.7 yards) per side and the area of the base is 5.30 hectares (13 acres). Through careful observation of the stars, the Great Pyramid was oriented more accurately than any other; it is off only one-tenth of a degree of present-day true north. Its original height is estimated to have soared to 147 meters (481 feet). Today it is about 138 meters (450 feet) high with its capstone and some tiers missing. Its volume is 2,562,576 cubic meters (90,496,027 cubic feet). It contains approximately 2.6 million building blocks and has an overall weight of approximately 6.5 million tons.

It is difficult to appreciate the enormous size of the Great

Pyramid by reading statistics. Perhaps a better illustration is this: if all of its blocks were cut into pieces one-foot square and laid end to end, they would reach two-thirds of the way around the world at the equator. Notwithstanding all of the problems of pyramid construction already raised, if the blocks of the Great Pyramid were carved and their carving waste taken into account, the total weight of the stone used would have been close to 15 million tons—placing an enormous burden on the accepted theory.

The carving and hoisting theory indeed raises questions that have been insufficiently answered. Using stone and copper tools, how did workers manage to make the pyramid faces absolutely flat? How did they make the faces meet at a perfect point at the summit? How did they make the tiers so level? How could the required amount of workers maneuver on the building site? How did they make the blocks so uniform? How were some of the heaviest blocks in the pyramid placed at great heights? How were twenty-two acres of casing blocks all made to fit to a hair's breadth and closer? How was all of the work done in about twenty years? Experts can only guess. And no Egyptologist can deny that the problems have not been resolved.

Theories of construction are many and continue to be invented. All are based on carving and hoisting natural stone, and none solves the irreconcilable problems. Only the casting theory instantly dissolves all of the logistical and other problems.

What direct evidence of molding is to be found in the Great Pyramid? The casing blocks are clearly the product of stone casting. As mentioned, most were stripped for construction in medieval Cairo after an earthquake destroyed the city in AD 1301. Those that survive are at ground level, buried beneath the sand in 1301. Joints between the casing blocks are barely detectable, fitting as closely as 0.002 inch according to Petrie's measurements. The casing blocks are smooth and of such fine quality that they have frequently been mistaken for light-grey granite. The English scholar John Greaves (1602–1652) thought, at first sight, that they were marble.

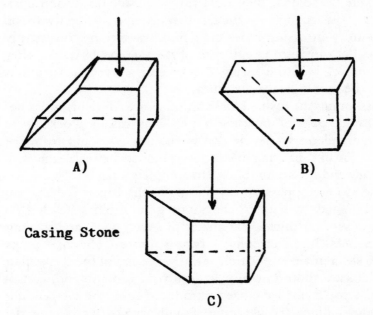

FIGURE 45. *Of the three possible positions for casting, only B and C are feasible for casting concrete.*

The casing blocks were angled to produce the slope of the pyramid. Because of their shape, casting them was more complicated than casting rectangular blocks. **Figures A, B, and C** show three casting methods: casting from the top, casting upside down, and side casting. Only B and C are feasible when making concrete. If workmen used only water, filling a mold using method A would be easy; but if workmen used concrete, it would be more difficult to fill the oblique part of a mold because the slurry would have to be pushed constantly against the inclined lid to eliminate gaps from forming.

In 1982 the German Egyptologists Rainer Stadelmann and Hourig Stadelmann-Sourozian discovered that the inscriptions on the casing blocks of the Red Pyramid of Sneferu were always on the bottom. This applies to the Great Pyramid as well and indicates that the casing blocks were cast in an inverted position (method B) against neighboring blocks. Once they hardened and were demolded, they were turned upside down and positioned. This accounts for the fact that inscriptions are always on the bottom of casing blocks. To find inscriptions consistently on the bottom is good evidence of the method by which they were made. Had the casing blocks been carved, inscriptions would be found on various surfaces.

Positioning the casing blocks was the most difficult and time-consuming part of building a tier. The casing blocks were inverted and set while the rest of the tier was built from the inside. Finally, packing blocks were added between the core masonry and the casing blocks to complete a tier.

The ascending passageway leading to the Grand Gallery had been plugged with three enormous granite blocks each 1.20 meters (3.9 feet) thick, 1.05 meters (3.4 feet) wide, and totaling 4.34 meters (14.3 feet) long. Edwards wrote, "The three plugs which still remain in position at the lower end of the Ascending Corridor are about one inch wider than its mouth and, consequently, could not have been introduced from the Descending Corridor." Since the plugging should have occurred after the funeral ceremony, Edwards continues, "No alternative remained, therefore, but to store the plugs somewhere in the pyramid while it was under construction and to move them down the Ascending Corridor after the body had been put in the burial chamber." Egyptologists have hotly debated where the plugs had been stored but have offered no satisfactory answer. Although no analyses have been made of the granite plugs in any of the pyramids, it is logical to suggest that these plugs in the Great Pyramid were agglomerated in the Grand Gallery and later slid into position.

Evidence of molding appears also in the ascending passageway. The blocks in this passageway are alternately set in either an inclined or vertical position. Although the inclined blocks have no structural function, the blocks set vertically support the passageway itself. There are large monolithic gates, consisting of two walls and a ceiling, made in a reverse-U shape. The evidence that these gates were molded are the mortices, later filled with cement, in the floor beneath them. Poles were inserted in these mortices to support the part of the mold needed to form the ceilings of the gates.

In addition, the sample provided by Lauer was from the wall of the Ascending Passageway. I have already described the sophisticated geopolymeric binder I detected, the stress bubbles, organic fibers, and wood-grain impressions exhibited in the sample.

The Grand Gallery is the most spectacular masonry feature of the interior of any pyramid. It measures 47.5 meters (156 feet) long, 8.5 meters (28 feet) high, and 2.1 meters (7 feet) wide at the floor level. Its walls are corbeled. One of Jomard's comments about the Great Pyramid was, "Everything is mysterious about the construction of this monument. The oblique, horizontal, and bent passageways, different in dimensions, the narrow shaft, the twenty-five mortices dug in the banks of the Grand Gallery. . . ." Jomard was referring to the mortices carefully plotted on the drawing (Figure XIV.8, XIV.9) made by Cecile for *Description de l'Egypte*.

Jomard did not notice that each square mortice in the floor corresponds with a vertical groove in the walls. The two French architects, Gilles Dormion and Jean-Patrice Goidin, who drilled a hole in the wall of the Queen's Chamber in 1987 in their search for hidden chambers, proposed that the purpose of the mortices was to stabilize poles that supported a wooden floor leading to a hidden passageway, which they failed to find. Any hidden chambers, which may be found, would add to the complexity of building the pyramid with the accepted theory.

It is obvious that these mortices and grooves were necessary for casting blocks. To produce a rectangular block, the mold must be oriented horizontally because, like water, a liquid slurry will seek its own horizontal level when poured. If a block is cast on an incline, a misshapen block would result **(Figure 45).** The blocks for the corbeled gallery were cast, therefore, in the horizontal position. The support mechanism was a wooden plank secured to the appropriate groove in the wall. The top of each groove is horizontal to the next mortice up. The plank was weighted, perhaps with a sandbag. Removing the weight disen-

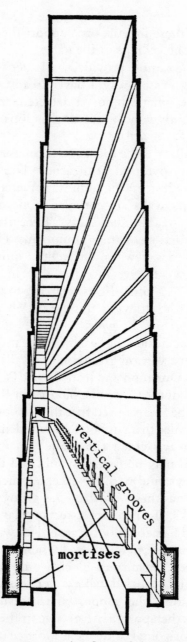

FIGURE 46. *Each mortice in the floor of the Grand Gallery of the Great Pyramid corresponds with a vertical groove in wall.*

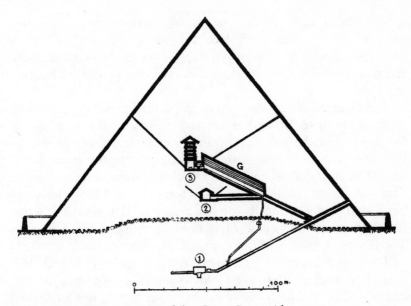

FIGURE 47. *Cross section of the Great Pyramid.*

gaged the wooden structure so the finished block could be
lowered and pushed into position **(Figure 49).**

The French architects previously mentioned used special devices provided by the French electricity company E.D.F., to
measure the whole density of the pyramid. They found a bulk
density twenty percent lighter than expected for limestone. An
Associated Press article published in December 1986, titled
"480,000 Stones Unaccounted for in Pyramid," reported the
team as saying, "Holes. We have holes. Maybe the size of a fist;
maybe the size of Notre Dame. . . . Or the answer might be
that some of the stones are of a lighter rock than the predominant limestone or that spaces appearing empty in the readings
are filled with rubble."

Though they found no chambers or enormous holes, that
core blocks are lighter than the bedrock was recognized in 1974
by the SRI International team. SRI International found the
density of the blocks of Khafra's pyramid twenty percent lighter
than the bedrock. Lighter density is a consequence of ag-

glomeration. Cast blocks are always twenty to twenty-five percent lighter than natural rock because they are full of air bubbles, which, though unavoidable during antiquity, in modern times can be eliminated by vibrating the molds with heavy machinery.

The Grand Gallery leads up to the so-called King's Chamber, deep in the interior and about two-thirds of the way up the pyramid. The blocks composing the flat roof of the King's Chamber are impressive, among the largest in the entire structure. The roof consists of nine monolithic slabs weighing about fifty tons each, totaling about 450 tons. These blocks have not been analyzed chemically or texturally to determine whether they are synthetic, made of granite aggregates from Aswan. The floors and walls of the King's Chamber are made similarly of finely jointed red granite that appears to be polished. It is logical to suggest that these blocks and the large granite sarcophagus, too large to be removed from the King's Chamber, were cast in place. The sarcophagus was cast after the pyramid was completed, as opposed to having been carved and hoisted up the pyramid during construction as is advocated.

If one considers size, design, and construction time limits, it becomes clear that if the Great Pyramids were dependent on primitive methods of carving and hoisting, they would not exist. In the Great Pyramid, hundreds of blocks that make up the core masonry weigh twenty tons and more and are found at the level of the Grand Gallery and higher. We have examined how the first pyramids were constructed of blocks weighing only a few pounds apiece. As engineering methods and design improved, casting stone directly in place in larger and larger units resulted in, to a civilization in the final phases of the Stone Age, monuments that stun modern observers, monuments that cannot be sufficiently explained today by experts or effectively duplicated within the appropriate amount of time by carving and hoisting natural stone. Now, we will examine the reason that, like the extinction of a mighty species, pyramid building in the sands of Egypt ceased.

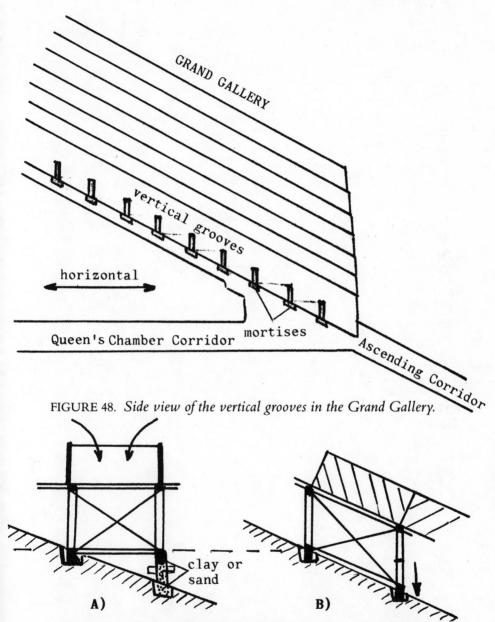

FIGURE 48. *Side view of the vertical grooves in the Grand Gallery.*

FIGURE 49. *Blocks were cast horizontally (A), and after setting, they were moved into the inclined position (B) to build the walls of the Grand Gallery.*

CHAPTER 15

The Decline

THE PYRAMID BUILDING DECLINE WAS BARELY NOTICEABLE at first. Khufus's son, Djedefra, was enthroned and built a monument about five miles north of the Great Pyramid, at Abu Roash. He named it the Pyramid Which Is the Sehedu-Star. Because Djedefra reigned only eight years, the monument was never completed, although substantial progress was made. The causeway was probably the most elaborate ever, measuring 1.5 kilometers (1640 yards) long. The base of the pyramid measures 100 meters (109 yards) square, and was planned to be considerably smaller than the Great Pyramid.

Several blocks of red granite remaining on the eastern face suggest that the pyramid was at least partially cased with this material, which would help to make any low, unfinished structure even more attractive for exploitation. Today the pyramid is mostly dismantled. The site was used as a quarry even in modern times. In *Pyramids and Temples of Giza* Petrie reported that he was told that as many as 300 camel loads of stone were being removed from the site daily. This gives us additional appreciation for the difficulty that quarrying stone with primi-

FIGURE 50. *Pyramid of Pharoah Khafra, the Second Pyramid of Giza.*

FIGURE 51. *From Khafra's mortuary temple to the east are (A) back of the Great Spinx, (B) causeway leading to gallery temple, and (C) Khafra's valley temple.*

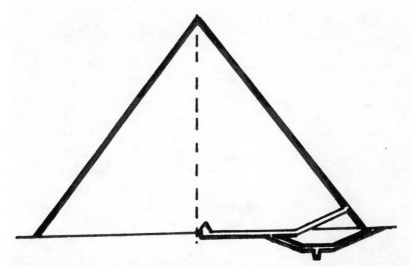

FIGURE 52. *Cross section of Khafra's pyramid shows interior far less elaborate than Khufu's Great Pyramid.*

tive tools poses. Even in modern times it has proved far easier to remove and transport pyramid blocks than to quarry hard stone from bedrock close to a building site and dress it.

The next pharaoh to reign was another son of Khufu named Khafra (also Ra'Kha'ef, and, in Greek, Chephren), who built the second largest pyramid. Today it is usually called the Second Pyramid of Giza, but the pharaoh named his monument the Great Pyramid. Its interior is not as elaborate as that of Khufu's pyramid, although, the complex, with its impressive features, is the most well preserved of the Giza group. In the Valley temple south of the Great Sphinx, two levels are made of blocks weighing fifty to eighty tons apiece and assembled with tongue-and-groove joints. As mentioned, some blocks weigh up to 500 tons. And Jomard, in *Description de l'Egypte,* remarked, "Because of their size, I first thought these blocks were protrusions of bedrock, rough-cut and squared. I would have remained ignorant about this if I had not noticed the mortar which joins the layers."

Despite these joints, the stones are considered to have been cut *in situ* because of their great size. The issue of the transport and placement of these stones is, therefore, conveniently

195

FIGURE 53. *Davidovits examines enormous blocks of first step on east side of Khafra's pyramid. The curved angle joint at A suggests stones were cast against bare neighboring stones to produce a close fit. B shows thick mortar sealing the bottom of mold.*

avoided. However, the joints, there to reduce stress, are per-fectly obvious and are filled with mortar. Their presence indi-cates irrefutably that these blocks were not carved *in situ*. Fur-thermore, these blocks are clearly defined from the bedrock, or, in other words, unattached. Certainly, the transport and place-ment of these blocks would pose enormous problems with means available to the Egyptians of the Fourth Dynasty. This entire issue is settled by the use of cast stone.

Indeed, as discussed in Chapter 8, the lift lines in these blocks are not horizontal like the strata of Giza. They are instead wavy, caused by construction interruptions. The heights of the lift lines do not match the strata of Giza. And these blocks exhibit the same erosion pattern as do the pyramid blocks. Although the causeway might contain some protrusions of natural bed-rock, for the most part, this same argument can be made for the blocks of the causeway.

The Valley temple was first excavated by Mariette in 1853. He found the famous diorite statue of Khafra in a well in the entranceway. The Valley temple was originally cased inside and out with finely jointed granite blocks, most of which have been removed from the outside. Inside, the granite blocks are in perfect condition, exhibiting the fabulous jigsaw joints, already described, which go around corners.

These and many other features in the pyramid and complex support the use of cast stone. The two-ton portcullis mentioned in Chapter 1 is positioned in a narrow passageway and requires the efforts of at least forty men to raise it. The passageway itself has room for no more than eight men to work together. In light of the evidence for cast stone already presented, it makes sense that the heavy portcullises of this and other pyramids were cast in place.

Too, features such as the uniform widths of blocks of the Second Pyramid demonstrate overwhelming evidence for stones cast in molds, and like the Great Pyramid blocks, the heights of the Second Pyramid blocks are staggered.

Several tiers of casing stones remain at the summit of the pyramid. Some are mottled and discolored by the growth of large patches of small, red lichen plants. Most, however, still maintain their smooth surface after thousands of years and reflect sunlight and white moonlight. The casing blocks fit together with tongue-and-groove joints. Certainly, casting these blocks makes more sense than carving them with primitive tools.

The pyramid itself measures 143.5 meters (157 yards) high and has a square base of 215.5 × 215.5 meters (235 square yards). Though not planned to be as large as Khufu's pyramid, the Second Pyramid is built on higher ground, making the two superstructures appear as gigantic twins from a distance. No Egyptian pharaoh would ever again come close to building on this tremendous scale.

Suddenly, the decline becomes dramatic. The next king was Menkure (Mycerinus in Greek). His pyramid, called by him the Divine Pyramid and today the Third Pyramid of Giza, was built of blocks of staggered dimensions, similar to the pyramids of Khufu and Khafra. It measures only 108.5 meters (118 yards) square and originally stood 66.5 meters (72 yards) high. It is seven percent the size of the Great Pyramid.

Menkure reigned for eighteen years, from 2490 to 2472 BC. Considering the amount of construction work accomplished during Khufu's twenty-year reign, Menkure would certainly have had time to build a larger monument, and yet, a sudden, dramatic decline occurred.

Menkure's small pyramid is no aberration. The last king of the Fourth Dynasty was Shepsekaf, who reigned a little over four years. He did not plan a large pyramid. Instead, he built a different type of royal monument that was neither a pyramid nor a true mastaba. The structure he called the Purified Pyramid is today called Mastabet Fara'un, and it looks instead like a giant, rectangular sarcophagus of fine-quality stone. The struc-

FIGURE 54. *The three great pyramids of Giza, from left, are of Khufu, Khafra, and Menkure.*

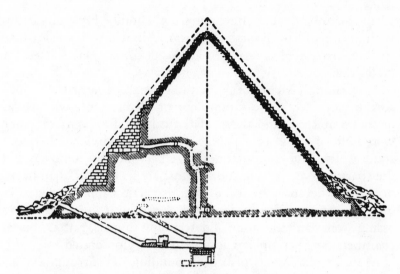

FIGURE 55. *Cross section of Menkure's pyramid.*

ture measures 100 × 72 meters (109 × 78 yards) and is only 18 meters (19.6 yards) high.

The Fifth Dynasty (2465–2323 BC) marks the end of the Pyramid Age. In the order of their reign, Fifth Dynasty kings known to have built pyramids were Userkaf, who built at Saqqara; Sahur, Neferirkare, Niuserre, each of who built at Abusir; and Djedkara-Isesi and Unas, who also built at Saqqara.

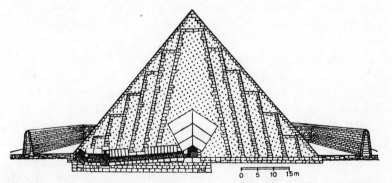

FIGURE 56. *Sahure's pyramid shows burial chamber of massive beams increasing in size as they ascend.*

Their pyramids were much inferior, shoddy by comparison with those of the Fourth Dynasty. All were planned to be smaller than Menkure's pyramid except for the one started for Neferirkare at Abusir.

Even though Menkure's pyramid is small, it consists of solid-core masonry, but the monument of Neferirkare, which was never completed, and those of the other Fifth Dynasty kings were built of loose stone rubble and sand, sandwiched between stone walls. The casing stones have been mostly removed and the structures are in ruin today. Most are little more than heaps of rubble, because this type of construction rapidly degrades once the casing is badly damaged or removed. The remaining casing stones and the stone of descending tunnels, rafters, burial chambers, and sarcophagi appear to be agglomerated.

More emphasis was placed on building the surrounding funerary complex, in this period, of both stone and sun-dried mud brick. These once elegant structures also are in almost complete ruin. The funerary complexes required far less stone than did pyramids and, therefore, do not compensate for the reduced size of the pyramids. Causeways, which require a great deal of stone, were sometimes altered to accommodate more than one pyramid, and advantage was taken of the bedrock in causeway construction. Sahure's causeway, for instance, changes direction twice to take advantage of natural features. It also contains blocks taken from Zoser's complex. This relates to what I have termed the sixth false proof of Egyptology, discussed in Chapter 4, which discusses the blocks hauled to Unas's pyramid.

Certain building blocks are much larger than those used in earlier pyramids. The burial chambers, for instance, have pointed ceilings made of enormous limestone support beams, sometimes measuring from 10 to 15 meters (11 to 16 yards) in length and weighing from forty to eighty tons apiece. The design of the ceilings consists of three layers of massive beams that support one another and increase in size as they ascend.

Though these are not great pyramids, some have notable features. Userkaf's pyramid complex, located about 200 meters

(218 yards) from the northeast corner of Zoser's complex, exhibits beautiful reliefs in stone walls of the mortuary temple. And this type of fine artwork typifies Fifth Dynasty funerary complexes. Reliefs in the complexes of Sahure and Niuserre are even more elaborate. The reliefs in Sahure's complex alone were estimated originally to have covered about 10,000 square meters (2.47 acres) of wall surface.

Egyptologists cannot explain why the Egyptians of this period dedicated themselves to lavishing decorations on temple walls instead of concentrating on building great pyramids, nor can they explain why the workers resorted to removing blocks from previous monuments to complete their construction work. The reason, however, will become obvious. In Sahure's complex at Abusir, an interesting feature of the Valley Temple, now in ruin, is an underground drainage system. Copper pipes, more than 1,000 feet long, run under the paving of the temple, court, and entrance hall, then down the length of the causeway, 200 meters (218 yards), to an outlet on the southern side.

The remarkably small pyramid of Unas is notable for the thousands of engraved hieroglyphs, painted blue, that cover the vestibule and white limestone walls of the burial chamber. These inscriptions, known as the Pyramid Texts, constitute the world's oldest surviving religious writings. Egyptologists surmise that these sacred texts date to the earliest Egyptian times. The writings, compiled by the priests of Heliopolis, contain such archaic word forms, indicating extreme antiquity, as those praising Khnum, which are far more remote than the reign of Unas. Many portions preserved in Unas's pyramid are not repeated on the walls of later monuments.

The power of the king began to dissipate after the Fourth Dynasty. The Fifth Dynasty kings could not hope to command the same degree of power and prestige as predecessors who had built the Great Pyramids. The governors of nomes gained local power and this is believed to have diminished central authority. Kings started marrying the daughters of these rich, powerful governors apparently in an attempt to strengthen their own royal power.

Still, the times were prosperous, and despite some minor border skirmishes, the period was not characterized by war. Instead, the Fifth Dynasty is characterized by a revolution in art and literature. Trade flourished and there was an Egyptian fleet in the Mediterranean. At least four of the Fifth Dynasty kings are known to have sent expeditions to the Sinai. And royal expeditions sent to Nubia and Punt (Somaliland) brought back exotic goods. Why, with all of the prosperity, combined with the Egyptian's accumulated expertise in engineering, organizational, and other skills, was there a great decline in building?

It is difficult for Egyptologists to pinpoint the reason that Fifth Dynasty pyramids were built inferior to former structures. Most advocate that the reduced size is attributed to a decline in the civilization itself. This is not a valid explanation because scholars evaluate the decline of the civilization not by hard evidence, but by the lack of building. Some scholars conjecture that the building trend was due to the consumption of something that leaves no trace. All agree that there is no one simple explanation.

A simple, logical explanation comes to light with an understanding of how the pyramids were really built. The building decline was caused by a depletion of mineral resources. Industrial quantities of mafkat minerals were removed from the Sinai mines during the Third and Fourth Dynasties, especially by Sneferu and the next few kings to follow. The mines of Wadi Maghara had been exploited by such kings as Zanakht, Zoser, Sekhemkhet, Sneferu, and Khufu, who proudly planted their reliefs there. The only surviving record of Khufu's activities are the reliefs at Wadi Maghara, indicative of important mining expeditions. Sneferu heavily exploited the nearby mines of Serabit el-Khadim, where he was later worshipped by the local Sinai people. The decline was caused by the consumption of something quite traceable after all.

How else can the tremendous quantity of mafkat excavated in the Sinai be accounted for? The existence of great desert mining industries is well established. Expeditions yielded gold and silver, and semiprecious gems such as jasper, carnelian, and rock

FIGURE 57. *The only surviving record of the activities of Khufu are scenes engraved in the Sinai indicating vigorous mining expeditions.*

crystal. The major mineral outcrop in the Sinai was mafkat ores. The town of Gebtu (Coptos in Greek and Quift in modern times) was prominent throughout Egyptian history because of its geographical location closest to the Sinai. Mining operations were conducted by the army dispatched from Gebtu. The task force labored under Egyptian foremen in fortified camps along with the Sinai bedouins. Huge shipments of turquoise, green and blue malachite, and the other mafkat minerals listed in **Table II** were transported to Gebtu.

The exhaustive quantity of extracted mafkat is unaccounted for. Did it disappear through trade with other nations? Certainly the number of surviving jewelry items, amulets, and other artifacts made of or exhibiting turquoise and other blue or

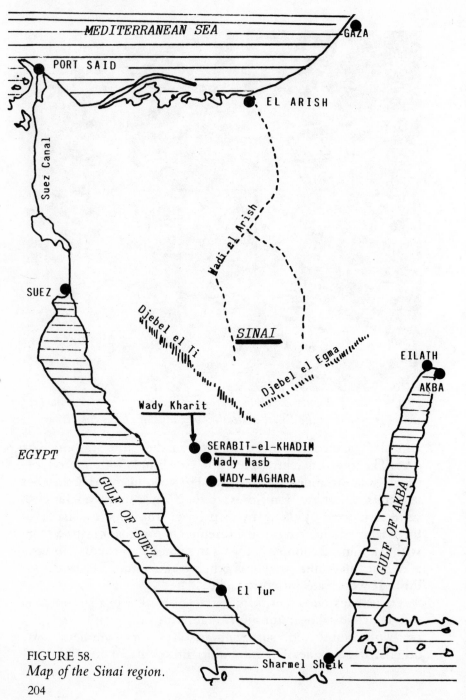

FIGURE 58.
Map of the Sinai region.

blue-green minerals is disproportionate to the amount of mafkat that was excavated. And artifacts found in regions known to have ancient trade with Egypt cannot account for the unusually high amount of mafkat extracted.

It has been estimated that more than 100,000 tons of mafkat ore were extracted, roughly the same as the amount of copper ore. If one assumes that mafkat made up ten percent of the cement, then the 100,000 tons would yield 1 million tons of cement. If one assumes that as much as ten percent of the pyramid limestone concrete is cement, then 1 million tons of cement would have yielded 10 million tons of limestone concrete. Because mafkat was only needed for high quality stone such as protective casing, the minerals from the Sinai mines would have served to build all of the pyramids and related stonework, such as interior and exterior casing stones, temples, capstones, and statuary.

If other minerals which react at ambient temperatures, such as opal (hydrated silicon oxide), flint, volcanic glass, and amorphous materials were added to the mafkat, a surplus of cement making material was certainly available. Copper slag from smelting also reacts at ambient temperatures with alkalis, for example, a combination of natron and lime. Slag could also have been used to increase cement yield.

By the Sixth Dynasty, Egypt was less powerful and the power of the kings seems no longer to have been absolute. The decline of architecture worsened and even artwork was adversely affected. Statues dating to the Fifth and Sixth Dynasties are relatively rare, and the finest date from the early Fifth Dynasty. In contrast, it was estimated through an analysis of fragments that almost 500 statues originally adorned the three Great Pyramid complexes at Giza, collectively. Sixth Dynasty kings were Teti, Pepi I, Merenre, and Pepi II. Their pyramids were constructed like those of the Fifth Dynasty kings. The surrounding funerary complexes and their reliefs, however, were far less elaborate.

High officials of this period undertook very ambitious, continuous foreign expeditions and quarry activities for which they

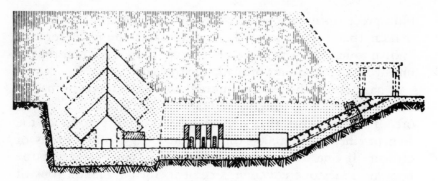

FIGURE 59. *Cross section of the pyramid of Teti shows enormous support beams.*

were better rewarded by the kings than were their counterparts in earlier times. The foreign expeditions, which yielded various goods, may have been motivated by the need for new mineral sources. If this were the case, the pharaohs would indeed have been extremely dependent on their administrators, explaining why such officials were allowed increased privileges and far more lavish tombs.

Accounts of ambitious foreign enterprises are inscribed in many tombs. Teti's officers visited Byblos, Nubia, and probably Punt, and exploited eastern desert quarries. Pepi I carried on these activities and extended forces to Palestine. Menenru recorded a visit to Elephantine to meet with Nubian chiefs to develop further trade. Menenra and Pepi I left their inscriptions at the depleting Sinai mining sites and apparently found sufficient minerals for producing stone for the most vital parts of their pyramids.

Objects found in Lebanon and bearing the name of Pepi II suggest a long, continuous trade in timber suitable for molds. Pepi II's pyramid was built better than most of this period, and it is relatively well preserved with some large limestone casing blocks still remaining on the western side. Of all the pharaohs, Pepi II would have had time to become Egypt's most prolific builder had the means been available. Extraordinarily, he reigned for ninety-four years, the longest reign in history.

Pepi II was to be the last great pharoah of the Old Kingdom.

Within a few years after his death, Egypt was no longer a united nation. The country was in a state of anarchy, lasting more than 200 years. Political and social revolution and high mortality rates characterize the epoch.

Having no proof, scholars speculate that the fall of the Old Kingdom was from long and continuous governmental mismanagement. Some scholars conjecture that erratic changes in climate produced food shortages against which the kings were powerless. Though such elements may be valid, consider that Egypt's economy became increasingly more depressed because of the erosion of its once enormous construction industry, which in time would jeopardize faith in government. Instead of the decline in the civilization causing the building decline, the opposite is more likely accurate.

The social disruption persisted from the Seventh through Tenth dynasties, called the First Intermediate Period. It appears that during the Seventh Dynasty ephemeral nobles of Memphis attempted to restore order and authority. According to inscriptions found at Gebtu, Eighth Dynasty kings of Memphis, also reigning for brief periods, extended control in Upper Egypt. Petty monarchs defended the nomes in which they resided not against foreign invaders, but against the many perils accompanying a breakdown in civilization.

The sparse monuments built during this era were made of poor-quality materials. Pottery replaced stone, metal, and faience in vessels. Structures never stood higher than 10 meters (10.9 yards), and most were left unfinished or have perished.

The town of Henen-Hesut (Heracleopolis) was the seat of government in Middle Egypt in the Ninth and Tenth Dynasties; the Thebans held control in the south. There was intermittent but intense fighting by these two factions until a Theban victory reunited Egypt in the Eleventh Dynasty, founding the period known as the Middle Kingdom. Thebes was established as the capital of Egypt and a king named Muntuhotep was enthroned.

He ambitiously reorganized the land and sent expeditions to Sinai, Nubia, Syria, and Lybia. It was in this time that a new royal building tradition was first effectively and dramatically used to bury a king.

CHAPTER 16

The Great Conflict

LIKE THOSE OF PREVIOUS STRUCTURES, THE SACRED MONO-
lithic sarcophagi, canopic chests, and rooms of limestone, granite, and other varieties of stone were often found intact in
Middle Kingdom pyramids and are of superb quality. In the
Twelfth Dynasty yet another remarkable feature was introduced
into pyramid construction. Egyptologists are hard pressed to
explain it.

All technologies have some degree of historical impact, and
the great stonemaking technology is hardly an exception. A
severe decline in any important technology strongly affects
social evolution. To understand how the abatement of stonemaking technology affected Egyptian civilization, one needs
only to imagine how radically a prolonged shortage of oil
would affect us in modern times. The decline of one technology
yields to the rise of another. In ancient Egypt, metallurgy, used
to produce improved stonecutting implements, gradually replaced alchemical stonemaking. In light of the abatement of the

old science, once misunderstood historical developments make perfect sense.

The Heracleopolitan dynasty was defeated around 2000 BC. It is generally assumed that no rival ideologies were involved in the power struggle that led to this war. A statement to this effect can be found in an authoritative *Encyclopaedia Britannica* discussion of Egyptian history. The Heracleopolitan defeat marked a critical point in history between factions fostering two distinctly different ideologies and also two different technologies. An overview shows that the history of Egypt actually takes on a whole new dimension.

The ruling family of Heracleopolis claimed to be the legitimate successors of the last great pharaoh, Pepi II. As such, their plan was to perpetuate ancestral religious traditions. Their goal was thwarted when the rival Theban prince, Mentuhotep, became the first king in more than 200 years to rule over a united Egypt.

The new king, born in the south, was devoted to southern culture with its Nubian influence. At this point in history, Mentuhotep's royal residence was a small provincial town, Waset, which the Greeks later called Thebai or Thebes. Memphis, the capital of Egypt since Archaic times, was replaced by this small, underdeveloped community. Mentuhotep concentrated building operations at Thebes and other parts of the south during a lengthy reign of fifty-one years. Though only a few monuments of Thebes can be dated to the latter part of the Old Kingdom, the town would rise to prominence during the Eleventh Dynasty.

As Mentuhotep's administration restored tranquillity throughout the land, the cult of the minor, local, Theban god, Amun, gained in influence. Though Thebes was Amun's only significant center of worship during early times, great antiquity could be claimed for the god. In line 558 of the Pyramid Texts of Unas's pyramid, Amun's name is surrounded by those of gods of remote antiquity, placing Amun among the primeval gods.

The Heracleopolitan rivals of the north preserved the ancient worship of Khnum. Various forms of Khnum were revered in Egypt, including Khnum-Ra, Khnum-Hapi, and Hershef. Heracleopolis, the setting for a number of significant mythological events, was the center of Khnum worship in the form of Hershef.

The doctrines of Khnum and Amun fostered fundamentally different religious philosophies. Documents dating from the Old Kingdom depict Khnum's doctrine, comparable to the biblical tradition advocating that humankind was created through an agglomeration of earth. In Khnum's tradition, the eternal bodies, or *kas,* represented by the king's statutes, were produced like the sacred eternal pyramids and temples, through an agglomeration of stone.

Nothing is known about the attributes or the form of Amun worship during the Old Kingdom. The doctrine of the Amun clergy, which was either preserved or which developed and emerged as the priesthood became Egypt's most powerful in later times, advocated a creative process different from that of Khnum, carving. Passages attributed to a Book of Thoth recount the relevant mythology:

> In the beginning, there was only the darkness of a watery abyss. There was only the darkness of the waters, and darkness lay over the waters, and there was no sign of life. Then out of the darkness of the waters oozed a mound of mud. The mound swelled, bubbled, and struggled, and took the form of the first god, Amun. And Amun tore off his limbs and all parts of his body, and these parts of the body of Amun were transformed into men, animals, and all of creation.

According to Theban mythology, sandstone and pink granite represented the body of Amun. Blocks of sandstone were quarried with great care so as not to injure the body of the deity. Obelisks made of Aswan granite were sometimes referred to as The Finger of Amun. After the introduction of bronze tools by the New Kingdom, statues were so piously quarried that the vivid chisel impressions in the quarries actually allowed Egyptologists to match statues to their place of origin.

In the soft sandstone hills of the western bank, opposite Karnak (el-Tarif), the Theban princes of the First Intermediate Period emulated their ancestors as they hollowed out their tombs. In the Memphite tradition, only common people were buried in a hollowed-out pit tomb. With Egypt under Theban rule, the common custom was followed to bury the imporant new king elaborately. Mentuhotep's chief architect selected the royal burial site in the northern part of the Theban necropolis at Deir el-Bahari. In a large, deep bay in the cliffs, the workers began hollowing out a vast tomb. Architects altered the plans several times until the final outcome was a new form of royal tomb, a mastaba temple.

The monument was approached by an open causeway about 1,200 meters (0.75 mile) long, extending through a formal grove of sycamore and tamarisk trees planted in rows of circular pits. A ramp approached the temple. Basically a large, rock-cut platform with some masonry filling, the temple rises in three terraces, the first two of which are partially furnished on the exterior with colonnades. The third terrace is surmounted by the remains of the most predominant feature, a ruined structure believed to have been a mastaba. It consisted of a core of rubble and flint boulders and was cased with two outer layers of limestone.

Initially, the structure was assumed to be the remains of a pyramid devoid of chambers or passages. Calculations by Dieter Arnold, however, determined that the terrace could not have withstood the weight of a pyramid. The mastaba temple style can be classified as a synthesis of Theban portico tombs and the ancient mastabas of Abydos. Abydos was an important burial ground beginning in the early dynastic period. It bordered the two rival territories and changed hands several times during fighting until recaptured by Mentuhotep.

Unlike Memphite burials, no mastabas were built for officials and nobles. Their tombs were hollowed from the soft rock of the vicinity. Instead of limestone, the statues of the king are sandstone. Certain features, including the mastaba, indicate a carry-over of the old tradition. This suggests a certain amount of religious compromise between the Thebans and Heracleopolitans and perhaps explains Mentuhotep's expeditions in the Sinai. Reliefs adorn the base of the temple, and some are crude whereas others are sophisticated, the latter believed to have been done by Memphite artisans. It is likely that some of the reliefs were carved and others agglomerated. The king's burial chamber was hollowed out of the hillside, yet it is lined with granite. No current data exist on the mineralogical composition of the limestone and granite to determine whether agglomerated stone is present.

Towering above the site is an unusual feature. On top of the western cliffs stands a pyramid said to be formed naturally. Anciently the pyramid was called the Holy Mountain or the Peak of the West. Today it is known as el-Quern, meaning "the horn" in Arabic. The curious pyramid overlooks the tombs of Deir el-Bahari and the Valley of the Kings.

No other tombs of the dynasty were completed. After the death of Mentuhotep's successor, a brief dark period of history passed when Egyptian again opposed Egyptian. When the confusion cleared, it appears that the last king of the Eleventh Dynasty, also named Mentuhotep, employed a man named Amenemhet (Amenemmes in Greek) as his vizier and as commander of the army. There are few clues about Amenemhet's knowledge and affiliations. However, he may have been associated with alchemical stonemaking, because he was chosen to obtain hard stone for the king's sarcophagus and its lid from quarries at Wadi el-Hammamat. He is believed to come from a prominent family of Elephantine and, therefore, would have been devoted to Khnum.

Almost nothing is known of the circumstances that brought him to the throne, although 10,000 men were under his command and the change was accompanied by some violence. Although his name shows an association with the Theban god, Amun, it appears that Amenemhet took the name to gain political acceptance. Once he was crowned king, Amenemhet I immediately reestablished dominion over most of the nome governors and moved the royal residence to a town near the old capital of Memphis called Ithtawi, not far from modern el-Lisht, which is in the vicinity of the Faiyum. He mined in the Sinai and built his pyramid in the nearby necropolis, returning as far as politically possible to Old Kingdom traditions.

His classical pyramid and complex are highly decorated in Old Kingdom style. The pyramid is called a museum of Old Kingdom art because it exhibits so many decorated blocks removed from monuments of Saqqara, Dahshur, and Giza. Some Egyptologists surmise that certain blocks were taken from the valley temples of Khufu and Khafra. The mortuary temple was decorated with relief drawings copied from the Old Kingdom.

Like the Sixth Dynasty pyramids, Amenemhet I's pyramid is made of masonry walls and a loose filling of rubble and sand, all reinforced with a casing of fine agglomerated limestone. Today it is in ruins with its enormous granite plugs remaining *in situ* and its burial chamber hopelessly submerged in water, caused by a significant rise in the level of the Nile bed.

Amenemhet I apparently promoted religious compromise, and Egyptologists recognize in his pyramid layout an influence of Mentuhotep's tomb because the causeway has no roof and the pyramid was built on rising ground. Its buildings are on two separate levels, the upper level supporting the pyramid itself. The levels have rows of tombs. About 100 mastabas of nobles and officials were built around the pyramid in the age-old tradition.

In addition to the design compromise, which in any case economized on the amount of stone required, Amenemhet I founded the great temple of Amun at Thebes and greatly increased Egypt's internal development. His name remained associated with Amun. Even with this level of compromise, the power struggle was not over.

In about the thirtieth year of his reign, Amenemhet I was murdered in his sleep one night by his chamberlains. At the time, his son, Senusert (Sesostris in Greek), was on a campaign in Libya. Realizing the conspirators' attempt to overturn the dynasty, Senusert gave orders to silence the news, then raced to the capital. Senusert successfully halted the takeover through swift action. After twenty years of rule, Amenemhet I had made his son co-ruler, and they had already ruled together for ten years. Amenemhet was the first to enact such a policy, which was adopted by Twelfth Dynasty successors and also by New Kingdom kings to help safeguard the dynasty during these times of political rivalry.

Senusert I, who would reign for another thirty-five years, sent expeditions to the Wadi Kharit mines in the Sinai and had his pyramid built near his father's at el-Lisht. The causeway was built of fine white limestone and the mortuary temple replicated those of the Sixth Dynasty. The remarkable interior of the pyramid is made of walls that radiate like spokes from the center of the structure to form compartments. These are reinforced with mud brick and stone rubble. Two layers of heavy casing of fine agglomerated limestone reinforced the entire structure, some of which remains on the western side. The passage descending to the burial chamber, also submerged in water, is lined with perfectly fitting red granite slabs. Near the pyramid are two interesting mastabas belonging to high priests of Memphis and of Heliopolis; the latter carried forth the name Imhotep and was probably a descendant.

Sensusert I carried on the religious compromise. He beautified Heliopolis with a magnificent Sun temple and obelisks. One of the latter is the only thing standing at the site. His architects energetically built monuments throughout the land, not neglecting Thebes. Investigations to determine which monuments were carved and which were cast would provide relevant insight about this political period.

His son, Amenemhet II, also maintained the old traditions, but there was further critical decline in stonemaking technology. Amenemhet II's pyramid at Dahshur appears to have been made almost entirely of mud brick. It is believed that casing blocks were taken from the Northern Pyramid of Seneferu in the vicinity, because roads dating from Amenemhet II's time link the two monuments. However, not a single casing stone was found during excavation. The pyramid is in such total

215

ruin that its dimensions can only be estimated. It is striking that 1,000 years after Imhotep, Amenemhet II, during times of prosperity, found it necessary to resort to building almost entirely in mud brick.

The next ruler was Senusert II, who built a mud-brick pyramid at el-Lahen, now in ruins. Entering the granite burial chamber, Petrie found an exquisite red granite sarcophagus that amazed him. He called it one of the finest pieces of work ever executed in such a difficult, hostile material. He calculated its parallelism to be almost perfect, with errors in form equaling no more than 0.01 cubit (⅙ inch).

The king's successor, Senusert III, was one of the greatest pharaohs of the Middle Kingdom. He built his mud-brick pyramid at Dahshur. The structure, now in ruins, was cased with limestone blocks and red granite was used for its exquisite burial chamber and sarcophagus.

This pharaoh energetically expanded Egypt's southern territory and completed several projects started by his great- great-grandfather, Amenemhet I. In the First Cataract region, Senusert III expanded channels for the passage of ships, and in the region of the Second Cataract he enlarged a series of mud-brick forts to help secure the southern borders. Above the Third Cataract, he established permanent garrisons and customs ports. He fortified Egypt's usual routes in and out of the country along the northeastern frontier with large mud-brick walls to regulate the entry of foreigners.

Since the beginning of the dynasty, the kings' envoys made regular trading missions to Syria. Contact with Syria, Palestine, and parts of Asia were mostly peaceful. Trade flourished, but there was also some conflict. The need arose for the pharaoh to enact sweeping government reforms, which secured the power of the throne and the administrative capital at Ithtawi.

It was a time of prosperity when literature and the arts flourished. Agricultural progress increased, with much effort spent on irrigating large tracks of land in the Faiyum. The land recovery program converted the district into one of Egypt's most bountiful. Like his father and grandfather before him,

Senusert III mined vigorously in the Sinai, expending more
effort but obtaining far less mafkat even though during this era
metal tools replaced flint for ore extraction. Documents show
that several expeditions were unsuccessful.

Senusert III is also known for defeating a stronghold of rival
monarchs at Hermopolis, the town where Amun was one of the
primeval group of eight deities, or ogdoad. Like the pharaohs,
the defiant monarchs of Hermopolis dated Egyptian events to
their own years of rule. They maintained fleets of ships and
armed forces. Artisans of this town, carrying on their religious
tradition, carved the great colossus of their ruler Djehutihotep
from soft alabaster quarried at Hatnub. It is a bas-relief in the
tomb of this ruler, depicting the transport of the great colossus,
that I call false proof of Egyptology 2. We see that the techniques of rivals of the pyramid-building pharaohs have been
used as proof of how the pyramids were built.

Favorable conditions had been set up for the brilliant forty-
six year reign of the next pharaoh, Amenemhet III. This great
pharaoh is not remembered for campaigns or reforms but for
outstanding art and construction. The classical historians credit
him with producing the large Lake Moeris in the Faiyum region. Though it is not as large today, the lake gleamed silver
with fish and was so large that it tempered hot winds blowing in
from the west, creating a balmy climate. The lake transformed
the surrounding area into a garden paradise of lush vegetation.
Scholars wonder if the lake existed earlier, but they don't question the pharaoh's involvement with one of Egypt's truly great
memorials, the fabulous Labyrinth in the Faiyum, at Hawara.

This monument must have been one of the most intricate,
splendid design wonders of Egypt, with its many doors and
confusing maze of winding, connecting passageways that
would have confounded any visitor. In modern times only
scanty remains of limestone rubble covering an enormous surface area represent the Labyrinth. Every stone has been broken
up and removed.

Fortunately, its confounding intricate maze of passages and
other features were described by both Herodotus and Strabo,

who saw it. Strabo described it as a vast, one-story building with huge pillars and massive, monolithic blocks making up the roofs of its numerous rooms. Herodotus said the building surpassed description and was astonished as he passed from the courts to the chambers, from the chambers to colonnades, and then to other rooms and courts. He viewed only the ground level, for he said he was not allowed to see the galleries below ground. He saw twelve vast-walled courts, six facing north and six facing south, and claimed that the building comprised 3,000 rooms, half above and half below ground.

Possibly, to construct the Labyrinth, the builders carved the soft, white limestone found at Tura. If, however, the monument was made of hard limestone, it is doubtful that the blocks were carved. Bronze was just beginning to appear in Egypt. A statue of Amenemhet III is bronze, but bronze apparently had not been used for tools. In a subsequently built pyramid, models of copper tools were found. Instead, the blocks probably were removed from older structures to build the Labyrinth. Stone monuments and artifacts remaining today are a mere fraction of what was produced in Egypt's long history, so there is no question that sufficient ready-made stone would have been available. Instead of using the available blocks to build the king's pyramid, which would require heavy lifting to great heights, for which there were no easy means, the architects constructed the single-story Labyrinth.

At the end of the Labyrinth was the finest pyramid ever made of mud brick, the pyramid of Amenemhet III. This pyramid has a truly remarkable feature. Unlike other mud-brick pyramids, Amenemhet III's pyramid at Hawara has not decomposed, although 3,800 years have passed. Why? Because there was an innovation in Khnum's technology. Khnum was held in the highest religious regard by Amenemhat III, as shown by a text attributed to one of his administrators:

> . . . I am addressing these important words to you and I count on you to understand them. . . . Venerate the King in your body, that he might live forever, and be faithful in your souls to His Majesty.

He is the intelligence in the hearts (of men) and his gaze penetrates all bodies. He is Ra by the rays by which one sees. It is he who illuminates the two earths (better still than) the solar disc. . . . He feeds those who serve him and he submits to the needs of those who follow his road. The King is Ka and his word is life. Whosoever be born is his work, for he is (the god) Khnum from whom come all the bodies, the progenitor. . . ."

At this point in history, Amun's clergy had not gained sufficient power to proclaim Amun as the progenitor. It was Khnum who created mankind, through an agglomeration process. To perpetuate the ancient rite of agglomeration, bricks were made for the eternal pyramid by mixing caustic soda (natron, lime, water) with mud from Lake Moeris. Partly because of the mineralogical composition of the mud, their efforts were most effective.

In the interior of the pyramid, a complex system of galleries concealed access to the burial chamber. The architects designed uncanny corridor arrangements, with dummy corridors leading to dead ends. Enormous sliding slabs, a trap door, and false burial shafts were incorporated to hide any structural clues that could reveal the true burial chamber entrance.

Petrie entered the pyramid and made his way through the devious maze of corridors. Much water had entered the pyramid and the passages were so blocked with mud that he had to slide through naked, all the time feeling for artifacts with his toes. He was astounded at what he found when he reached the burial chamber. This extraordinary structure was made of a single piece of yellow quartzite. If the block was carved, it would have weighed originally about 110 tons. Petrie wrote:

> The sepulchre is an elaborate and massive construction. The chamber itself is a monolith 267.5 inches [6.8 meters] long, 94.2 inches [2.4 meters] wide and 73.9 inches [1.9 meters] high to the top of the enormous block with a course of bricks 18.5 inches [0.5 meters] high upon that. The thickness of the chamber is about 25 inches [0.6 meters]. It would accordingly weigh about 110 tonnes [metric tons]. The workmanship is excellent; the sides are flat and regular,

and the inner corners so sharply wrought that—though I looked at them—I never suspected that there was not a joint there until I failed to find any joints in the sides.

Petrie was referring to the original mass when he estimated the weight of the block, because the chamber itself weighs seventy-two metric tons. If this chamber was carved, the work would have required precision tooling, inside and out, on a solid mass of hard quartzite, the hardest type of rock. This is the type of artifact that has added fuel to theories advocating the existence of ultramodern machinery and super Space Age sciences during antiquity. Petrie could not explain its manufacture. Lowering the enormous structure into the confined space would have been the least of the difficult problems. If the mass was quarried, the quarry site should remain. Egypt's quartzite quarries show no signs of quarrying blocks or statues according to members of the Napoleonic expedition, who made a thorough investigation of Egypt's quartzite ranges. On the other hand, loose, weathered quartzite is available in great quantities near all quartzite quarries, and was ready for agglomeration.

Another mud-brick pyramid with a complex interior arrangement, called the Unfinished Pyramid, was built nearby and is tentatively assigned to one of Amenemhet III's successors. If carved, the monolithic block used to produce the burial chamber would originally have weighed a massive 180 tons. Yet, it is this pyramid that contained the small models of copper tools mentioned earlier.

Amenemhet III also built a mud-brick pyramid at Dahshur with a similar interior design, which is now in ruins though still standing. Its summit was crowned by a magnificent pyramidion made of lovely dark-gray granite and now in the Cairo Museum. Some Egyptologists surmise that because of structural weaknesses, Amenemhet III abandoned the structure and built at Hawara, where he was presumably buried. His death marked the end of the Middle Kingdom.

At Mazghuna, about three miles south of Dahshur, two ruined mud-brick pyramids are attributed tentatively to

Amenemhet III's Twelfth Dynasty successors. Reasons for the Twelfth Dynasty overturn are uncertain. Pharaohs of the Thirteenth Dynasty maintained their capital in the north, and a few managed to build mud-brick pyramids. One pyramid attributed to Khendjer, built at Saqqara, contains a monolithic burial room made of hard quartzite that would have weighed about sixty tons if it were carved from a single block.

In the Thirteenth Dynasty, which lasted about 150 years, about seventy kings ruled in rapid succession. At the end of the Thirteenth Dynasty, or perhaps a little later, the land again passed through a severe, dark time, known as the Second Intermediate Period. This period differed from the former anarchical period. This time trouble erupted from political division coupled with foreign intrusion.

The nebulous history of the period leaves the method of takeover unclear, but the enemy, a vast ethnic movement, came to be known as the Hyksos or Shepherd Kings. Some historians describe them as an avalanche of conquering, nomadic Semitic hordes, basing themselves in Palestine or Turkey and finally sweeping into Egypt in the hundreds of thousands. In this scenario, their front lines advanced in horse-drawn chariots carrying troops wielding weaponry made of hard bronze, all of which (bronze weapons, horses, and wheeled vehicles) were viciously introduced to Egypt for the first time. Memphis was seized and thousands of armed troops spread out, swarming the land, demolishing the temples, and wreaking destruction everywhere their chariots rolled. The Jewish historian Josephus (Flavius Josephus AD 37?–100) reported the Egyptian plight, based on an account by Manetho:

> During the reign of one of our kings, whose name was Timarus, it came to pass, I know not how, that God was displeased with us, and men came from the eastern lands and were bold enough to enter our country and subdue it by force, without our daring a battle with them. Once they subjected our rulers, they burned our cities and demolished the temples of the gods. They treated all of our inhabitants barbarously; they slew many men and led their

children and wives into slavery. At length, when they had proclaimed one of themselves king, whose name was Salatis and who lived in Memphis, they made both the upper and lower regions pay tribute, and they built garrisons where ever they pleased. . . . He [the Hyksos king] rebuilt Avaris with very strong walls around it and an enormous garrison of two hundred and forty thousand armed men guarding it.

Many historians consider Manetho's account to have been inspired by Persian and Assyrian invasions of his time, so they largely discount it. Instead of a sudden victory, they see the takeover as evolving from a confederation of tribes encroaching the power of Egypt after continuing to concentrate in the Nile delta in ever-increasing numbers.

We know that as early as the First Intermediate Period, Semites from Palestine started settling in the delta region. Their numbers mushroomed in the Twelfth and Thirteenth Dynasties. The immigrants were absorbed into the lower levels of Egyptian society and gradually advanced socially. By the Thirteenth Dynasty they saturated the eastern Delta, and at least one pharaoh, Khendjer, was of this ethnic stock.

During the critical period, the north and south were divided, with one dynasty ruling at Thebes and another in the western Delta. Perhaps this split eliminated the possibility of resistance, or perhaps the Thebans simply looked the other way while the Hyksos overtook the north. Whatever the case, Thebes was spared injury and the Hyksos allowed the Theban kings to coexist. Historians suspect, based on surviving names of princesses, that the Hyksos and Thebans were related by marriage.

Once established, the Hyksos kings adopted the formal trappings of an Egyptian king. Like the Egyptian pharaohs, they enclosed their Egyptian throne names in cartouches but maintained their distinctive personal names, such as Jacob-El, Khyan, and Anath-her. They maintained the worship of Ra of Heliopolis and revered Sutekh (Seth), an Egyptian war god comparable to their Baal.

Over time, bronzeworking was adopted by the southerners, and they acquired the horse-drawn chariot, composite bow, new types of swords, scimitars, daggers, and other items introduced by the Hyksos. As Theban kings grew more confident, they also grew less tolerant of foreign rulers and became more and more ready to use the Hyksos own type of weaponry against them. By the Seventeenth Dynasty, they rose in battle, resuming their former struggle to dominate Egypt. For many years, intermittent skirmishes with the Hyksos were futile. Finally, around 1570 BC, the Hyksos fell under the fury of Thebes.

The death blow was dealt by Amosis, the liberating pharaoh who virtually founded the Eighteenth Dynasty and the New Kingdom with his victory. His troops attacked the Hyksos by surprise, pursuing them all the way to Palestine. There, barricaded Hyksos were besieged with an unmerciful vengeance for three years, until Egypt was satisfied that they were either destroyed or captured. It was clear that Egypt was again a mighty power.

At home, Amosis quelled a rebellion, and put his Hyksos captives to work cutting stone in the quarries of Tura with their own bronze implements. The stele of Amosis, formerly at Tura, is qualified as False Proof of Egyptology 4. It depicts the first known instance of quarrying stone with bronze tools.

Amosis extended Egyptian territory from the Second Cataract to parts of Palestine, and Thebes became Egypt's primary town, with Amun the hero god of Egypt. As the Eighteenth Dynasty progressed, the Egyptian civilization reached its zenith, and Thebes became the commercial and cultural center of the world. The Amun clergy became so powerful that they acquired for Amun all of the attributes of Egypt's other gods, and he was usually depicted as Amun-Ra.

All New Kingdom kings were buried in rock-cut tombs, with the most important ones hidden in the Valley of the Kings. For the sixty-two persons found buried there, only one pyramid was associated with their burial. But it was theirs only to share. Dominating their tombs from 1,000 feet above, stands the curious pyramid, the Holy Mountain (el-Quern).

Neither the religio-political struggle nor the stonemaking

technology came to an end during the New Kingdom. For the most part, however, New Kingdom temples were built with carved soft sandstone, and regardless of the political gains of New Kingdom pharaohs seeking to revive Khnum worship, no pyramid was ever again erected in the sands of Egypt.

CHAPTER 17

Closing the Knowledge Gap

HOW MUCH MORE ADVANCED OUR CIVILIZATION MIGHT BE today if there had been a continuum of science from antiquity instead of the destruction of knowledge by war, civil unrest, religious intolerance, and other circumstances. The burning of the Great Library of Alexandria, reputed at one time to hold about 900,000 manuscripts, is a classical example of the destruction of information. Most written works by pre-Socratic scholars have not survived. A few of the scholars are remembered only by their great reputations, and some are represented through fragments in classical literature.

In our own "Information Age," even general knowledge is not flawlessly transmitted. For example, most contemporary history books credit Pythagoras with discovering that the earth is round, but, as shown by Herodotus's *Melpomene,* this knowledge existed in ancient Egypt during the reign of Pharaoh Necho II (610–595 BC), who lived before Pythagoras (c. 582–507 BC):

. . . As for me, I cannot help but laugh when I hear the people who have given descriptions of the circumference of the Earth, claiming, without allowing themselves to be guided by reason, that the Earth is round, as if it had been shaped on a potter's wheel; that the ocean surrounds all of its parts. . . . As for Libya [during Herodotus's time the entire African continent was known as Libya], it is surrounded by the sea except for where it is joined to Asia. Nechos, the king of Egypt, was the first to our knowledge to have demonstrated this. When he ceased the construction of the canal joining the waters of the Nile to the Arabian Gulf [Red Sea], he sent a Phoenician crew with orders to sail around and return to Egypt through the Mediterranean Sea by way of the Pillars of Hercules [Strait of Gibraltar]. The Phoenicians navigated from the Red Sea to the Austral Sea [Indian Ocean] and every autumn they docked on the Libyan coast and sowed wheat, then waited for their harvest. Having collected their grain, they returned to sea again, and after two years they passed the Pillars of Hercules and in the third year returned to Egypt. The men had claimed, though I do not believe the statements they made, that in sailing westerly around the southern extent of Libya that the Sun was on their right.

A true historian, Herodotus documented the report of the circumnavigation of Africa and its cosmographic implications despite his own belief in the possibility of a spherical world. The reported position of the Sun, which rose on the right once the fleet passed the equator, upholds the authenticity of the voyage and affords an accurate calculation of the shape of the earth. It was not until 2,000 years later that the general European populace slowly began to realize that they were living on a spherical world after the New World was discovered by Columbus in early Renaissance times.

The knowledge may have been taken for granted by learned astronomers and cosmographers of Babylon and Heliopolis. The Greeks held extraordinary reverence for the Egyptian sages, and Pythagoras, who visited Egypt and Babylon as a young man, may have been tutored in these lands. Today, some contemporary encyclopedias suggest that the dimensions of the Great Pyramid incorporate information on the spherical shape and size of the earth.

Other lost or obscured knowledge is exemplified by ancient products and processes that are little understood today. Some were mentioned in Chapter 1, and those not already explained will be covered in this chapter. The products of antiquity in question are the result of ancient chemistry or alchemy. Understanding them helps to close the knowledge gap between ancient and modern science, and some of the recovered technology can help solve complex modern problems. This is our main objective at the Institute for Applied Archaeological Sciences (IAPAS), which I founded at Barry University near Miami, Florida, in 1984. Before considering the ancient technology, let us take a brief look at the history of alchemy from a broader historical perspective than ever before possible.

History recognizes that the birthplace of alchemy was ancient Egypt and that alchemy flourished in Alexandria in the Hellenistic period. Though Arabic, Indian, and other forms of alchemy are outgrowths of the old Egyptian science, scholars have been unable to approach the origins of alchemy with certitude. It now becomes clear that Hellenistic alchemy and its outgrowths were descendants of the alchemical processes of Khnum. This opens new avenues for exploring the relationship between the alchemy of pre-Alexandrian Egyptian and western Europe. The root of the word alchemy, "chemy," is uncertain but can be traced clearly to Khnum. Hellenistic alchemy was especially kindled by documents such as the Famine Stele relating to Imhotep and Khnum. The rise of alchemy that historians recognize in Alexandria was actually the rebirth of alchemy under the Ptolemies.

Why is the founder of alchemy considered to be Hermes Trismegistus, the Ptolemaic equivalent of the Egyptian god Thoth, instead of Khnum? The influence of Khnum made a brief resurgence during the New Kingdom, but the power of Amun was paramount. The knowledge of Khnum, however, was retained in the Books of Thoth. And Thoth gained prestige under the dominion of Amun, because Thoth was the god of Hermopolis, where Amun was one of the primeval ogdoad. This explains why the knowledge of Khnum was held in the library of Hermopolis, the seat of political rivalry during the Middle Kingdom.

As Amun became more powerful, his clergy usurped for him all of the attributes of the other Egyptian gods, and the influence of Amun is seen even in alchemical literature. The name Amun, for instance, is the root of the word ammonia. Sal ammoniac (ammonium chloride), a product crucial to alchemists attempting to transmute baser metals into gold, literally means the salt of Amun. The whole notion of transmutating baser metals to gold may reflect the extent of the influence on alchemy of Amun, the god presiding over metallurgy. In addition, translation errors from old Egyptian texts into Greek or Arabic may account for the belief that base metals could be transmuted into gold.

Is the legendary Philosopher's Stone, the agent believed to transmute baser metals into gold and to prolong life indefinitely, synonymous with the pyramid stone? The Philosopher's Stone had various names in many languages. Zosimos of Panopolis, an early Hellenistic alchemist, called it The Tincture. Some Hellenistic alchemists also called it The Powder. The Arab alchemists called it the Elixir of Life. With science and philosophy united as one body of knowledge, the substance later became known to western European alchemists as the Philosopher's Stone and sometimes just The Stone. But its various names always characterize the pyramid stone, because they are usually associated with some form of minerals, liquid, or stone.

There is no doubt about its inorganic nature, and mysterious descriptions in alchemical literature, such as "a stone which is not a stone," now become perfectly clear. It also becomes clear why alchemists commonly ascribed alchemical works to Khufu or another great personality of Egyptian antiquity who was involved with alchemical stonemaking.

When Empedocles influenced the alchemical doctrine by proposing that air, earth, fire, and water composed all matter, he recognized these elements in the primeval Egyptian gods of creation. The link between the creation beliefs of the Old Testament authors and the mythology of Khnum were pointed out in Chapter 9. Other profound esoteric implications involving alchemy will be discussed in the future.

Perhaps, slightly before the full-blown rebirth of alchemy in Alexandria, a school of alchemy was developing in China. There alchemy was practiced mostly by Taoists who believed that physical immortality was possible through alchemical means. There are many Chinese stories of immortality. Centuries before minerals were used for medicinal purposes by alchemists in western Europe, Taoistic alchemists prepared medicines with minerals in an attempt to prevent aging.

Experiments made in an attempt to discover the Elixir led to the discovery of porcelain and gunpowder. Too, alchemical methods for preserving the deceased were clearly in an advanced state by the second century BC, as exemplified by the Lady of Tai's coffin mentioned in Chapter 1.

Mysteries of the ancient world unfold as we understand more about ancient technology. The challenge to the age of the Sphinx, which centers on the question of the damaging water's source is an example. The large amount of water at the site can be explained easily by the fact that the limestone of Giza was disaggregated *in situ* with water to construct the monuments of Giza.

The so-called pyramid power issue is also settled. Wheat, which is thousands of years old, has been found in good condition stored in stone vessels within pyramids. Though germination was unsuccessful, researchers attempted germination because of the excellent condition of the grain. Well-preserved flowers and other organic materials have also been found. The popular theory of pyramid power, which attributes preservation, in part, to the shape of the pyramid, resembles teachings of the Pythagorean school, which ascribed special attributes to numbers and geometrical shapes. The real secret lies in chemistry.

The principle is this: the pyramid stone is based on the synthesis of zeolites, secondary rock-forming minerals that readily gain and loose moisture. The water absorbed, ten to twenty percent by weight of the zeolite, is easily released when heat is applied. The zeolites, therefore, allow pyramids, or any vessel made of geopolymeric material, to store organic material through harmony with natural atmospheric heat and moisture.

The Nile valley is characterized by extreme dryness during the day. At night the humidity level rises. The zeolitic pyramid stone absorbs humidity at night or any time the humidity rises. During the day, the material absorbs calories from the atmosphere, which has been heated by the Sun, and the previously absorbed humidity evaporates. In the stored material, this exchange maintains a temperature that is constant with that of the atmosphere. It eliminates sweating on the inner walls of the structure and, therefore, mold growth. The material provides for an exchange of humidity from the interior of the structure to the exterior—in other words, automatic humidity and temperature control. There is no renewal of oxygen in a hermetically sealed vessel or chamber, and the material has more than adequate strength to prevent invasion from gnawing insects and rodents. These parameters combined with the longevity of geopolymeric materials provide ideal conditions for storage.

The zeolitic makeup of geopolymers also explains the method of desalination attributed to the pots described by Pliny. He called the method "remedying unfit water," but the chemical process involved is called ion exchange today. A more sophisticated method of ion exchange is widely used in water softening today. In the chemical reaction at work in the vessels, ions, electrically charged atoms or groups of atoms, were reversibly transferred between the vessel and the salt water, allowing only salt-free water to enter the vase.

The vessels Pliny described would have behaved in exactly the same manner as would the 8,000-year-old white lime vessels from Tel-Ramad, Syria. The fragments I examined contain up to forty-one percent of analcime, one of the many zeolites capable of ion exchange with solutions.

Zeolites were synthesized in the Near and Middle East 8,000 years ago and more to produce chemical reactions now known as geopolymeric. Why were geopolymeric chemical reactions not developed by modern science earlier? The reason is that mineralogy has been neglected by industry. Until developments in recent years, there were no extraordinary breakthroughs in the cement, glass, and ceramic industries for 150 years.

Since the synthesis of urea in the 1800s, industry invested in research and development of organic chemistry, yielding dye stuffs, drugs, plastics, synthetic fibers, and the like. Industry considered mineralogy useful mostly for classifying rocks and minerals and for producing synthetic jewels, but though analysis of rocks serves to classify them, their major elements were studied primarily. About ten percent of a stone is made up of mineral elements that bind that stone together. This ten percent is what interests me, and when I first began my chemical research in mineralogy, there was absolutely no competition. The five to ten percent of mineral elements binding the pyramid blocks, though different from the micritic cement in the bedrock, is every bit as effective.

Another explainable issue is the discrepancy between the dates provided by the recent carbon-14 dating of the pyramids with those historically established. Mortar sampling was carefully performed by the ARCE team for the project sponsored by the Edgar Cayce Foundation. The latter group hoped to date the pyramids to 10,000 BC, the date provided for the construction of the Great Pyramid by Edgar Cayce, a well-known reputed psychic.

The November/December 1985 issue of *Venture Inward* carried an article describing how the samples were taken and other aspects of the project. In a follow-up article titled "The Great Pyramid Reveals Her Age," appearing in 1986 in the same publication, ARCE team member Mark Lehner remarked:

> You can look at this almost like a bell curve, and when you cut it down the middle you can summarize the results by saying, "Our dates are 400 to 450 years too early for the Old Kingdom pyramids, especially those of the Fourth Dynasty." . . . . The discrepancy here is in hundreds of years, not in 8,000 years, but it's really significant and everybody is excited about it.

When asked if he thought established chronology was wrong, Lehner said he thought they could be wrong within 400 or 500 years, dating the Great Pyramid to about 3100 BC instead of to the Fourth Dynasty at 2650 BC. Lehner, et al, have since published a report in the *British Archaeological Report International,* Series 379, in which the average difference is 374 years older, instead of 400 to 450 years.

When these articles were brought to my attention, I realized their problem, which I explained in a letter sent to three administrators of the Edgar Cayce Foundation, though I never received a reply. The problem is one of contamination, not through careless sampling, but because of chemical makeup. One of the ingredients used to make the mortar is natron (sodium carbonate), which contains carbon. The actual date of the geological formation of the natron in the samples is uncertain, and very small quantities dramatically affect the age evaluated by carbon-14 dating. Carbon dating could only produce such illogical results as the mortar at the top of the Great Pyramid dating older than that at the bottom. The illogical dates obtained for some of their samples suggest that established chronology is off from 200 to 1,200 years. Although the charcoal and reeds found in the mortar were subjected to acid leaching to remove carbon contamination prior to the dating process, there is no pretreatment that can eliminate contamination due to a concentrated alkaline solution of sodium or potassium carbonate. The scientific literature describes several cases of error in dating aquatic plants that grew in hard water lakes similar to the Egyptian lakes where natron was harvested. Calcined trees and reeds from a natron lake typically date older. In addition, cellulose fibers are known to chemically react with the highly alkaline sodium carbonate. Because it is highly porous, charcoal absorbs not only a great deal of natron solution, but also a lot of carbon dioxide, resulting from the decomposition of natron.

How are Egyptologists reacting to my theory of pyramid construction? Will this presentation convince them? Have all of the mysteries of pyramid construction been solved by my research? The examples of Egyptian artifacts previously presenting baffling problems are numerous: the man-made sandstone statuettes of the Thinite epoch examined by Le Chatelier; hard stone vases with long, thin necks and bulbous bellies that no known tool could have produced; the diorite statue of Pharaoh Khafra supposedly carved with stone or copper tools; other hard stone statues with inlaid eyes; monolithic stone sarcophagi situated in confined spaces disallowing their ingress and egress; heavy portcullises situated in spaces in pyramids too small to accommodate the manpower required for lifting them; huge, perfectly formed monolithic burial rooms made of extremely hard stone materials in Twelfth Dynasty pyramids; the seven-story high Colossi of Memnon exhibiting inscriptions that are impossible to produce through carving and which, though originally monolithic were not (based on de Roziere's examination of the quartzite quarries) quarried in monolithic form; coatings and cements lasting for thousands of years though some were exposed to blistering sunlight and harsh sandstorms through the ages; great temples with blocks too enormous to move; and most popular and conspicuous of all, the massive Great Pyramid structures themselves, each built during the reign of a pharaoh, with their casing stones exhibiting no tool marks and fitting as to closely as 0.002 inch. The problems these and other artifacts posed became increasingly more baffling and complex as scientific methods of investigation improved.

The quantity of popular books generated in the last fifteen years about the mysteries of the pyramids and other ancient feats of engineering demonstrate the ongoing quest for a solution. Few Egyptologists take part in this quest. They are willing to accept standard, inadequate explanations of the enigmatic artifacts and are mostly satisfied with logistical studies on the pyramids. However, the problems of logistics accompanying the carving and hoisting theory prove to be larger in scope than has been studied so far. In fact, based on the uniform sizes of pyramid blocks and Klemm's study concluding that the stone used for the Great Pyramid was quarried from all over Egypt, the problems are insurmountable.

Klemm's study is only a few years old, and my study of Khafra's pyramid is preliminary and should be verified with on-site measurements, so neither has been considered in a logistical study. The measurements of Coutelle and le Pere of the Napoleonic expedition, however, show that many of the largest stones in the Great Pyramid are situated thirty stories high. These measurements, obtained 150 years ago are rarely acknowledged. The problems calculated by Dieter Arnold, who proposed doubling or tripling the life span of pharaohs, merely leave the subject open for debate among Egyptologists, that is, debate based on the carving theory. And Le Chatelier's revelation of 100 years ago was never applied to other artifacts, even though the use of man-made stone should have been considered as a possible explanation to the age-old riddle of pyramid construction.

Though the standard theory is speculative, with no scientific merit, from every perspective, engineering logistics, geo-chemistry and geology, Egyptology and other history, feasibility and common sense, all of the mysteries of pyramid construction dissolve when the casting theory is applied.

Engineering and Logistics

Every so often we read about another clever lifting device being proposed as a solution to the riddle of pyramid construction. Demonstrations of simple, effective methods of pounding or otherwise tooling stone also arise. Interesting in and of themselves, such devices and methods are inapplicable if scientific analyses of the stone in question indicate a man-made agglomerate. My research has established a whole new criterion for evaluating stone artifacts, which is especially applicable for those exhibiting no tool marks.

From an engineering perspective, when applying the casting method, we understand how enormous blocks were placed at great heights to build the Great Pyramids using the technology of the Pyramid Age. We understand how the tiers of the Great Pyramids were made level and their faces absolutely flat, each meeting to form perfect summits. We understand how 500-ton blocks were placed in temples. We understand how casing blocks were applied with great precision in the Great Pyramids without even slightly chipping the corners. We can dismiss from our minds the absurd scenario of numerous thousands of workers crowded onto the work site at Giza shoulder to shoulder, with many struggling to raise enormous blocks to great heights.

Geology and Geochemistry

From a geochemical viewpoint, we understand why the pyramid stone does not and could not possibly chemically or mineralogically match the stone of Egyptian quarries. We understand the unusual textural characteristics and density pattern of the pyramid stones, the lift lines in enormous blocks, and why the rough core blocks in the Great Pyramids of Giza do not conform to the local strata even though petrographers can show that the stone originated at the site. We also know that the jumbled nummulitic shells in the pyramid blocks cannot be accounted for geologically and, therefore, indicate that the pyramid blocks are concrete.

Feasibility and Logic

Whereas the carving and hoisting theory is a dead, impractical theory that leads only to riddles, we understand why casting stone satisfied all issues of feasibility and logic. It makes good sense.

Egyptology and Other History

In 1978, I discovered that Pliny's description of the murrhine vases was mistranslated. That was 145 years after the publication of the Panckook edition of *Natural History* in 1833, resulting from the translations of the French Academy of Sciences. How long it will take for my corrected translation to be ac-

235

cepted remains to be seen. And Pliny's text is in Latin, a language used and understood by many scholars. With fewer expert Egyptian hieroglyphic linguists, identifying and redeciphering relevant texts will take longer.

I am certain that, other than the Famine Stele, hieroglyphic texts exist and contain information about the alchemical stone-making process of Khnum, but are mistranslated. As is stated in the Hermetic writings, "Hermes . . . used to say that those who read my books find them clear and very easy to understand . . . whereas they will become absolutely abstruse when the Greeks translate them from Egyptian into their language, and this will yield a complete distortion of the original text and a complete misunderstanding of its meaning."

When hieroglyphic and cuneiform texts describing metallurgic processes were first translated, thanks to the decipherments of Champollion and Grotefend, metallurgists and chemists were consulted to ensure correctness of technical words and information. Whereas careful translations were carried out with the help of experts from appropriate scientific disciplines, such translations may not be possible for a long time with texts involving geopolymerization because of the time it will take to produce experts in this field. In fact, it may take several years before experts and organizations involved with Egyptology recognize projects dealing with this topic as valid.

Historians must depend on information derived from Egypt's ecology, geography, artifacts, and inscriptions, the latter of which are known often to be ritual. Very little of Egypt's actual history is known until Ptolemaic times. The historian Manetho compiled a chronological list of pharaohs which sheds some light upon some more ancient history. Egyptologists must, therefore, qualify and conditionalize their historical writings. They have never found a historical document that they recognize as describing their theory of how the Great Pyramids were built. But the Famine Stele supports the alchemical method of construction, and the historical reports by Herodotus and Pliny, previously ambiguous, now make perfect sense.

We have reached back into the history of science at its roots.

We have followed the evolution of alchemical stonemaking in Egypt from the production of the prehistoric stone vessels of Khnum to a probable transition of door jambs and floors in royal mastabas, to an entire building made of cast stone, the first pyramid. We know that pyramids were built entirely of man-made stone during the Third and Fourth Dynasties, when the Sinai mines were abundant in minerals.

The Fifth and Sixth Dynasties are characterized by a dramatic decrease in the amount of cast stone used in the pyramids, corresponding to the depletion of the mines. It is easy to see why during the Fifth Dynasty kings began to remove stone from the monuments of their ancestors, though this has never before been adequately explained, and why, with less material to work with, they concentrated on building surrounding funerary complexes, paying special attention to making exquisite bas-reliefs. By the Sixth Dynasty stone was conserved for the most vital parts of pyramids, such as casing stones and burial chambers.

Little stone was used in the Twelfth Dynasty pyramids. During the reign of Senusert I, the discovery of a small vein at Serabit el-Khadim in the Sinai provided only enough stone for the royal burial chamber. The end of pyramid building marked the end of any appreciable amount of mineral quarrying in the Sinai.

We understand the evolution of pyramid construction and why these great structures were no longer built. The use of man-made stone explains why, as tools improved, the dimensions of pyramid blocks were made continually larger, though the opposite would have occurred had the blocks been carved. In the broad perspective, we understand what had remained the technological paradox of Egypt.

Too, we see the transparency of the evidence for the standard theory of pyramid construction presented by Egyptology. Additionally, unaware of the two different masonry methods, Egyptologists recognize only a few stylistic alterations in the monuments of Theban kings, which they attribute to differences in Theban ideas about the afterlife from those of

Memphite predecessors. Egyptologists have never fully understood the sudden rise to preeminence of the Amun clergy. With the abatement of alchemical stonemaking, the pyramid tradition became increasingly less practical. The Amun clergy, however, could endlessly perpetuate their religious tradition by carving very soft stone.

We have gained precious insight into the old religion of Khnum and also into the religious objectives for producing faience, stone, and glass. Mystery upon mystery is solved. After thousands of years, the secret of the pyramids is revealed and their true story told.

But do Egyptologists see me as the visionary who solved the pyramid riddle? So far, the reaction appears to reflect the NIH (not invented here) factor, if we are to judge by comments appearing in magazine and newspaper articles. Some Egyptologists have commented in the press that my theory is "a hunch carried too far" and is "against reason and logic." Their only knowledge, however, of my research comes from the press.

No Egyptologists have ever contacted my laboratory in Europe or my offices in the United States or Canada for copies of my papers on the topic or other information. No requests have ever been forwarded to me by the American Chemical Society (ACS) or other scientific bodies for which I have given presentations. Certainly it is unprofessional and intellectually unfair to criticize research without first reading related materials. Of those who have attended any of my presentations at international conferences over the past years (e.g., Grenoble, France, 1979; Toronto, Canada, 1982; Manchester, England, 1984; Denver, Colorado, 1987), at the time of this writing none has ever volunteered to work with me to critique or endorse my research, and not one actively follows its progress. Most Egyptologists view alternative explanations of pyramid construction a threat to their own expertise.

The fact is that when my research is endorsed by geologists and other scientists, it will be up to Egyptologists to reconcile the method of pyramid construction with Egyptian history.

This leads to another question. Why is this book not endorsed by geologists? There are two reasons. One is that the samples loaned to me by Lauer are very small, and he requested their return. Further cutting for tests would have destroyed the samples, which are the only official specimens or proof that I have. Even though I was denied permission to sample the pyramids, I have declined several pyramid stone samples gathered by unauthorized people because such samples are not recognized as valid for research. The second reason is that for the last several years the chemical reactions that I have developed have been highly confidential. Any disclosure of in-depth chemical information would have been a violation of corporate secrecy agreements with the manufacturer of geopolymers. It would hardly be possible to debate a limestone geologist determined to show that the pyramid stone is natural without countering his arguments with technical information. Until the manufacture of geopolymeric cement was under way, my corporate agreements prevented me from publishing papers in scientific journals as well.

A criticism of me by the general public is that I have taken all of the fun and mystery out of the pyramids. My response is this: carving and hoisting stone is grueling labor that is in no way glamorous or romantic, but ingeniously building pyramids through chemistry, and thereby fooling even brilliant modern minds, is a great credit to the researchers of antiquity.

Whether or not this presentation will convince anyone who does not want to be convinced is hardly predictable, especially since this work has not had the benefit of peer review before publication. This issue, however, is a matter of hard science, which must be confirmed or disputed by qualified scientists. It is not ultimately for Egyptologists, who are specialized historians, to approve or reject. Right now, several expert geologists are seeking samples of pyramid stone for their own textural analysis and further examination. Scholars from many disciplines, petrographers, sedimentologists, engineers, concrete specialists, logistics experts or arithmeticians, mathematicians, physicists, logicians, chemists, architects, theologians, linguists, and Egyptologists recognizing the validity of my research can and will further prove my theory from their own research perspective.

The German philosopher Schopenhauer (1788–1860) wrote, "There are three steps in the revelation of any truth: in the first, it is ridiculed; in the second, resisted; in the third, it is considered self-evident."

APPENDIX 1

The Ancient Alchemical Inventions

BEFORE DISCUSSING THE FIRST ALCHEMICAL INVENTION, enamel, let us look at Le Chatelier's experience with the self-glazing enameled sandstone statuettes. After Le Chatelier discovered that the statuettes of the Thinite epoch were agglomerated sandstone, he had to convince his colleagues. He used microscopy to prove his point, and wrote:

> The basic material of which the statuettes are made is fine angular grains of sand, indicating careful grinding. Some claim that this indicates that the objects were carved of natural sandstone and enamelled. I have shown that the statuettes contain numerous spherical bubbles, which means that, irrefutably, they are made of an artificial ceramic matrix.

A natural sandstone matrix does not exhibit bubbles. Only when either ground sandstone or loose sand is mixed with a binder do air bubbles appear. Le Chatelier carried out bulk chemical analysis in an attempt to demonstrate how the statuettes were made. The mineralogical composition follows:

Silica	(SiO_2)	93.3 to	95.3%
Iron oxide	(Fe_2O_e)	0.1 to	0.4%
Aluminum oxide . .	(Al_2O_3)	1.0 to	2.5%
Lime	(CaO)	0.6 to	1.7%
Magnesium oxide .	(MgO)	0.4 to	0.8%
Soda	(Na_2O)	0.6 to	2.5%

Assuming that the small amount of aluminum in the analysis constituted the binder, he tried to reproduce the formula by blending:

Modeling clay	10%
Ground sand	30%
Fontainebleau sand.	60%
Total	100%

His formula contained twice the alumina as the statuettes, and his opponents were therefore not impressed. Because of the fine, angular grain structure observed in the statuettes, they continued to argue in favor of natural sandstone. Le Chatelier, however was not alone. His colleague Pukall made several trials in an attempt to reconstitute a siliceous ceramic paste comparable to the matrix of the statuettes.

After long deliberations, Le Chatelier and Pukall finally reached an agreement with their opponents. Pukall proposed the use of soluble sodium silicate (water glass) and the appropriate amount of aluminous clay. Pukall's proposal seemed plausible, but the opposing scientists were still not willing to concede that this formula was used during antiquity. It seemed more likely to them that an intermediate product was used, which, when ground and blended with water, would produce soluble sodium silicate. This intermediate product became known as alkaline frit (sandy frit), a partly fused combination of fluxes and sand. With vague data, the opposing scientists estimated that alkaline frit was invented in the Nagadian epoch (c. 4000–3600 BC). With regard to the statuettes, *Dictionaire des Techniques Archeologiques* states:

> The basic material was natural hard stone (quartz) or natural soft stone (steatite), or more generally, any hard stone (sandstone, flint, or quartz sand) powdered finely and agglomerated with an adhesive.

By whatever chemistry it was assumed produced the statuettes, it was established in the early 1900s that the Egyptians produced man-made stone.

Le Chatelier also performed bulk chemical analysis on blue ceramic tiles from the subterranean chambers of Zoser's pyramid at Saqqara. His analysis shows raw materials involved in geopolymerization:

Silica	(SiO_2)	92.5%
Alumina	(Al_2O_3)	1.2%
Lime	(CaO)	0.6%
Soda	(Na_2O)	2.5%
Manganese oxide	(MnO_2)	2.4%
Copper oxide	(CuO_2)	0.8%

This analysis is useful for pinpointing the origin of raw materials used to make the statuettes and tiles. **See Table III** on page 244.

First Alchemical Invention
Enamel, a By-product of Copper Smelting, Invented 6,000 Years Ago

Before the statuettes were made, blue enamel had been invented and applied to beads and pebbles, such as those found in neolithic tombs of about 4000 BC. Scholarship maintains that the discovery of enamel was accidental. It is assumed that malachite and natron, ground together on large, flat sandstone millstones to make eye paint, happened to mix with silica debris from the millstones themselves, producing a layer of enamel.

This explanation, however, does not conform to analysis. Silica is anhydrous and requires a temperature of 1,300° C (2,370° F) to melt, because only in the molten state can it mix with a flux (natron or other). This temperature was not achievable in Egypt in 4000 BC. To reach it, large bellows were needed, not yet invented in 4000 BC. It is much easier to fuse natron and chrysocolla than natron and silica, malachite, or other copper carbonates. Chrysocolla, in its natural hydrated state, mixes easily with a flux.

Chemists might assume that a combination of natron and chrysocolla would not fuse because sodium carbonate melts at 850° C (1,500° F), a temperature higher than achievable in 4000 BC. This temperature must to be reached before natron can act on either silicate or silica. By the time it is reached, water in the crystalline structure of chrysocolla has evaporated, eliminating the possibility of a reaction with natron for the production of enamel.

Table III. Sources of Raw Materials for Statuettes

Chemical substance	Raw material	Source
silica	quartz	Nile sand
silica	sodium silicate from opal/ calcedoine or chrysocolla	reaction of silica with caustic soda Sinai mines
alumina	turquoise	Sinai mines
soda	natron (plus lime)	Natron is abundant in deserts and lakes
manganese oxide	pyrolusite	Sinai mines
copper oxide	turquoise/chrysocolla	Sinai mines

244

The assumption would be correct if the sodium carbonate were manufactured by the modern Solvay process, which produces a pure product that melts at 850° C (1,560° F). This is not, however, the case with Egyptian natron. The invention of enamel was possible because of the composition of Egyptian natron, which is:

Hypocarbonate of soda	23.35%
Sufate of soda	11.29%
Muriate of soda	51.66%
Clayish and siliceous sand	02.90%
Carbonate of lime	.89%
Oxide of iron	.20%
Water	9.71%

Egyptian natron possesses a particularity that is not generally known. Its composition of sodium carbonate, sodium sulfate, and sodium chloride produces a fortunate eutectic point. When mixed together, two pure substances can have a melting point that is lower than they have individually. The melting point of sodium chloride is 800° C (1,470° F), and melting point of sodium sulfate is 850° C (1,560° F). But a eutectic mixture of sodium chloride and sodium carbonate melts at 634° C (1,173° F). The eutectic point of sodium chloride and sodium sulfate is 628° C (1,162° F). The eutectic point of all three salts combined is only 612° C (1,133° F). This affords a reaction with chrysocolla, allowing the invention of enamel to have occurred not at 850° C (1,560° F), but at only 612° C (1,133° F).

Second Alchemical Invention
Caustic Soda Used for Enamel Production 5,600 Years Ago

Today caustic soda is made using electrolysis (the action of electric current on sodium chloride). Anciently, a simpler method was used. Namely, natron was mixed with lime (calcined limestone) and water.

Less material is required for enamel production when using caustic soda. This is because caustic soda is more reactive than natron. Caustic soda, when made with natron, lime, and water, always retains a small amount of lime and, therefore, reacts with various siliceous materials between 50° C (122° F) and 150° C (302° F). This type of caustic soda was also used by the chemists of the nineteenth century to produce alkaline frit and soluble sodium or potassium silicate (water glass), which they called stone liquor. In ancient Egypt, caustic soda was the main part of the reaction for agglomerating stone.

Third Alchemical Invention
Sodium Silicate Produced 5,600 Years Ago

Archaeologists, assuming that alkaline frit was anciently used to agglomerate stone, used the term agglomeration to imply a process capable of yielding sodium silicate (water glass). To manufacture sodium silicate today, a mixture of quartz sand and sodium carbonate is fused at 1,300° C (2,370° F).

Quartz sand has a compact structure and reacts with difficulty at moderate temperatures. On the other hand, hydrous siliceous mineral varieties, because of the water in their crystalline structure, are readily attacked at moderate temperatures by caustic soda and therefore easily form sodium silicate. Some of these are diatomaceous earth; opals and flints; chalcedony, such as carnelian, agate, and onyx; volcanic glasses, such as obsidian; chrysocolla; and allophanes (typically as stalactites or as encrustations on chalk and sandstone).

Amorphous (having no definite crystalline structure) silica, opal, flint, and chalcedony are found in considerable quantities in Egypt. De Roziere commented:

> A multitude of agate pebbles, either oval or rather flattened, were spread over the surface of the ancient town of Thebes. . . . All of the pebbles seem to have a common origin. They could not have been transported to the rather high ground of the ancient towns by any natural means, and they are found mostly on the heaps of ruins and debris of ancient monuments, sometimes even in the isles of the

Nile, such as the Isle of Philae, and especially the Isle of Elephantine, where they seem to be strewn in very considerable quantities over the site where this Egyptian town stood.

Agate is just one form of amorphous silica abundant in Egypt. Plant ashes and diatomaceous earth are also abundant. Because caustic soda reacts easily with these materials, there were numerous possibilities for producing sodium silicate for cement.

Fourth Alchemical Invention
Agglomeration Using Turquoise, 5,600 Years Ago

Le Chatelier was unable to recreate the formula composing the statuettes partly because he assumed that a binder based on clay was essential. While it is true that kaolin clay was used in some cements, the binder for the statuettes was based on sodium silicate.

It is relatively easy to cause a thin layer of sodium silicate to set in open air. It is more difficult in a closed mold, such as required for statuettes. This is because neither sodium silicate nor lime are hydraulic binders. Hydraulic setting takes place only if the water in the mixture evaporates, and even then, the resulting product is not water resistant unless geopolymerization is introduced. Geopolymerization produces a water-resistant cement in a humid environment by transforming sodium silicate into a synthetic zeolite. This is achieved with an aluminum phosphate, which, for ancient Egypt, was turquoise.

Fifth Alchemical Invention
Agglomeration with Aluminous Limestone by Imhotep, 4,700 Years Ago

The aluminous limestone of Saqqara reacts with caustic soda (natron, lime, and water) to yield a basic geopolymeric cement, which is not as strong as that obtained using turquoise. The

247

alumina and silica in the clay binding the bedrock is activated by caustic soda, forming a sodium alumino-silicate, a basic geopolymeric cement.

Sixth Alchemical Invention
Arsenic Used to Speed Setting 4,600 Years Ago

As long as only small limestone bricks were being produced, a slow rate of hydraulic setting did not present problems because small bricks dry rapidly. From Sneferu's time forward pyramid blocks became larger, and hydraulic setting was modified to avoid shrinkage and cracking. Sodium arsenate is an activating ingredient that could have been used to induce rapid hydraulic setting. In ancient Egypt, this product was obtained by reacting an arsenic mineral ore, such as scorodite and olivenite, with caustic soda.

Seventh Alchemical Invention
Borax Slowed Setting Time 4,600 Years Ago

Borax slows the setting time of geopolymeric binders. It was probably used to fabricate enormous temple blocks and the beams forming the roofs of the burial chambers of the Fifth and Sixth Dynasty pyramids.

Glossary

amulet: object, usually worn on the body, believed to possess magical powers and used to ward off evil or harm.

Amun: primeval god ushered into prominence by the Theban kings of the 18th Dynasty, who drove out the Hyksos. The name Amun is believed to mean "hidden."

architrave: beam that rests on top of columns.

Atum: name for the Sun, also known as Ra (Re).

bas-relief: sculpture produced in such a way that figures protrude slightly from the background surface.

Ben Ben (benben): primeval mound that rose from the waters of Chaos during the creation of the world in Egyptian mythology. A representation in the form of a pyramidal stone was worshipped at Heliopolis.

Bennu: mythological bird identified with light that dispelled the darkness over the waters during the creation of the world.

Book of the Dead: Egyptian funerary texts, usually placed in a tomb of the wealthy, comprised of lists of incantations and drawings believed to ensure the deceased a safe, happy afterlife.

Books of Thoth: forty-two books divided into six classes, according to Saint Clement of Alexandria (AD 150?–220?). The Books of Thoth concerned laws, gods, priestly education, worship, history, geography, astronomy, medicine, among other topics.

canopic chests: wooden chests, usually painted black, for holding canopic jars, the latter of which held the viscera of the dead removed during mummification.

cartouche: hieroglyphic sign in the form of a loop or oval shape with a knot at the base, representing all that the Sun encircles. In the sign, the two most important of five royal names of the pharaohs were written.

casing stone: blocks of high-quality stone finishing applied to beautify and protect monuments.

corbelled masonry: masonry in which layers protrude further as they ascend; the appearance is like upside down steps.

cuneiform: wedge-shaped inscriptions of ancient Akkadian, Assyrian, Babylonian, and Persian writing.

Egyptian royal linen: fine, translucent linen made by ancient Egyptians.

faience: any of a variety of beautiful materials, often made into tiles, beads, vessels, and amulets, which the Egyptians named "brilliant." In general, Egyptian faience was made of a friable nugget of quartz coated with siliceous glass in a wide variety of colors.

First Time: term used by the ancient Egyptians to describe the most monumental events of their history.

funerary boat: large boat designed for use by the souls of the pharaohs during their death journeys.

Geb: a male deity who personified the earth. Geb was the husband of the goddess Nut.

Gnostics (Gnosticism): advocates of salvation through gnosis (knowledge), Christianity, Greek philosophy, and Oriental mysticism.

Hapu: highly honored god, a fertility symbol who personified the Nile.

Hermes: son of Zeus and Maia, Greek mythology, depicted as a young, athletic god. Hermes was the messenger and herald of the other gods. The Romans identified Hermes with Mercury.

Hermes Trismegistus: name meaning Hermes the thrice greatest. Hermes Trismegistus was the Greek name for the Egyptian god Thoth; identified with Hermes.

Horus: son of Isis and Osiris, a complex god with many attributes and forms. Horus was commonly represented with the head of a hawk.

Hyksos: foreign kings of Egypt ruling from about 1700–1550BC.

Ionic Greek: branch of the ancient Greek language that includes the dialect of Attica, a province of ancient Greece dominated by Athens.

Isis: sister and wife of the god Osiris. Isis became the supreme and most popular Egyptian goddess. In the Late Period Isis was worshipped at temples throughout Egypt. Festivals and temples dedicated to Isis were also prevalent throughout the Roman world.

Jupiter: god of Roman mythology prevailing over man and gods, identified by the Greeks with Zeus.

Ka: the vital energy which both sustains and creates life, depicted as a duplicate of the physical body. Funerary rites were spoken to the ka of the deceased.

Khnum: ram-headed technocrat god of very ancient origin. Khnum, most prominent during the Pyramid Age, was worshipped in numerous Egyptian towns under various attributes and forms.

labyrinth: complicated maze structure.

lintel: weight-supporting threshold or horizontal crosspiece over a doorway.

mastaba: oblong, flat-roofed tomb with sloping sides.

Medusa: one of the three Gorgons of Greek mythology slain by Perseus.

mortuary temple: temples built east of pyramids in which ceremonial funerary offerings for the dead pharaoh took place.

nilometer: rock-cut staircase entering the Nile with cubit markings next to it for measuring the level of the water.

Nut: sky goddess, daughter of Tefnut and Shu, and wife of the earth-god Geb, according to Heliopolitan mythology. Also, at Heliopolis, Nut was the mother of Osiris, Isis, Nephthys, and Seth. Nut was equated with Rhea in Greek mythology.

obelisk: tall, stone pillar with four sides that taper to form a pyramidal top.

Ogdoad: name of the elemental forces or group of eight gods that were responsible for creating the world in Hermopolitan mythology.

Ptah: ancient Egyptian creator god of Memphite mythology. A god of artisans, tradition credited him with inventing crafts.

Pyramid Texts: basis of subsequent Egyptian funerary literature. The Pyramid Texts were inscribed on interior walls and chambers of some pyramids and were used in the priests' liturgy.

pyramidion: pyramid-shaped capstone placed at the top of pyramids.

Ra (Re): the Sun, worshipped since early times. The main center of Sun worship was Heliopolis, where Ra was also known as Atum.

Roman Colosseum: enormous amphitheater of Rome built at about 75 AD.

Rosetta Stone: ancient black basalt tablet bearing Greek, demotic, and hieroglyphic characters. It was found at Rosetta,

Egypt, in 1799, and it provided the key to deciphering ancient Egyptian writing.

sarcophagus: stone coffin, usually ornamented and inscribed.

scarab: winged dung beetles, or their images, prepared with inscriptions on their underside and used as a seal or amulet.

Seth: god of disorder, war, and storms, brother and murderer of Isiris, defeated by Horus.

Shu: symbolic deity of atmosphere, space, or void who separated Nut (sky) from Geb (earth). Shu was identified with Atlas in Greek mythology.

sphinx: statue usually fashioned with the body of a lion and the head of a man.

stele: a boulder or slab bearing inscriptions or designs, usually used as a marker.

Talmud: collection of writing concerning Jewish religious and civil laws, consisting of text and commentary.

Tefnut: female twin of the deity Shu, usually depicted with the head of a lioness or uraeus.

Thoth: lunar god depicted with a human body and the head of an ibis or dog. The god of magic, wisdom, and knowledge, his main center of worship was Hermopolis, where Thoth incorporated with the ogdoad.

Valley of the Kings: wadis in the Theban necropolis in which New Kingdom kings from Thutmosis I to Ramses XI were buried.

Valley temple: temple in which, starting in the 4th Dynasty, the dead pharaohs were washed, purified, and underwent the ceremonial processes of mummification.

Waters of Chaos: primeval waters of Egyptian mythology from which the creator arose when creating the world.

References

Davidovits, J. 1979. Synthesis of New High-Temperature Geopolymers. PACTEC IV, Society of Plastic Engineers, Brookfield Center. pp. 151–155.

Davidovits, J. 1979. La fabrication des vases de pierres au V et IV Millenaires. Second International Congress of Egyptologists, Grenoble (France). Abstract in the *Bulletin of the Geopolymer Institute, Archaeology,* Apr. 1982, p. 17.

Davidovits, J. 1979. Les offrandes de natron et le symbole de l'incarnation divine dans la pierre. Second International Congress of Egyptologists, Grenoble. Acts of the Second Congress of Egyptologists, and the *Bulletin of the Geopolymer Institute, Archaeology,* Apr. 1982, pp. 19–25.

Davidovits, J. 1980. Determination de la provenance des ceramiques, par l'analyse des geopolymeres. Twentieth International Symposium on Archaeometry, Paris. *Revue d'Archeometrie,* V. III, 1981, pp. 53–56; and the *Bulletin of the Geopolymer Institute, Archaeology,* April 1982, pp. 7–10.

Davidovits, J., and Courtois, L. 1981. Differential Thermal Analysis (D.T.A.) Detection of Intra-Ceramic Geopolymeric Setting in Archaeological Ceramics and Mortars. Twenty-First International Symposium on Archaeometry, Brookhaven National Laboratory, New York. *Bulletin of the Geopolymer Institute, Archaeology,* Apr. 1982, pp. 11–15.

Davidovits, J., and Aliaga, F. 1981. Fabrication of Stone Objects by Geopolymeric Synthesis in the Pre-Incan Huanka Civilization (Peru). Twenty-First International Symposium on Archaeometry, Brookhaven National Laboratory, New York. Abstract in the *Bulletin of the Geopolymer Institute, Archaeology,* Apr. 1982, p. 29.

Boutterin, C. and Davidovits, J. 1982. Low Temperature Geopolymeric Setting of Ceramics. Twenty-Second International Symposium on Archaeometry, Bradford (G. B.). Proceedings of the 22nd Archaeometery Symposium, Bradford, 1982.

James, C., and Davidovits, J. Apr. 1982. Avebury Stone 101, Tertiary or Neolithic?. *Bulletin of the Geopolymer Institute, Archaeology,* Apr. 1982, pp. 27–28.

Davidvoits, J. 1982. Fabrication of Stone Vessels. Third International Congress of Egyptologists, Toronto, Sept. 5–11, 1982.

Davidovits, J. 1982. Bio-Tooling and Plant Extracts. Third International Congress of Egyptologists, Toronto, Sept. 5–11, 1982.

Davidovits, J. 1982. No More than 1,400 Workers to Build the Pyramid of

Cheops with Man-Made Stone. Third International Congress of Egyptologists, Toronto, Sept. 5–11, 1982.

Davidovits, J. and Boutterin, C. 1982. Utilisation des Terres Lateritiques dans les Techniques de Geopolymerisation, Proceedings, Colloquium Acutalite de la Construction de Terre en France, Plan Construction, French Ministry (Urbanisme et Logement), Paris/Ecole Nationale des Travaux Publics de l'Etat, Vaux-en Velin, 1982, p. 5.

Davidovits, J. 1983. Geopolymer II, Processing and Applications. *PACTEC 83*, Society of Plastics Engineers, Brookfield Center, 1983, pp. 222–230.

Davidovits, J., Thorez, J., and Gaber, H. M. 1984. Pyramids of Egypt Made of Man-Made Stone, Myth or Fact?. *Abstracts,* Symposium on Archaeometry, Smithsonian Institution, Washington, D.C., 1984, pp. 26–27.

Davidovits, J. 1986. X-Ray Analysis and X-Ray Diffraction of Casing Stones from the Pyramids of Egypt and the Limestone of the Associated Quarries. *Science in Egyptology,* Manchester University Press, 1986, pp. 511–520.

Davidovits, J. 1986. Le calcaire des pierres des Grandes Pyramides d'Egypte serait un beton geopolymire vieus de 4,600 ans. *Revue des Questions Scientifiques,* (Brussels), V. 157, No. 2, 1986, pp. 199–225.

Davidovits, J. Apr. 1987. Pyramids Man-Made Stone, Myth or Fact III: Cracking the Code of the Hieroglyphic Names of Chemicals and Minerals Involved in Construction. Eighth Symposium on Archaeological Chemistry, Denver, Apr. 1987, American Chemical Society (Washington, D.C.), Paper No. HIST 37.

Davidovits, J. Dec. 1987. Ancient and Modern Concretes: What is the Real Difference?. *Concrete International: Design and Construction,* V. 9, No. 12, Dec. 1987, pp. 23–28.

Morris, M. Dec. 1987. Archaeology and Technology. *Concrete International: Design and Construction,* V. 9, No. 12, Dec. 1987, pp. 28–35.

Davidovits, J. Apr. 1987. Antique Mortars and Antique Man-Made Stone Artifacts, Answer to the Chernobyl Syndrome. Eighth Symposium on Archaeological Chemistry, Denver, Apr. 1987, American Chemical Society (Washington, D.C.), Paper. No. HIST 38.

Comrie, D., and Davidovits, Jan. 1988. Waste Containment Technology for Management of Uranium Mill Tailings. One Hundred Seventeenth Annual Meeting of the American Institute of Mining Engineers and the Society of Mining Engineers, Phoenix, Jan. 25–28, 1988.

Davidovits, J., Comrie, D., and Paterson, J., and Ritcey D. 1988. Application of Geopolymer Technology in the Prevention of Ground Water Contamination. Second Annual Hazardous Materials Management Conference, Toronto, May 10, 1988.

Index